Helen lives in West Yorkshire with her husband, son and three mischievous cats. In the past, she has been a palaeontologist, a scientific research assistant, a translator and a medical administrator. In 1996, she came to the United Kingdom which she now regards as her home country.

Helen Leeds

The Missing Marathoner

H&W Investigations

Austin Macauley Publishers™

LONDON ★ CAMBRIDGE ★ NEW YORK ★ SHARJAH

A CIP catalogue record for this title is available from the British Library.

ISBN 9781035806577 (Paperback)
ISBN 9781035806584 (ePub e-book)

www.austinmacauley.com

First Published 2023
Austin Macauley Publishers Ltd®
1 Canada Square
Canary Wharf
London
E14 5AA

I would like to thank my family for their great support and belief in me.

Prologue

Early morning, end of September. Sounds like a line from Leonard Cohen lyrics. It gives you a certain sorrowful mood of anticipation. It has been raining all night, now a clammy white shroud of thick fog has descended on the road. Covering everything under its ethereal embrace, distorting the reality. It's like a Giant's child who decided to play with his colossal eraser and rubbed nonchalantly away as many trees and bushes, fields and hills, as he could reach, leaving only occasional tufts of withered grass or a few awkwardly stuck out coal-black boughs.

Only a small patch of the glistening tarmac can be seen.

Tap-tap-tap!

Lime green Nike trainers are moving like two synchronised pendulums. There is a wet surface underneath. Slippery. Full of deceitful bumps and potholes. But he is confident, he is obviously a good runner. Experienced. Professional. He is a long-distance runner.

The fog is getting thinner, or she is getting used to this murky scene. She notes that the runner is well prepared for the weather and his uneasy task. He is dressed in a high-visibility lemon yellow jacket and a pair of thick thermal tights. He can easily be seen in the unlikely case of any traffic passing by on this country road. It seems to her that a running outfit is jogging on its own, cladding a famous Invisible man, perhaps.

Tap! Tap! Tap!

She doesn't feel good anymore, she feels danger, this place is dangerous. The fear sets its serrated claws deeply in her soul. The premonition is unbearably heavy. It is palpable.

There is a distant sound of an approaching car. It is rapidly growing. The car is coming fast. Too fast for this misty, bumpy road. The lonely runner is not the slightest worried, though. He just moves even more to the edge of the road. He is cautious. As always. But it will not save him. She knows this, but cannot do anything. This notion drives her mad. She is desperately frightened now. For him. She wants to stop what is coming, freeze the picture, press the 'pause' button...

It is strangely quiet, except for muffled footsteps and an engine roar. Powerful headlights cutting through the mist. The murderer is getting close.

The runner turns back. He recognises the car. He stops and waves his hand boldly. The car doesn't show any signs of slowing down. Soon his friendly smile, together with all his confidence, will be wiped away for ever.

The car is fast and determined like Nemesis herself. The runner is doomed, and in the last seconds of his life he fathoms this. Then she hears an inevitable blow and the body, like a broken marionette, is thrown up in the air and already falling down, not even having a slight chance to enjoy the freedom of the flight.

Chapter 1

It was the aroma of Autumn she liked the most in the Austrian Alps. A tantalising mixture of bonfire and ripe apples. Lady Arina Holroyd-Kugushev was finishing her long and exhausting walk, descending rapidly down the steep forest path. It was getting dark fast, only the peaks were blissfully lit by the last rays of the setting sun, their whitewashed sharp jags against the indigo sky reminded her of placoid scales which belonged to some extinct shark. She tried hard to reminisce the name and… it came to her at once—Elegestolepis! Silurian primitive shark, elusive and intriguing species, whose appearance was still a mystery for scientists. Arina chuckled with relish, her late husband's legacy hadn't gone down the drain. A famous palaeontologist who was awarded a peerage just before his sudden and premature death.

Lady Holroyd gave out a little sigh and ordered herself to think about something else. For goodness' sake, almost twelve years had passed since he had contrived to be caught by the rock avalanche in the Tian Shan Mountain range. Anyway, sometimes Arina was even doubting his full departure, imagining him to become a kind of restless spirit, the Wandering *Palaeontologist*, forever hovering over the most hidden and unapproachable fossil sites.

But one thing had happened for sure since his disappearance—Arina had started seeing strange dreams, a sort of prophetic visions. Sometimes they were very frightening, very frightening indeed. Lady Holroyd shivered when she suddenly remembered last night. A tiny, but sharp needle was piercing through her heart. She had to stop walking to catch her breath. *Poor long-distance runner…*

Of course, it might had been just a *normal* dream…She smiled wearily. Deep inside she knew that it had not been an ordinary nightmare, so somewhere the young man was savagely killed, and her new goal will be simple enough—no more no less than to find the murderer.

Arina was very much aware how deceptive was her petite and slightly fragile appearance. But she was not exactly young anymore. As she bitterly had to admit several times in public, she was not in her thirties, or even forties anymore (Lady Holroyd had turned sixty-two recently, to be precise). But she shouldn't be really poignant about her age. Lady Holroyd was fortunate enough to keep her original beauty almost intact. Age didn't wreck her fine, chiselled features, neither had it ravaged her piercing eyes of a very unusual turquoise shade. Yes, her hair had gone grey, but their thick, unruly bob gave her a more mature, sophisticated charm.

The *Guesthaus* where Arina was staying symbolised a typical Tyrolean house with bleached walls, a blunt triangle for the roof and hanging from ornate carved wooden balconies were flower baskets, full of colourful petunias and geraniums. As soon as Lady Holroyd came in, she was welcomed by the familiar, somewhat comical figure in a Tyrolean hat, hanging askew on the perfectly bold, rugby ball shaped head. The wrinkled face, tanned to the stage of a ripe aubergine, was bowing enthusiastically.

'Usual?' inquired Herr Maier.

Arina nodded, the question was purely rhetorical. For the last seven years her taste for Martini Bianco with two cubes of ice and a slice of lemon had not changed a bit. She took off her battered but still the most comfortable walking boots, and started ascending the wide wooden staircase which led to her room on the top floor.

Lady Holroyd was looking forward to having a hot bubbly bath, followed by a drink at the bar and a nice local meal to round off the evening. She was very fond of this small, family hotel. The guests (not mentioning the owners themselves) were eccentric enough for her taste, also the dinners, which were served at seven o'clock sharp, were authentic and scrumptious.

It was so cosy in her 'Eagle nest', as was noted on the ornamented name plate hanging outside the massive antique panelled timber door (every room had its own original name). She herself preferred to call it 'The Room Under the Roof'. She didn't mind the low, sloped ceiling with thick stained oak beams, covered in grooves and holes, like they had been brought from an old pirate vessel.

Arina poured two cups of a Bergamot and Jasmine foaming bath cream into the running hot water and added two handfuls of Dead Sea salt. She did take her bath-soaking procedure seriously. Waiting for the bath to fill, Arina changed to her favourite violet plush bathrobe. Tiredness was catching up with her and a chill was seizing every single bone of her ageing body. She couldn't wait to immerse herself into the relaxing steaming water.

At last everything was ready to her satisfaction. The bath was full to the brim with scalding water, blanketed with a thick, heavily scented froth, which was sparkling and crackling lively. Arina smiled and carefully plunged her right foot. Unfortunately, the left one never had a chance to join in.

The deafening booming of the Skype ringtone burst its way into the bathroom. Lady Holroyd uttered a rude exclamation sounding more like an angry lioness growl. Still cursing under her breath, she retreated from the bathroom and rushed to the bursting its guts laptop.

Of course, it was her nerdy secretary, also known as her agent, companion and so on, in other words, chief cook and bottle-washer. Damn him, he couldn't choose a better time! She clicked the 'Answer with video' button (though, if it was not for her innate curiosity, she would have opted for the 'Cancel' one) and slumped into the chair.

A face with spiky, sandy hair filled the screen. Then she heard a heart-sinking thump, and the connection was lost. When, a few minutes later, Luke Weir reappeared blissfully smiling, Lady Holroyd was at her highest boiling point.

'You'd better come up with something really important, because, you know…you've just successfully dragged me out from my hot relaxing bath after a long and tiresome walk! You should be ashamed of yourself, young man!'

'Oh, I am so sorry,' managed to interject Luke, but his shining excited green eyes behind square rimmed spectacles betrayed him. Even his whole thin face, with a dash of freckles, together with quite a long nose didn't show any signs of remorse.

'And this crash….' suddenly Arina became suspicious, 'you're not in my place by any chance, are you?'

'Hm…I'm just passing by, you know…and your cats, they need a lot of attention, they are missing human company…'

'They're definitely not missing your company, Luke, thanks a lot for creating havoc in my house!'

'Anyway, I've got superb news for you, we've got a new case! Yes, a missing person, hm…a missing marathoner, sounds good, what do you think?'

'I knew it! I had my vision last night! Yes! He is not missing, my friend! He's been brutally killed while running his… whatever how many, miles.' Arina clasped her hands in excitement, once again her prophecy had proved to be right.

Luke Weir looked unsure, however.

'Erm…What I actually meant it's that Aaron Statham…who's disappeared, it's our case now, erm…of course, if you agree…'

'Can you get to the point?'

'Sure! He *was* a long-distance runner, but *in the past*, I mean. He is…was a proper marathon runner once, taking part in all sorts of championships, even winning some bronze or silver medal in the Olympic games. Unfortunately for him, four years ago he had a horrible accident. I'm not one hundred percent sure what sort of accident it was… but, as a result, he had lost the use of his legs!'

'That's really bad,' Arina mumbled almost inaudibly and added louder, 'so he was an invalid after all, was he? He couldn't possibly be on the road running anymore…bloody hell, I was wrong again!'

'Wrong?'

'Precisely! If he had his legs cut off, how could he possibly be running again in his posh shining Harlequin trainers?'

'Harlequin trainers?'

'Trainers the colour of a very bright and equally annoying shade of green. Sometimes I have my serious doubts about what they teach you at university nowadays.'

Luke tapped his forehead with his long fingers and laughed heartily.

'You've seen this again…ha-ha…it's astonishing how can you believe in such nonsense…ha-ha-ha! Especially after the last…'

At this instance Luke's face disappeared from the screen, and a black and furry snout, which resembled very much a chubby bear cub, appeared gaping at Angelina in a thoughtful way.

'Chernomor, my sweet, sweet cat, you definitely have got more intelligence and understanding than this bumpkin!'

There were some shoves and pushes in the background which resulted in a very disturbed picture and crackling noise. Then a sepulchral voice emerged informing her about sending the case digest by email, and the Skype call ended.

Of course, the bath was long forgotten. Arina was glued to the screen scrolling through pages of what appeared to be a concise and clear chronicle of the events which had happened a year ago. Luke Weir had his uses after all, he was gifted with a rare ability to grasp the key facts and display them in a plain comprehensible manner. This, however, referred to his written skills exclusively. His oral manners left a lot to be desired.

It was getting really late. If she wanted to have dinner tonight, she had to hurry. Arina didn't regret any more about the missed and so much awaited hot soak. She was already engrossing herself in a new case.

****

The dinner was over, it was probably good, but if Lady Holroyd was asked to describe her dishes, she would find it difficult. She retired to the hotel bar, flanked with rows of differently shaped and coloured bottles, sparkling welcomingly from the glow in a large fireplace. Arina hunched there in the corner, near the fire, like a small bird, clasping in her thin, slightly crooked fingers a crystal tumbler filled with her favourite Martini.

She was deep in her thoughts, doubting herself once again, disputing her own ability to solve this new mystery. It was true, she had cracked a few cases in the past. But others had been different, this one was standing out as a particularly awkward one. She didn't have time to read through Luke's briefing thoroughly, she will have to do this tomorrow. But what she had absorbed so far didn't look too promising.

Arina sipped her drink and didn't taste it. She put her glass down with a clink on the small table, full of marks and scratches left by years of hard service. She was gazing at the burning logs, hypnotised by the flames dancing vividly, revealing strange figures and shapes.

'Hmm…you don't mind me joining you?'

Arina gave a startled flinch, but immediately frowned at her intruder.

'Sorry, if I've frightened you…'

She snorted in insult.

'You have NOT frightened me. I was just thinking, you know, Klaus. I do think from time to time!'

The retired German general and NATO commander with his sagging jowls would have reminded her of a sad, placid bulldog, if it was not for his shrewd, icy-cold eyes of a pale blue and high forehead, weathered and sewn with furrows.

'Good evening, Lady Arina. Did you have a good walk *today*?'

Despite his impeccable English, practically without a trace of any accent, his accentuated, almost caricatured *Germanness* was written all over him. A leather waistcoat and a pair of short trousers with bracers, a stentorian laugh and hearty consumption of beer contributed to this image. But perhaps, a dash too obvious, too bold, thought Arina. She was getting suspicious of people who preferred to hide their intelligence behind a façade of dim-wittedness.

'Hmm, yes, better than yesterday,' she replied bluntly.

'Ha-ha! I guess, yesterday's stroll was too much for you. You know, we are like mountain goats, we enjoy heights and ravines, we are blessed with steady feet and steady heads, ha-ha!'

Lady Holroyd managed to produce a wry smile. Yesterday's walk was a disaster, a total fiasco. Klaus and his infantile daughter, who at the age of twenty-seven was still behaving like an unruly toddler, persuaded her to join their "morning stroll". From the very start Arina had bitterly regretted her hasty decision.

'I simply don't take a shine to galloping up and down like... like a reckless... *goat*.'

The ex-general slapped his meaty thighs and exploded with his usual guffaw. Arina reckoned that her evening was irretrievably spoiled.

Klaus roared and snorted, his voluminous belly was shaking, his ruddy face got even more flushed. Is it possible, that I was wrong in my judgement of him, that he is as he actually seems to be, thought Arina until she met his eyes. At this instance her qualms have been swayed away. These eyes lived their own life, apart from the rest of Klaus's face and body. With a Basilisk's cold detachment, they were observing Arina. Even a touch of amusement could be visible in their expression.

Lady Holroyd-Kugushev shivered unintentionally. An invisible iron fist hit her inside with such power, that she was out of breath for a moment. So, her instinct was right. This man was up to no good. No good at all.

'What, er...what are you saying?'

'Have you seen a ghost? Ha-ha-ha-ha,' this time the old soldier managed to stop himself reasonably quickly. 'You are so pale, are you not ill or something?' he looked concerned now, 'would you like me to take you out in the fresh air?'

'No, thank you very much. I'm just tired. That's all.'

'We cannot leave her like this, Krista! Hey!'

To Arina's great dismay, they had been joined by the notorious *baby-girl*. She tramped towards them and was now towering over Arina with her usual dim look.

'Our noble lady is not very well, you see, my duckling.'

Krista uttered a grunt which could be interpreted in many different ways.

'We are going to take her out, you and me. For a sip of fresh air. No, no, I don't take no for an answer! C'mon, duckling, give me a hand.'

Krista's face didn't look unpleasant, far from it, she would be considered quite attractive with her high cheeks and short regular nose, if it was not for her still, robotic features and apathetic eyes. She is dangerous, suddenly thought Arina, she could have killed me yesterday. Both of them could have done this.

It had all started badly. They had wrongfooted her from the beginning. The route they had chosen was unfamiliar for Arina, though she knew the area pretty well. The narrow uneven path ascended sharply through the spruce woods, the pace was too fast. The former general and his daughter had gone out of sight in minutes. Arina was breathing heavily, trying to keep up with them. She didn't want to slow down, she didn't like to show her weakness.

Exhausted and sweaty she had reached the flat clearing and slumped by the massive trunk. Her heart was thumping so hard that its beats were reverberating in her ears. That was why she had not heard this laugh at first. Nasty little giggle. Smirking. Offensive. Humiliating.

Lady Holroyd looked around. She took a handkerchief out of the fleece pocket and wiped her face. Squinted. The dazzling morning sun was blinding her vision. She felt a little giddy, she had missed her breakfast.

They obviously decided not to wait for her, so after a while she got up and continued her walk, but slower this time. It's not bloody racing, for God's sake. The path was not going so steep now, winding around colossal pine trees and spruces, thick blueberry bushes and mossy boulders, the silent witnesses of the Ice Age.

It was very quiet now. No other ramblers, tourists or locals were seen nearby. Even birds kept sepulchral silence. It looked like this way had been long forsaken. This thought was unsettling and Arina frowned. May be, they've got lost? Or, perhaps, it was only *she* who has got lost…

Then she heard something. Two voices. At last! She sighed with relief. The wood was thinning out, the voices were getting louder. The ex-general and his daughter. Lady Holroyd couldn't have been happier if she had met her best friend. Anticipation of traditional cuisine served in this mountain inn—the rewarding purpose of their morning walk—made her swallow hard and speed up. For this brunch she would, probably, opt for a couple of thin *Frankfurters* with mustard and a slice or two of fresh bread. In addition, may be, a bowl of spicy soup with dumplings and, certainly—a glass of red wine.

'Grüss Gott!' Klaus welcomed her teasingly.

'Grüss Gott!' replied Arina and looked around in confusion.

Something was not right. A small open area with a few wooden tables and benches scattered chaotically around was deserted. Framed by grooved, jagged rocks, blocking the sun at this time of the day, this place was far from welcoming. Surprisingly, it didn't affect the incongruous gaiety of her German guides.

'Bad news!' Krista informed her brusquely.

'Bad news, indeed!' echoed her father.

'Wh…what do you mean?' Arina suddenly felt very tired. She detested their vagueness, she was repelled by the whole situation. She wished that she had never gone ahead with their idiotic idea of a Tyrolean picnic. Too late to lament now, just clench your teeth and survive these few bloody hours, Lady Holroyd ordered herself but didn't feel better.

A frigid waft of unforeseen wind had brushed her neck. Like an omen, a death warning…

'I just hope that you managed to have a good breakfast before…'

'Why?' Arina frowned.

'Proper English breakfast,' this time it was Krista who parroted Klaus.

'I don't understand! Can you kindly explain me what is going on?' Arina was losing the rest of her patience, which was not great even at the best of times.

Klaus pointed towards the mountain tavern with one of his walking sticks. The words were not needed, actually.

'Is it closed?' The question sounded silly and irrelevant, as for 'Alp Nook', how it was pretentiously called, looked as closed as it could be. With its shutters on the windows and the massive padlock on the door, not mentioning a big notice 'GESCHLOSSEN'.

'Very sorry, my dear lady, I am deeply and sincerely sorry that we dragged you up here for nothing.'

The ex-NATO-general looked really upset, but Krista was barely bothering to conceal her smirk, which seemed to glue to her large wet mouth like frayed chewing gum. She was obviously not giving a toss about their hungry and exhausted noble friend.

'The bright side of all of this is that we still have a wonderful, picturesque walk ahead of us.' The general's optimism proved to be limitless.

And there they were, trotting back. Arina was surprised how fit both of them were. And this, despite their large frames and Krista's apparent laziness, in addition to Klaus's age. They were also both appropriately equipped with a pair of walking sticks, high walking boots and even expensive looking knee braces.

'Are we going a different way?'

'Yes! This way is shorter, as we all need to fortify ourselves, you know, compensate our missed meal, ha-ha,' roared the former general leading the small group down the overgrown track.

The view was truly magnificent. They had left the conifer woods behind and were walking down the grassy slope, fully enjoying the sunshine and the warmth it brought with it. At least, Lady Holroyd-Kugushev did. The snowy glowing peaks with the almost transparent blueness of the clear autumn sky and, a crisp scent of the pristine highland air. She was so submerged, that she didn't realise at first that the path had changed.

When she did, she gasped and leaned heavily over the rocky surface. She would have dropped her walking stick if it had not been fastened with a leather loop around her wrist. Her palms had gone cold and clammy, her heart was racing madly, the whole world was spinning in front of her eyes.

Arina had a phobia, to be honest she had a few phobias, but this one was the worst. She could easily cope with heights, and she really enjoyed mountain walks but under one condition. She must be more or less enclosed, having a sort of a barrier between her and the drop, whatever its depth might be.

But now she was just a meter away from the edge, and nothing was there to protect her from falling into the bottomless void.

'Problem?'

Klaus was standing almost at the edge of the path, with his back to the sheer drop, smiling nonchalantly. He must be utterly insane, thought Arina and embraced the cliff even tighter.

'Are you okay?'

'I'm just fine,' she managed to emit a chuckle. 'Is there…hm… any other way down?'

The old soldier looked puzzled. 'What do you mean, my lady? I don't follow you…'

'I mean,' Arina's anger gave her more strength, 'is there any *other* way apart from this crappy path? Where you don't risk breaking your neck any second?'

'Ha-ha, are you not afraid of heights by any chance? That's really funny! Such a keen and experienced hiker like you frightened of slopes and drops! Ha-ha!'

Lady Holroyd wanted to slap him, but she couldn't detach herself from the only stable object within her reach. She closed her eyes and started counting. She must calm down, she must regain herself before falling hopelessly apart.

****

Arina emerged from her thoughts with a bad taste in her mouth. The taste of fear. She was not usually so easily manipulated. Some of her friends would not even believe that it was at all possible.

'Thank you so much for your kind offer, but—no!'

'Are you sure?' Klaus tried again.

'Absolutely! And I am going tomorrow anyway.'

'Going where?'

'Home, of course!' Arina was surprised herself, because up to this minute she hadn't thought about cutting her holiday short. She had another week to stay and even the new case wouldn't stop her from enjoying the last days of her favourite vacation. But now this sudden decision seemed to her to be the only right one. Lady Holroyd wanted to go home. To her nice cosy cottage, to her animals, to familiar faces and comforting habits. She didn't want to admit even to herself that the main reason was slightly different.

'Hh…home? I thought you were saying that you have another week or so…' the former general looked confused. He frowned. A glimpse of concern flashed through his eyes, 'can I ask you why?'

'I've got a new case. I need to go back to my duties. The holiday is over, unfortunately.'

'Really?' Klaus looked like he'd lost the plot. Transfixed Krista convincingly played the role of a Greek chorus.

Lady Holroyd stood up and departed majestically. Back to her room, flinging absentmindedly her things into a capacious suitcase, she felt very clearly that she'd just escaped great danger. She couldn't discern why they wanted to kill her yet. But she would find out sooner or later. Like she had always done.

Arina froze. Somebody had knocked at the door. It was a delicate, discreet knock. Almost inaudible. Arina stood very still, grasping tightly whatever she was going to pack. Her heart was galloping again, she forgot to breath.

'Ahem…'

'Who is there?'

'Lady Holroyd, I am so sorry to disturb you at this time…but as you are leaving so suddenly…ahem…'

'It's you, Herr Maier,' she said too loudly and drew a sigh of relief.

She unlocked the door and let the owner of the guesthouse come in. After they'd discussed all the details of her unplanned departure and he'd left, Lady Holroyd went to bed. Despite her immense exhaustion she couldn't sleep.

As soon she closed her eyes, she was back at the rock. She hated herself for such pathetic weakness, she would have slapped herself if she could free her hands. Klaus left to fetch his daughter, though Arina asked him in no uncertain terms not to do this. She had only a few minutes to escape this embarrassing situation. She would rather die than allow herself to be dragged like a whimpering wretch.

So, step by step, facing the outcrop, tracing with her palms the craggy limestone surface, she managed to partially retreat her way back, when a large boulder fell with a crushing thud exactly where she had been stuck for the last quarter of an hour.

Her legs turned to jelly, shaky and unsteady, but the final twenty meters she covered with remarkable speed. She was back into the safety of the bucolic pasture in no time. The whole situation seemed ridiculous now.

If it was not for the boulder. It was too much of a coincidence. She understood it clearly. The thought tasted bitter like rowan berries. And like their flavour stuck to your teeth forever.

She heard them calling for her, of course. She didn't reply. She walked back the same way quietly and carefully, full of sadness. She passed locked up 'Alp Nook' with its air of decay, she only hesitated a few seconds before choosing the right forest path. She was always good at orientation.

Arina felt so lonely, so vulnerable. She missed her late husband so much. His scientific integrity, his dry sense of humour, his sharp razor-like mind. And most of all—his kindness. She uttered a tiny sob, like a small animal which has been brutally captured.

Alexander was his name. Sir Alexander Holroyd. When he'd received his peerage, he mocked her a lot over her double-barrelled title, asking, with the most serious expression on his long clever face, how would she prefer to be addressed—Lady Holroyd-Kugushev or Princess Kugushev-Holroyd. He never did take nobility seriously.

Arina would never have shown her weakness in front of anybody. Except for her husband or her father. Both of them who had gone. Forlornness came down heavily on her shoulders. She shuddered and had to stop for a moment. Maybe she should have stayed there? Let it go…let her pointless empty life to end at least!

I'm nobody! I'm an amateur, dilettante in all aspects. I'm a pathetic old woman lost on her own in the modern world. I forfeited everyone I loved. I've had enough of this!

Then she thought what Alexander would have said. And at once Arina smiled involuntarily. 'Silly woman, get hold of yourself. You have so much going for you. To start with, there are three cats waiting for you at home. Three poor souls, spoiled rotten by Luke. Don't forget about the latter, by the way. How will he solve all these crimes, which are jumping out like peas from pods upon your nonsensical head, without you? Have you thought about this? Of course, not! The years have not changed you, not a bit! And there are still some people left in this world who need you, don't cast them away.'

Arina didn't have anything to say back. Anyway, is it not pointless to argue with a ghost? Instead, she drew a deep breath and blew her nose. His presence was so tangible, like he was just next to her, hiding from her behind trees and silently laughing. *Alive.*

He was going now. The distance between them was growing wider, his voice was sounding duller… The last words she heard from him were so cheeky that she blushed immediately and shook her fist. 'A trail of your admirers will be sad to lose you too…he-he…'

Arina turned onto her other side, trying vainly to get some sleep. It was no wonder that after such a horrendous day she had a nightmare. Of course, it must be a nightmare. How silly it was to confuse it with anything else. She was fuming with annoyance that she had let her guard down while speaking to Luke. This smart arse could see straight through her giving him a chance.

The morning was creeping in, depriving her of the last chance to have any rest before a long tiresome journey. Feeling groggy and frustrated, with bloodshot eyes and dishevelled hair, Lady Holroyd got up and went to the window. She shuffled the curtains and peeped through the parting.

She recoiled almost immediately. Her nightmare of the past two days was continuing.

Down there, in a small parking area surrounded by dog rose bushes, so exquisite in their autumn attire, wearing regally their jewels of bright, shiny carmine hips, scattered over the pale-lemon, translucent lacy foliage, stood Klaus. Despite the early hours he was not alone. He was talking to one of the taxi drivers employed by their hotel. He actually might be the same driver who was going to take her to Salzburg airport a few hours later. Unlike his usual manners, Klaus was speaking very quietly. Secretly. In Arina's eyes it looked very much like a conspiracy.

Chapter 2

Luke Weir was staring at his laptop screen. Staring back at him was Aaron Statham. It was his last photograph taken by his fiancée Lisa, just a few days before he had disappeared. Aaron was not exactly handsome, or cool, or trendy as many men of his age would try to be. Instead, he looked older than his twenty-seven, in some way, old-fashioned or like somebody who didn't care very much about his looks.

Luke liked Aaron's face. There was something positive about it. His grey eyes were clever and kind. A few thin wrinkles were gathering in their outer corners, like he was about to burst out laughing and trying very hard not to do this. His fair hair had not been cut for a while, and a long strand was falling boyishly over his forehead. He looked happy and mischievous, and nobody would guess in a million of years that he was a crippled invalid, depressed and lost. Maybe, because he was not, Luke thought.

That was the police version. That the man had gone away of his own free will. Threatened by the wedding and his bleak future as an impaired husband.

Luke pushed his rectangular glasses encased in a heavy black frame up on the top of his head and puffed out his cheeks meditatively. He squinted and tapped his prominent chin with his long artistic fingers.

No, it's not possible, said Luke aloud and shook his head. Somebody giggled. He put back his glasses and looked around.

A girl of about ten or eleven, with long blond hair and freckled face, was gawking at him with poorly concealed amusement. She was sitting with her family at the table next to his and obviously thought it was hilarious to see a mad person talking to himself.

To his great annoyance, Luke felt that he'd started blushing. He quickly bent down over his laptop trying to go back to his train of thought but couldn't concentrate anymore. It was a beautiful clear autumn day, and all sorts of aircraft, parked, taking off or landing, could be seen through the full-length windows at the Leeds-Bradford airport waiting area.

Luke was very excited about this case. They hadn't come across anything serious for a while, so he'd had to divide his time between the mundane routine of tracking unfaithful spouses or business partners and even more boring translation work, with which he was involved occasionally. Luke Weir was a very gifted scholar, fluent in German (thanks to his granny from the mother's side, who was originally from Munich and had a habit of speaking to her grandson only in her native language), he also achieved a great success in teaching himself Polish and Czech. Above all, Luke Wier had read History at Cambridge and later had obtained a PhD for his thesis 'The short reign of Paul I'. That was how he'd met his future boss and a senior partner in their sickly detective business, Lady Holroyd-Kugushev.

Luke wanted to learn the language of his latest passion—Russian history, to be able to absorb sources in their original form, not distorted by the translation. As he was a man of action, the next step for him was straightforward: he needed a Russian teacher. Preferably, a native speaker. He'd tried three different tutors before finding Arina.

By then, he was fed up with the "highly qualified, professional teachers of Russian language tailored for all ages, stages and abilities". He was almost ready to tackle the language by himself, when he'd by pure chance run into a lapidary advert in the Local Pages: Directory of local tradesmen & businesses. He was actually looking for a plumber—trusty, experienced and not madly expensive. Obviously, Luke lived in a different era, such a person didn't exist anymore.

Instead, he'd found a new tutor for himself and what was good about this one—the teacher lived very close to him. Luke had expected to meet another of these ladies from the former Soviet Union, totally isolated from modern Britain, surviving exclusively in their nostalgic time capsules, still and stiff like they had just emerged from an ancient sarcophagus.

His new tutor's house was even closer to his small semi than he thought. It was a very nice stone cottage with a magnificent view of the large reservoir lined with pine trees. He knocked at the door and was let in almost immediately.

'Luke, I presume, come in please.'

She didn't have even the slightest touch of an East European accent, instead she spoke the poshest English he'd ever heard. She was also a stunning looking woman with laser-sharp turquoise eyes and a sardonic smile. And she didn't look Russian at all.

'I came erm…to learn Russian…you know…on your advert…erm…are you a…'

'Yes, it's me, my name is Lady…damn…just Arina. Why do you want to learn such a difficult and not very useful language? Aha, I assume, you've got a Russian lady friend or something like this? Anyway, I want to know the reason.'

Luke was lost for words under such intense interrogation, his first thought was to run away as fast as possible. But then, somehow, he'd managed to edge in a word or two, which Lady Holroyd found amusing. This was how it all had started. A friendship… sort of…a companionship…

Luke Weir smiled and scratched his chin thoughtfully.

Four years had passed since, four amazing, unforgettable years. He hadn't succeeded in Russian a great deal, though. And he honestly could admit to himself that it was not due to the lack of diligence or desire to conquer a new challenge from his side. His new teacher had simply lost interest in taking him through the labyrinths of complicated grammar and the lexicon. She also wouldn't win a prize in patience.

Luke forced himself to unglue from this exciting view and pleasant memories and started packing his laptop into an expensive looking suede shoulder bag, specially designed to be a vessel for this sort of portable device He didn't want to be late as he tended to be usually.

Arina's plane has landed five minutes ago. Luke had plenty of time. He strolled down the large, glassed waiting area, bathed in a weak autumn sun, squinting like a happy cat. He was looking forward to plunge fully into their new case.

Luke Weir was waiting in Arrivals among a sparse crowd of others meeting the flight from Salzburg. Luke was pleased with himself. He thought he looked great today, in his beige corduroy slim-fit trousers and a short red and black checked coat. Elegant and professional. A good representative of their 'H&W private investigation agency'. He failed to hide a conceited smirk. He took off his satchel and adjusted its strap a little.

The people around him started shuffling. The first arrivals were coming through the double swing doors. There was a small group of businessmen armed with shining attaché cases, all wearing identical dark suits, white shirts and unnaturally wide smiles. They were met by their obviously identical twin, who ushered them outside. Two lively girls, loaded with enormous hiking backpacks, were greeted by their happy parents. There was an elderly couple, fit and tanned, who walked past speaking loudly in German. There were other people, on their own or not, old or young, but there was not a trace of Lady Holroyd-Kugushev.

Luke felt like an iceberg had hit his solar plexus with almighty power and crushed it to pieces. Something bad had happened to her, something really bad. In their brief early morning conversation, she had vaguely hinted at some evil people wishing her harm. He didn't take this very seriously then, he was more concerned about changing plans and meeting arrangements. Meeting arrangements…

This iceberg was killing him now, he forgot how to breath, his lungs turned to a punctured old football. His throat went dry. His ears were full of superfluous sounds. Women's laughter, a loud talking, a rattle of suitcases being pulled carelessly, a screech of the shutters being rolled up in the nearby newspaper kiosk. His head was about to explode.

Luke went into his pocket and with shaking hands fished his mobile out. Not surprisingly, he didn't hear anything from it, he'd prudently muted it before entering the airport. There were dozens of missed calls and an equal number of texts. All of them were from Lady Holroyd.

Luke went outside. He was not admiring the sunshine anymore, instead he was staring at his smart phone like it was a cobra intending to launch its venomous attack. How could he have forgotten that this time she was flying back to Manchester, not to Leeds?

She'd called him very early in the morning, so early that she'd had to wake him up. He was still half asleep when she told him to meet her at the airport. That she was coming back today, that there had been a change of plans. That she was in danger and she was also desperate to occupy herself, meaning that she wanted to embark on their new investigation immediately. And, of course, because of rebooking the flight, he had to drive to Manchester airport.

He inhaled deeply and tapped "Call back".

****

After two days Lady Holroyd was still very cross with Luke's mess-up. She couldn't easily forget that she'd had to be squashed into a very crowded train with a lack of fresh air and any basic comfort for almost two hours, instead of travelling in style in the fast, spacious car driven by her personal chauffeur—Luke.

Today they were for the first time meeting their new client Lisa. Luke had spoken to her on the phone, but they had never actually met face-to-face. The appointment was set at twelve o'clock at Lady Holroyd's house.

Since they'd stopped renting an office in the city centre, which was too expensive, too small and too stuffy, their main headquarters had been moved to Arina's house. She assigned for this purpose a long and narrow room on the ground floor, which used to be just a humble library recluse. Its walls were lined with bookshelves, and there were two large windows, which viewed the stone wall entwined with climbing white roses. A massive wooden door, always shut, at the end of the room led to the hall.

Arina was already sitting deeply in her special "detective" leather armchair, carefully positioned in the darkest corner of the room. She had all the necessary preliminary information in the form of different sizes and shapes of pieces of paper scattered, as it seemed, chaotically over the Long John table in front of her. Some of them were A4s with neat strings of printed text, some were photocopies of old newspaper cuttings, some were just her own scribbles.

Lady Holroyd looked a little apprehensive with the two vertical lines between her eyebrows more obvious than usual. Her left fingers were tugging large azure beads of her handmade necklace, the right ones were occupied with messing her silver mane. But there was nothing new about her behaviour, she always felt this way at the beginning of each new case.

Luke was well accustomed to this and tried not to get in her way, especially in light of the last unfortunate events. He busied himself with setting the scene for the interview. Basically, preparing his own "working environment" as he liked to call it. He unfolded a small portable desk and placed it in close vicinity of the comfortably padded swivel chair. It was his private observation post, strategically situated by the wooden panel separating the two half-circle leaded windows, so he could have a full view of their client from the right side, while Arina would cover the left.

'Have you finished at last?' Lady Holroyd-Kugushev was x-raying him with her enormously beautiful turquoise eyes.

Once again Luke Weir admired her appearance, so exquisite and fragile at the same time, like she'd stepped into their imperfect world from a different epoch of crinolines, powdered wigs, chandeliers and imperial balls. But he was also very aware how deceptive her façade was, there was a steel armour of an experienced warrior concealed behind.

'Yes, your Ladyship, all done and I am at your service!'

'Stop buffooning at once,' she ordered him in a stern voice, which didn't fool Luke, he knew too well that she was thawing rapidly.

The doorbell rang. Lady Holroyd perched her ultra slim reading spectacles on the top of her head and shovelled all the papers with her long, sharply nailed and impeccably manicured fingers into a big untidy pile. Luke went to open the door.

His heart sunk. Lisa looked even worse than on photographs, nor did the rain improve her look. Squat, plump, with a pastry heavy-set face and wet dark hair of an unidentified style. Arina, who had already almost made up her mind in favour of the police version of runaway Aaron, would be fortified in her tenets even more seeing his manqué fiancée.

Lisa came into the room, smiling tentatively. It was obvious that she was not at ease.

'Please, take a seat here,' Luke showed her to the "visitor" chair and added in his most welcoming voice, 'would you like some coffee or tea?'

'No, thank you, I would rather go straight to my business.'

Arina didn't say anything, she just nodded and continued to rustle papers on the little table.

'That's absolutely fine, shall we start from…'

'Why did you choose our agency?' Arina interrupted Luke sharply.

Lisa interlocked her hands and blushed a little.

'I was going through a few local agencies, a quite long list, actually, and then I saw yours. And it just clicked…H and W. You know, it reminded me of Sherlock Holmes stories. Holmes and Watson.'

'Really?' Arina looked sincerely astonished.

'Yes, and I always liked…loved these stories, I read them in my childhood, and then I read them again, and it was the happiest time of my life…and I thought it would bring me luck. To choose you, I mean.'

'How unusual,' murmured Luke.

Arina looked at her with more interest now. Lisa was blushing, and it made her look much nicer, not so plain, and her brown eyes were clever and sad.

'Do you mind us recording this session?' asked Luke taking out of his pocket his recent expensive toy which he was very proud of—an Olympus digital voice recorder—a sleek black stick with a lot of buttons.

'No, not at all.'

'All right, now tell us what happened,' Arina asked.

'Okay,' Lisa inhaled deeply, pressed her palms tightly down to her knees and started. 'It was supposed to be a very quiet wedding. Nothing pompous, a few friends, that's all. I'm older than him, you see…I'm thirty-six…so it makes eight years difference. Which is not a great deal if you are a bloke. Who is older, I mean…'

Lisa swallowed hard.

'Is it possible to have a glass of water, please?'

'Of course, would you rather have something hot?' asked Luke.

'No, it's fine, just water, please. My throat has got so dry.'

After she drank almost a full glass, she went on. Her voice was steady and controlled but her hands were clutched together in a moving, wrestling tangle again.

'So, this morning, the morning of our wedding, he vanished. Last time I saw him was the day before. And you know, it sounds really ridiculous, but we felt guilty to see each other on the eve of our wedding. We didn't spend a lot of time together, though. We were so looking forward to the future…' her voice broke.

Arina coughed and looked away uneasily. Luke thought that he could perceive the ocean deep, nonhealing sorrow with all his five senses.

'I knew from this moment that something had happened to my poor boy. Something really terrible. But nobody believed me,' she said with dry irony, 'nobody, not even my mother!'

'What about his parents?' asked Arina.

'Oh, he'd lost his parents when he was just a boy, fourteen or fifteen, I think…'

'Both?'

'Yeah, they died in a plane crash, you know, like a small private plane. It crashed in the mountains.'

'Mountains?' Luke looked confused.

'Oh, sorry, I didn't tell you that Aaron came from New Zealand originally. I mean…his parents were there working on a contract or something like that. And he lived almost all of his life there.'

'Okay, now, Lisa, please tell us what you know about Aaron, about his life, what sort of person he was, what made him tick, what he liked, what he hated, people who were close to him, you know…just let it go… Try not to miss anything, even a small or unimportant detail, as it might seem to you, could bring light on his disappearance.' Arina's voice sounded soothing and friendly, and convincing. When she wanted, she could be exceptionally amiable and winning.

'I'm afraid, my story won't take much time,' Lisa gave a small apologetic smile and continued. 'I'm a teacher of English literature, you know, at a small independent school. In the Harrogate area. It's called "Lombardy Poplar Grammar School", quite a pontifical name, don't you think? But, anyway, the school is nice and not far from home. And that was, of course, where we met for the first time.' Lisa stopped and sighed.

'As we've learned so far, Mr Statham had been employed as a PE teacher, but excuse my ignorance…erm…he was not…he couldn't run anymore…'

'Mr Weir…'

'Please, call me Luke!'

'Luke, I know what you mean,' a faint smile rippled across her lips, 'we were all puzzled. We knew that he was a very successful marathon runner in the past. He was a sort of celebrity, you know, winning all these international sports events. He had a great future ahead of him. At the last Olympic games, the last for him,' Lisa stumbled for a moment, brought her hand up to her big, lipstick free mouth and brushed away non-existent crumbs, then looked at them ruefully and went on. 'He came third, would you imagine, he won a bronze medal. An Olympic bronze medal!'

'So, what did actually happen to him?' asked Luke impatiently.

'Oh, that was silly, a very silly accident. Like all accidents, I suppose. Avoidable as well. He was repairing a roof. Just a small job, putting on a few new tiles. But he wanted to do it by himself. Why was he doing this? I don't know. Maybe, because he wanted to impress his new girlfriend. Yes, ironically, it was his girlfriend's house. And he was not afraid of heights, it was the very opposite, he was a very keen and experienced rock climber, you know.'

At this instance, Arina shifted her position nervously.

'Isn't it odd that he had never had any falls or traumas while climbing all these peaks and famous mountains? And there he was, on the top of the roof, smiling and whistling, showing off… and next moment—he was in the air, falling down. He woke up weeks later just to learn that he would probably never be able to walk and that this bitch, pardon my French, had left him.'

'What was his reaction?' Arina asked.

'Of course, he was totally devastated. Later, when we were talking about this, he admitted that the most upsetting thing for him was not that this dumb blonde shed him like tiresome, old-fashioned clothes; but that he didn't notice any hazard on this damn roof. That he fell like an amateur. He was still puzzling how it happened. He was going back to this moment again and again, asking himself what went wrong. Slippery roof after the rain? Rotten safety plank? Dazzling sun in his eye distorting the vision? It was his obsession for the next year.'

'What about you, what do *you* think caused him to fall?' queried Arina.

'What do I think?' Lisa mused for a moment, 'I think that he was cocky, that he was too sure about himself, he was just careless. And I think, no, I'm sure that he understood this himself. Not then, later, when his emotions had faded away and he had regained his usual coolness and steady headedness... Ohh! Who is that?' Lisa exclaimed pointing towards the window.

****

She had all reasons to be surprised. The massive shape of a ginger tabby materialised on the windowsill.

'Nero, you shouldn't be here' Arina rebuked this monstrous creature who was coldly observing Lisa with his impudent translucent eyes.

'Nero? What an unusual name...'

'Yeah, it suites him pretty well, he is a destroyer.'

'What do you mean?'

The answer to Lisa's question came immediately. One lash of his thick, peach and cream ringed adorned tail—and a pot with a small cactus went down with a nasty crash.

'What have you done! Luke you shouldn't let him in, how many times have I had to tell you!' shouted Arina.

Undisturbed in the slightest, Nero jumped down heavily and raced to the bookshelves. With the power of a professional athlete, he climbed up to the top shelf, dropping on his way one or two volumes, which looked equally old and valuable, and settled there comfortably for a long and peaceful siesta.

'He is a clever beast!' exclaimed Luke with a broad smile. 'He was hiding, who knows where. Honestly, I have tried my best!'

'You know the rest,' added Arina sarcastically. Then, addressing Lisa, 'Sorry for all this disturbance. Can we continue? So, can you tell us, to the best of your knowledge, of course, what did actually happen to Aaron, in medical terms I mean?'

Lisa smiled politely and rearranged her nervous hands.

'Yes, as a matter of fact, I can answer your question. He had a lumbar spine injury which affected the mobility of his legs. At first both legs were paralysed, then the left was slowly getting better, regaining some mobility back. So, you can say, he was lucky in the end. It could have been much, much worse.'

'So, he could actually walk?' asked Arina eagerly and cast a triumphal glance at Luke's direction.

'Yes,' Lisa replied pensively, 'the first year after his accident he had been confined to a wheelchair, but later on he learned to get by using a pair of crutches, or even only one crutch or a special walking stick occasionally. He was very good with them, deft, you know. Adroit. When you saw Aaron, you would never have thought about him as a cripple. He moved so swiftly, so easily, at least he gave you such an impression. He had this sort of aura about him.

'All his students adored him. It appeared to be that he was a naturally born teacher. And proved to all of us by his own example that you don't have to physically participate in all these games in order to involve students. He could make a proper career as a national coach, I am sure of this! But preferred to stay with us and train girls. He seemed so happy, you know. Especially when he was permitted to organise this running club for those who were interested in long distance running. He was over the moon then.'

'What you are saying about Mr Aaron Statham is all very positive. You also strongly believe that he didn't run away, right?'

Lisa nodded.

'Okay,' Arina continued, 'in this case, how do you explain all the police findings undermining your version?'

'You don't believe me?' Lisa asked desperately, 'why are you taking my…'

'We are not talking about believing or not believing here,' interrupted Lady Holroyd firmly, 'we are here to find the truth. What did actually happen to Mr Statham? We are not taking sides here. Do you understand this? Very well. May I continue? When you calm yourself down, I will repeat my question.'

Luke cleared his throat and looked at his boss reproachfully, then said to Lisa softly, 'You have to excuse us for our bluntness, but we have to ask these questions, some of them will be unpleasant, even hurtful. Without them it would be very difficult to help you.'

'I understand. And it puzzled me since I'd seen it. You are talking about this footage taken by video cameras at the cash machine?'

'Yes, by CCTV, that is correct. This footage, showing Mr Statham using his own Lloyds Bank credit card, withdrawing £200 from the cash machine outside the main branch of the named bank, in broad day light, in the centre of Leeds, in a calm and confident manner, just a week after his supposed disappearance, is indeed our main problem,' Arina's voice sounded detached and unemotional, but the effect of her words was unmistakably accusing.

'I don't know what to say. Really, what the hell! It is him, all right. It is Aaron.'

'Also, according to the police report, his passport, all his credit cards, his mobile phone and his laptop are also missing. And this is without mentioning the text messages you have received from him over the last year, not yet.'

Lisa seemed to shrink in size somehow, she was stooping in her chair, the mask of grief glued to her face.

'Let us look at this image again,' Luke suggested reassuringly.

'I haven't got it with me, I'd seen it at the police station, of course. This detective… I couldn't remember his name, one of the two who were dealing with my case, had shown me this photo.'

'No problem,' cheerfully replied Luke, 'we've got it on our computer, together with other relevant files, which had been kindly sent to us by DCI Crawnshaw.'

At this point Lady Holroyd sniggered discreetly.

Luke took his already opened laptop from the portable desk and placed it down on the coffee table. Then, with just a few clicks he found the required picture, enlarged it and positioned the screen so it would face Lisa. He had prepared well for this meeting and was not shy to demonstrate it in front of his quirky boss.

Lisa shook her head in disbelief. She brought her palms to her face like trying to shield her eyes, but with her fingers spread wide apart.

'I don't know, I'm really lost here. It's him, I agree, but at the same time he looks somehow different.'

'Why?' asked Arina leaning forward and craning her neck, so she could also see the paused footage, 'what is different about him?'

Now they were all looking at a grainy, black and white image of the missing marathoner. Even on this poor-quality shot Aaron Statham was easily recognised. With his tousled, lively blonde hair partly covering his right eye and his broad, healthy-looking face, which usually made him look boyish and nonchalant. Except for this time.

'He looks serious. There's no smile on his face. I've rarely seen him so serious, if ever...'

'But, surely, it's not a surprise, is it? Taking into account the situation,' Arina looked at Lisa hard.

'But maybe, he was *forced* to disappear, I don't know, some nasty people were after him. Pressurising him, threatening him to hurt me...and...and he was forced to run away.'

It was obvious that even Lisa herself didn't believe this bosh.

'All right,' said Arina wearily, 'did he have many enemies? No, I thought not. Any ex-girlfriends, except the one with the dodgy roof, who wanted to take revenge on him? No. Was he rich? No...sorry, what?'

'There was a question of money brought up by the police once. No, he wasn't rich himself, but what I mean is that his uncle is a real millionaire.'

'What?' Lady Holroyd and Luke exclaimed simultaneously.

'The police toyed for a while with this idea of kidnapping Aaron for ransom, that sort of thing. But nobody had actually contacted Lord Mount-Hubert, nobody had asked for money.'

'Excuse me, Lord Mount...' great interest flashed in Arina's eyes now.

'That's Aaron's rich uncle, Lord Mount-Hubert.'

'So, what you're saying is that Aaron had a very rich close relative? Why did you not start with this?' Arina couldn't conceal her annoyance.

'I don't know, I didn't think that it might be of any importance, the police had lost interest in him fairly soon.'

'We are not here to follow the police steps, no matter how many mistakes they have made,' the icy remark of Lady Holroyd-Kugushev was full of sarcasm.

'If Mr Statham had survived his uncle, would he have inherited some of his money?' Luke quickly barged in.

Lisa hesitated for a few seconds before answering the question, and when she did at the end, her voice sounded flat and lifeless.

'He was the only one who would have inherited everything. His uncle is very ill, terminally ill, that's the reason why I knew. He doesn't have more than half a year to live.'

Chapter 3

'Can we trust her?' Lady Holroyd-Kugushev asked thoughtfully, addressing mainly herself, 'was she lying to us? Was there any truth in what she had told us?' Arina knew too well that, when Luke Weir was driving his precious Jaguar F-Type of a frosted-cherry shade, he was deaf as a beetle. You could get more sense from any of her three cats than from him at these times.

'Erm…who?' Luke was driving fast, emerald hills and valleys, picturesque woodlands and sunlit openings with herds of spotted deer were flashing before their eyes.

'Lisa, of course. Can you slow down, Luke, please! I don't wish to join my late husband, not yet!'

It was the next day, and Lady Holroyd together with Luke Weir were on their way to interview a few people at "Lombardy Poplar Grammar School For Girls".

'I think…erm…you're wrong…bastard!'

'I beg your pardon?'

'It's this idiot in front of us, dragging his tractor in the middle of the road. We have to tail him for who knows how long now. Dammit!'

Luke's usually placid face was red as a beetroot and his hair was standing up in an aggressive porcupine way. When he was behind the wheel, he became a very different man.

'Why don't you believe her?' Luke asked in a while, when he had calmed down and could think about something else, other than the annoyingly sluggish vehicle in front of them. They turned into a country road and were driving along a narrow lane flanked by gigantic Populus nigra "Italica".

'Because she might be the one who killed Aaron,' answered Arina calmly.

Luke pulled over the car and killed the engine. It was a very quiet road, the car's windows were pulled down and they could hear the wind rustling somewhere very high up, where still green upright branches were brushing the bottom of the weak blue sky.

For the first time, since they had taken the case, he felt frightened. It was a very frightening idea to think, that this timid, shy and very plain woman they had met yesterday, could be a cold-blooded murderer.

'Why did she bother to approach us then?'

'There is a big sum of money involved, very big, Luke. If she had planned it through, and I'm inclining to the idea of premeditated murder rather than a crime of passion, then she could use us to help her to look trustworthy in the eyes of the police, law or anybody who would doubt her rights.'

'Rights? I am not getting…or I see, you mean that she will somehow benefit from all of this. If Aaron had left a will where he stated her as his prime inheritor, Ooh…that's horrible!'

'Luke, we are talking about millions of pounds here. Think! This money could change all her life. I admit that she is a brilliant actress. She'd managed to fool even me for a time. Before she'd mentioned the uncle-millionaire.'

Bang!

Arina and Luke both jumped. Bang! Bang! Bang!

A huge bumblebee was playing a kamikaze, ramming the car's front window. Luke uttered a nervous giggle.

'In this case, how do you explain this footage of him?'

'Easily,' Lady Holroyd replied confidently, 'say, they agreed to cancel, no, more likely to postpone their wedding. A clever, manipulative woman (as Lisa surely is) could come up with a lot of very reputable reasons. For example, not to upset his dying relative, let him pass away in peace.'

'Do you think that he was opposing their marriage?'

'Haven't you seen her, Luke? Wait! Maybe he didn't even know about this? Yes, of course! She'd threatened him with this, that he wouldn't get his uncle's money!'

'Arina, please! Who had threatened who? Explain! Please!' Luke exclaimed in confusion.

'It's so simple. Whether the uncle had known about their wedding or not, it doesn't matter for now. She…Lisa persuaded Aaron to postpone the ceremony. Until this Lord…what's his name?

'Lord Mount-Hubert.'

'Until his death. Then they can get married and live happily after. In the meantime Aaron should hide somewhere, possibly in her place. To avoid silly questions from friends and family and so on. After a week they need money. Lisa is sending him to a cash machine in the centre of Leeds. Say, to avoid people who know him. He is caught on the camera. Good! That is her alibi. Then she bumps him off. Details are not important now! What she needs, is to *make an impression*. That is where we come in.'

'Hm…I'm not so sure…'

'You are never sure, my friend! C'mon! Let's go and see what others will tell us. I need some proof, any proof before putting this *Dawn French* behind the bars.'

'Dawn French?'

'Yes! Because she reminds me of her.'

'And texts—she could have sent them to herself using his mobile.'

'Of course! Just give me a little time and I'll weave a thick spider web around her. She won't even notice before it's too late! Before I catch her.'

'This sounds cruel!'

'You should know by now that I'm merciless when dealing with murderers!'

****

"Lombardy Poplar Grammar School For Girls" looked disturbingly old-fashioned, surrounded by its thick red brick wall with wrought iron gates, which were decorated with sharp arrowheads along their top and a school coat of arms in the middle. The latter consisted of acorns, oak-leaves and a scholastic-looking rook with a pair of round glasses perched on his crooked beak and a manuscript tightly grasped in his claws.

'Wow!' Luke couldn't help himself.

Lady Holroyd didn't say anything but gave him a stern look.

They heard a rasping sound, and the gates started to open automatically. They were certainly not as old as they pretended to be.

They drove through in silence. The school was looming behind a massive ancient oak tree which partly explained the school's crest. They stopped by the main entrance. It was oppressively silent. The whole place resembled a dead city. A city after the Last war.

Luke came out of the car first. The building was huge, built to last centuries. Its large dark windows were staring at intruders with hostility, the walls, covered with a trembling crimson-red mass of Boston Ivy, evoked an impression of armour washed in blood.

Arina joined Luke. She looked serious, with her tightly pressed lips and sunglasses, fully hiding her eyes. Shoulder to shoulder, they walked to the side door with a clear sign "Entrance for parents and other visitors". Inside, before being shown to the principal's office, they underwent a thorough check of their credentials by a bald, scrawny man, well in his mid-eighties.

'I'm *tremendously* pleased that you are going to look into this sad case. We *all* used to be extremely fond of this unfortunate young man. And it was an unforeseen shock, yes, I assure you. Nobody had the tiniest idea,' the headmistress, or principal as they called her here, shook her head solemnly.

'What's the idea you are talking about?' asked Lady Holroyd briskly.

The principal squinted at Arina through her droopy, puffed-up eyelids with a well-noticeable disapproval.

'The idea about the shameful disappearance of the groom before his wedding, of course! A proper scandal, I say. And both of the people directly involved in it were members of our very own staff. This is unspeakable for our well-respected school. School with traditions!'

'So, you think that Mr Statham has just run away?'

'Absolutely! What else? All this business about marrying was simply ridiculous!'

'Why?' inquired Luke, regretting almost immediately.

The principal sighed heavily and pressed her lips together. Sometimes the silence could be much more significant than any words. And that was definitely the case.

Luke felt a stab of pity for Ann. Everybody just assumed that she couldn't be loved because of her colourless plain appearance. How unfair! The whole of her life was probably hard and unfair, dull and unadventurous, Luke thought philosophically.

The headmistress was holding out an A4 piece of paper to them.

'Eh?'

'Here is the list we've prepared, me and my deputy, a list of names. For your convenience,' she explained coldly.

Luke wrinkled his nose trying very hard not to sneeze but failed at the end and went on his usual sneezing fit. Both ladies were staring at him crossly. He didn't like the place. It was stuffy and reeked of old-fashioned lavender fragrance sachets, which would be more appropriate in a nursing home rather than in a 21st century school.

'Are you feeling all right? Are you allergic to something or what?'

It was like he was back in the posh private school his parents had sent him to, and which he hated so much. The same atmosphere, the same manners, and absolutely the same questions. He wanted to shout, to swear, to behave wildly and unruly, he was slipping back in time.

'Would you mind slightly opening your window? Just a crack? Please.'

It was Lady Holroyd-Kugushev, putting on her best aristocratic tone, who came to his rescue. The coldest and the most contemptuous smile was passing her lips.

The day had started badly; logically, it finished equally badly. It crawled slowly as a fat, slimy slug, purposelessly and endlessly. Despite the opened window Luke developed a splitting headache, which he occasionally suffered from. In addition to this, the staff interviews proved to be a total waste of time. So repetitive, so predictable, echoing the principal's words.

'Ouch!' Luke cried and tried to push away his boss's determined hand holding a boiling kettle. In vain, though.

'Is it too hot or what?' she barked pouring the scolding contents down into a large ceramic bowl with his two feet the colour of overboiled carrots in it jiggling madly.

Lady Holroyd was not in her best mood, she was impatient to discuss today findings (however insignificant they were) and plan their next move with her secretary, who was instead delaying this by being awkward and too sensitive to her approved treatment procedures.

'Stop behaving like a spoiled toddler! I'm doing my best to put you back on your feet!'

'Thanks...but...'

'Enough! No 'buts' anymore! Just sit still for a moment, would you?'

Easier said than done. Luke was jammed in the deepest and the most uncomfortable armchair in Arina's living room, so close to a live fireplace that he was constantly worrying about his hair going up in flames, as his head was tilted back—an ice bag rapped in a towel was balancing on his forehead. With one hand Luke tried to stop this cold, dripping compress from sliding down, with the other he was stroking a very hairy cat who was resting on his lap. The cat had an enormous bushy tail and a heavy look. Brahms, the third cat in Lady Holroyd's household, equally resembled his namesake and a European Wildcat, some blood of which was definitely running through his veins. He had a whim to start using his enormous claws effectively if not cuddled, brushed or just ignored. Luke was well aware of this nice habit.

'Now you need a drink.'

'Exactly!' Luke cheered up a little. But not for long.

'There you go,' Arina placed a steaming mug down by his side.

'What is that?' asked Luke suspiciously.

'Just a traditional herbal tea, which is good for your migraine.'

'I thought…a drop of whisky would be much more appropriate. And, anyway, I think my head is better. Honestly, Arina, can you, please take this forest creature away from me.'

'Brahms, my sweetie come on, come with your mummy, we are not welcome here.'

The rain was slashing its fat drops against the French windows now. The weather had changed dramatically and there was not a tiny patch of blue sky left to be seen anywhere. Arina was standing by the window, her elegant silhouette with Brahms hanging over her shoulders was just visible against the ominous darkness. The only light they had was coming from the fading fire and a dimmed floor lamp stuck in the furthest corner of this vast room.

Luke cleared his throat. He didn't want to admit that those draconic measures of hers made him feel much better. His head was clear and light, and he could function once more.

'Erm…'

'Yes Luke, are you feeling better? Are you ready to go back to our little investigation?'

'Yes, thanks. I am fine,' he tried to pass this subject over as quickly as possible. 'Do you want to go over the whole lot of interviews or hover over anybody in particular?'

Arina didn't reply, instead she carefully put Brahms in a comfy looking plush chair with a plump green cushion on its seat. Then she leaped quickly away, just escaping the sharp teeth of this beast who was obviously not impressed with his owner's decision.

'They all were saying the same, did you notice?' Arina broken the silence.

They were both facing the dying flames, leaning back in the matching armchairs, Luke's Procrustean bed long forgotten.

Luke thought that he had never seen so many chairs, armchairs, divans and sofas put together in one room. He frowned, checked his steamed glasses with his index finger and stated gloomily, 'I reckon that we are back to square one.'

'Let's see what tomorrow will bring. Hopefully, these girls of his will give us something more useful.'

'Are there ten of them? From his running class?'

'Ten or eleven, I am not sure how many we will be allowed to talk to. This is all a bit of a game, Luke, games of our prudish principal who is scared stiff to let any hint of scandal escape the premises of her precious school.'

'Okay. And then?'

'Then, I think we had better split up. We have already lost a lot of time. I'll go and see Aaron's flat and you will visit this medical centre or sort of... do you remember Mr Baxter mentioned it?'

'Oh, this poor bloke! The only man in the school now.'

'You've forgotten the other one—this mummified sentinel,' giggled Arina.

The only male teacher, apart from Aaron Statham, employed by this strongly feministic school was Tom Baxter, a tall, stooped man of about forty plus, who taught physics and mathematics.

'Seriously, Arina, he was really helpful.'

'Hm...helpful...yes, you can say so, compared to this spiteful bouquet of Gorgons.'

'Ha-ha, exactly! Against their background Lisa doesn't look too bad, actually.'

'Don't mellow again, Luke! Listen, I think we've just found something,' Arina's voice sounded so quiet, it was almost a whisper, but Luke was covered in goose bumps in no time.

'What do you mean?'

'Tom, Mr Baxter, he told us that Aaron went to this rehabilitation place...a private physiotherapy clinic in Harrogate, right?'

Luke nodded.

'He didn't just go there occasionally. He was sort of obsessed with the place, it became an important part of his life for the last half year, at least. We don't know why, we can only speculate. To improve his mobility? To reduce some pain? It's not the main question for us right now.'

'What...what is the main...'

'Has Lisa mentioned about this clinic to us? No! Why?'

'Maybe she's simply forgotten?' tentatively suggested Luke.

'Maybe. Or maybe not. We can easily check this tomorrow, can't we?'

****

The next day they were taken straight to a makeshift interview room without any delays. The ancient custodian even produced a thin and utterly false smile when directing them to a sports hall—their temporary headquarters.

A small group of slim and long-legged girls was shifting on their feet outside. They looked nervous and excited at the same time.

The first girl, Angel, was the prettiest of all. With long blond hair falling over her shoulders and big blue eyes, she was very sure of herself and her seduction skills.

'What can you tell us about your ex-teacher Mr Statham?' Lady Holroyd-Kugushev asked.

'A lot. I knew him *very* well,' she fluttered her long eyelashes at them, mainly at Luke, of course. With an infallible instinct she sensed his weakness and fully summoned her charm up.

'Tell us more, please. He was your coach we heard.'

'Oh…this…hm…of course, he was a brilliant coach,' she uttered a little sob. Then she took a deep breath, swayed her hair back, widened her eyes so her impeccably applied mascara would not be compromised and continued in a weak, unsteady voice, 'what I meant was that we were *really* close. Do you know what I mean?' the question was aimed directly at Luke but they both shook their heads.

'We were in love!'

Darkness was gathering by the corners of the sports hall, its hanging rings resembled the gallows, the silence, which followed, weighed them down heavily.

'In love?' asked Arina coldly, 'explain yourself, please.'

'Ha,' a bitter snigger escaped Angel's lips. 'You don't believe me, I can see!'

'How old are you?' asked Luke bluntly.

She held a long theatrical pause before answering.

'I am eighteen this year.'

'He was about to get married, you know,' Arina said.

'Oh! That was a joke! He and that…that…toad! You've seen her!'

'But the wedding was going ahead,' Luke added.

'No! He was going to marry ME! He promised me!' the girl cried out angrily.

'All right, calm down now,' ordered Arina. 'So, you are saying that Mr Aaron Statham was going to call off his wedding with Lisa, sorry, Miss Roberts. Is that correct?'

'Yes,' Angel replied quieter.

'And…' prompted her Arina.

'Marry me. After I finished school. In a year's time.'

'Instead, he has disappeared,' finished Luke.

'She must have killed him, what else?' Angel twisted her lips but didn't cry.

'There is another possible scenario,' Lady Holroyd said darkly.

The girl left, and they exchanged looks. The case was obtaining more colours, more depths. Angel rapidly joined Lisa in their list of suspects.

'Hi,' said the girl, called Olivia, with dull green eyes and a small button nose. She looked bored even before they started asking her questions.

'I dunno,' she replied on almost everything they asked her.

Next came in a tall dark-skinned girl with a face of Nefertiti and manners of a princess, which was not too far from the truth—she was the heiress of a very wealthy oil baron.

'You don't have to address me by my full name,' she said, clinking graciously her thin silver bracelets, 'Fairuza will be enough. Which means a woman of triumph,' she added casually.

'That was a very relevant piece of information, thank you…Fairuza,' Arina said sarcastically. 'But we need to ask you a few questions regarding the disappearance of your teacher, Mr Aaron Statham.'

'Oh, I know. Poor guy! He was *so unlucky*!'

'Unlucky…in what aspect?' Luke asked baffled.

Fairuza fixed him with her bottomless black eyes.

'He fell for the wrong girl,' she stated.

'Why do you think Miss Roberts was wrong for him?'

'Miss Roberts? What has she got to do with this?' Fairuza said scornfully.

'He was getting married to her! Somehow people here keep forgetting about their upcoming wedding,' Arina said crossly.

The "baron's" daughter laughed sonorously, confidently demonstrating her perfectly pearly teeth. Luke shook his head a few times, their interview was more and more resembling a mundane soap opera.

'He loved *me*, of course! But we couldn't get married. Is it not obvious? My family, you know, he was not good enough for me,' she gave out a little sigh.

Luke and Arina looked at each other. *Another one?*

'Hm…I am sorry to break the news to you…but we have been told that Mr Statham was involved with…another girl from your running group,' Arina informed her.

'Really?' Fairuza didn't sound too surprised or upset, 'is her name Angel by any chance? She's delusional, everybody knows that. Don't listen to her, that girl is full of lies up to her long nose!'

Arina had had enough by then and gestured to Luke that she was going to pop out for a few minutes.

Ms Kale, the principal, was leaning against her window, peering tensely through its thick glass. Her heart was leaping like a March hare, her face was red and hot. She was extremely confused. Why was he there? Down there, hiding in the bushes like a thief? Why was he back? She was not mistaken, it was definitely Aaron Statham under her window, spying on her. She shivered. She felt danger. Something was not quite right with him. About him?

Then she saw these two private detectives leaving the school. She screwed up her face. Lady…what was her aristocratic name? Arrogant little bitch! Snooping around, fishing for secrets. Secrets should be left alone!

At least the limping fugitive had enough sense to hide away. They passed him by a few meters without noticing. That is a modern sleuth for you! Ms Kale wrinkled her nose in disgust.

But really, she shouldn't be too worried. What could they find out? Nothing! The girls were a bunch of born liars. There was less than an ounce of truth in the ocean of their nonsensical blabbering.

How she hated them! Particularly the older ones. All of them groomed, sophisticated, well-travelled and well-spoken. They laughed at her all the time. She was very aware of this. She might be ugly and old, but not stupid. Sometimes she pleased herself with thoughts of how she would slap, and slap, and slap their pretty faces until they turned to a malformed pulp. The principal smiled lustfully. She did miss the old days of corporal punishment.

The intruders had long gone, as well as her students. The staff also left one-by-one. The cleaners came and went. Only she stayed. As always. As she did when her parents were still alive. And when they died. For a long time now. But she—stayed. No husband, no children of her own, no pets. Just the school, which she'd inherited and run for the last fifteen years. And had lived there. Since she was a little girl. Their big family flat, where she grew up, was actually on the top floor of the main school building. How gothic and how sad. She was chained to these Victorian red-brick walls, and nobody was going to come and rescue her. There were no knights on white horses left anymore...

Ms Kale blinked and wiped away a few scarce tears from her flabby cheeks. She clasped her hands together and got a grip on herself. Enough feeling sorry for herself! Back to reality!

How very right she was about Aaron! How could that ugly cow win his heart? Impossible! So, being a true gentleman, he preferred not to hurt her feelings. No, he had just gone. But why was he still there, lurking in the gardens? Did he want to communicate with somebody? Perhaps, with her? She was always very nice to him, very understanding.

The principal drew a deep breath. If she was younger... twenty years...or more...who knows? It was getting late, and she was struggling to see anything down there. Her poor sight didn't cope with the growing darkness very well.

Suddenly something caught her attention. At first, she took him for an outstretched oak's bough moving under gusts of a strong wind. Then she realised—the man with a stick was waving to her.

Ms Kale felt uneasy. She was not so sure anymore. In the huge dark building she was on her own. Surrounded by tall trees, which suddenly seemed so alien to her, and the howling wind. And not a soul except the crippled man with the white mask of a face which she could no longer recognise.

Diary 1

Your face has a funny shape, almost rectangular. Bony. Not very attractive. And you are not an attractive person, sorry. In Victorian times they would have described you as a plain woman with heavyset features. You don't smile often which is probably right, why should you?

And now...at first you looked surprised, then confused and now—you are scared. You are looking around, but you should know better—there is nobody except me and you. You prefer solitude and there you are. Only yourself to blame.

You are trying to say something, not very clear, but I understand.

'Is it you? But how...'

'Of course. It's me! Who else it could be but me?'

I suppose, it's a natural female reaction to lose her mind in a stressful situation. But I better stop dwelling on this subject, it's not a good time or place to do so. I will indulge myself later.

You don't like my answer, I can see it. I also can see how panic is shooting its roots through your entire body. Your, normally fairly small, eyes are getting really wide, their pupils are enormous, your face is pallid, it is noticeable even under its usual healthy ruddy colour. And you are trembling, like an aspen leaf.

But it's time now.

I'm looking behind you, I am waving my hand in a welcoming gesture, I'm smiling.

And, of course, you turn your head back. You don't have time to realise your mistake. I'm quick. I'm also well prepared. The rock in my hand is heavy but easy to hold on, it goes exactly where it is aimed, at your temple. You fall down.

I'm calm, composed, organised. It doesn't matter that you are still breathing. What is important is that you are quiet.

I open my backpack. Get a roll of Sellotape out of it. My multi blade penknife is always with me, it's been with me since my fourteenth birthday. I cut tape in short strips, but long enough to cover your thin mouth and both of your nostrils.

Criss-cross. Criss-cross. Criss-cross. Then a few longer strips—to go around your head, to secure the smaller pieces. I like order, tidiness.

I look at you. You look ugly. I don't feel pity or remorse. I think it's better this way. I am not a violent person, but I have to do this. Nothing personal, believe me. It is survival instinct.

Farewell!

Don't be worried—your body will not be left unattended. I will look after it. You will be safe for now. Safe and tranquil. It's not the first time I am doing this. And not the last. I am afraid.

Chapter 4

The first impression was that Aaron Statham, the owner of this flat, had just popped out and would be back any minute. The penthouse apartment in a five-storey modern block was airy and spacious, and through its glass walls gave a captivating view over the Leeds-Liverpool canal.

Lady Holroyd-Kugushev was sitting on the floor in a *Sukhasana* pose, with her shins crossed and legs folded, in the middle of the open-plan kitchen-living area and meditating. Using her usual method, she was trying to penetrate beyond the visible. To see deeper. To make inanimate things talk and reveal their secrets.

She inhaled deeply through her nose, then exhaled slowly. It felt like breathing in nicotine, she thought. Oh, how she missed her cigarettes on these occasions!

She was inhaling for a count of four, holding her breath for another four counts and exhaling the same way. She was trying to absorb, to sense the atmosphere of the place where Mr Statham had been seen in person the last time, the day before the wedding.

Unfortunately, nothing was coming to her mind right now. She put her hands with the palms down on the flooring, its bleached wood parquet bathed in the late morning sun, and felt pleasant warmth, but nothing else.

She got up and walked slowly around the apartment once again. The place looked very comfortable and expensive. Scarcely, but functionally furnished. Not many books on the shelves, which were mainly used to display Aaron's trophies or exotic knick-knacks from different countries.

A few huge modern pictures adorned the walls. One had a bunch of red and blue balloons stuck in a filthy looking passage between two garages. On the other picture there was a girl jumping in a health threatening position, bending backwards like a witch, against the walls covered in graffiti. An array of rainbow-coloured circles had inundated the third canvas. Arina wrinkled her nose; though she was not a great admirer of this sort of art, she was forced to admit that these pictures appended a certain zest to the decor.

Arina sauntered into the bedroom. The dark blue spread on the king size bed matched the shade of the curtains and walls. Above the bed head there was hanging yet another picture—an oil painting of some yellow and red sloppy objects dangling from black sticks. It would require an extensive imagination to recognise an autumn theme there, thought Arina and chortled nervously.

A shining dream-bathroom, with everything you can possibly imagine to be present in the modern washing place, and a second bedroom didn't arise any interest either. Except proving even more the very good financial status of the young flat occupant.

Musing on this, Arina returned to the living area. It seemed that her visit was fruitless. Arina went back to the transparent front and once again admired the view. She carefully pressed her index finger against the glass, it was so clear, almost invisible. And everything in this apartment was so clean, so pristine.

At this point she felt suddenly alarmed. She looked nervously around. Fatty, green leaves of houseplants were shiny and glossy, full of life. The shelves were free of any dust, even a speck of dust, to be precise. Above all, a tall crystal vase with a bunch of yellow roses was standing on the dining table in the kitchen area.

Lady Holroyd rushed there, annoyed with herself for missing out such important detail. As she feared, the flowers were real and fresh. The water in the vase was also fresh and didn't have the unpleasant, stale smell which follows any old water.

She froze. She stopped breathing. She listened.

A sound.

A sound which was coming from the front door.

Like a key moving in a keyhole. Like somebody trying to come in.

She understood it too late. She felt useless. She felt stupid. She *was* stupid! It was so obvious! Even a child would have noticed! But she…she was submerged in her own thoughts, locked in her own world. Imaginative world. As far as possible from reality. And now, she would have to pay the price.

Arina heard the sound of the opening door. Closing door. Some rustling. Then heavy steps. Heavy steps which stopped right behind her. She quickly turned around to face her enemy.

'Oh, hello there,' Lisa looked rattled, with flushed cheeks and wandering eyes. 'I thought…I though…it was silly of me…'

'Hi, Lisa,' Arina tried to sound calm, breathing in and out, in and out, restoring her composure, 'what did you think?'

There was a long pause before Lisa replied.

'I thought…for a moment…that Aaron had returned. Would you like anything to drink?' she went to a range of chrome wall cabinets and confidently opened up one in the middle. 'Tea? We've got a good selection of herbal teas.'

'Yes, please, green tea will be fine. You obviously know this place well…'

'Of course, I stayed with Aaron almost every weekend. From Friday until Monday, when we would go to work together, I would drive. It was convenient, he didn't have to be worried about his journey to work, at least twice a week. It had been a real problem for him before we became a couple. He was not used to public transport, he couldn't drive anymore and relying on somebody to give him a lift…hm… it was not his habit. You know, I offered him to stay with me on working days, but he refused. You see, I live very close to the school, but in a small house, tiny actually, which I share with my elderly mother. Aaron hated the whole idea, I am afraid.'

'I understand,' Lady Holroyd took a sip from her cup. 'Do you come here often?'

'Twice a week, sometimes three…I have plenty of time on my hands nowadays…I just want to keep his flat clean and nice, and ready for his return…if he returns, of course,' she added dejectedly.

'I see,' drawled Arina noncommittally. 'Do you mind me asking, why don't you just stay here, like before, rather than going back to your Harrogate house every time?'

'It's not easy to put into words…it's just…it belongs to him. It was never my place, oh, don't think that I felt unwelcome here, or something like that. No, no! Quite the opposite. It's that the apartment and me are not compatible, if you know what I mean.'

'I think I do,' Arina replied.

Lisa blushed but couldn't stop herself.

'The flat is very stylish and expensive, if I may say—swish… Now look at me! I have never had illusions about myself,' she smiled joylessly. 'I always knew that I wouldn't fit in here or be part of this world. As you can probably guess, I came from a pretty poor family. We are not used to luxury and never will be. But Aaron tried. Gosh, he really tried his best with me. And you know, for a while it became bearable. But now…I don't see any point to live the life of somebody else.'

Lady Holroyd finished off her cup, stood up from her chair and came over to Lisa. She touched her shoulders in a slightly awkward manner, which she hoped would be taken for a gesture of reassurance.

'It's okay, Lisa, you don't have to go on and on about this. You don't have to explain anything. It's very understandable that you don't feel comfortable here anymore, without Mr Statham it doesn't seem the same, does it?'

Lisa sobbed quietly.

'Can I do anything for you? Do you want me to stay with you for a little bit?'

'Thanks. Thanks a lot. I am really sorry for this pathetic behaviour. It is not the real me,' Lisa was patting dry her eyes with a piece of white tissue, which Arina pulled out of an elegantly carved wooden box and passed to her. 'And yes, if you don't mind…I need to show you something…Would you like some more tea or some wine, perhaps? I am going to have a glass myself.'

'I am not in a hurry,' lied Arina.

****

Sorry for everything. I know it is unforgiveable. I just cannot be with you. I don't deserve you. You will be much happier with someone else. Love. Aaron. 26 September 2015

Please, stop looking for me! It will not bring any good to either of us. I don't want to be found. There are a lot of things going on you don't know about. Xxx Aaron. 30 September 2015

I am alive and well, considering… That's what you need to know. Don't try to contact me! Anyway, you'll not be able to. I change my number all the time. Aaron. 23 October 2015

That is my farewell to you. I will try to explain why I did what I did. I became involved with nasty people, I had no idea who they really were. Now they are after me. The reason is not important. I feel awful about all this, but nothing could be done…It would be dangerous for me (and you!) if I didn't run away. You must put your mind at rest and try to forget me. I wish you a Merry Christmas and a much happier New Year. Forever yours, Aaron. 24 December 2015

Don't involve anybody! I've told you many times, I've gone off on my own free will. Don't forget about this! I don't want to be found by you or by anybody else! This is my decision—respect it! Aaron. 3 October 2016

Luke Weir frowned. He was not aware of any recent activities of the missing marathoner. He'd read previous messages, of course, and not once. But the last one…Lisa had been economic with the truth, at the very least.

'Mr Weir, our clinical director Mr Globe is ready to see you,' a blonde and very fit looking receptionist announced.

Luke jumped. It took him a moment to realise where he was. He gave another quick look at Aaron's messages displayed on his smartphone before putting it away and following the tall formidable blonde.

They walked fast, but Luke had seen enough to make his mind up about Physiotherapy & Pilates Practice "Better Life". It looked cheerful and properly managed. A long and wide corridor, with half a dozen therapy rooms to the left and rest areas with comfortable soft chairs, coffee tables and potted plants—to the right, led them to Mr Globe's office.

After Luke introduced himself and briefly explained the business of his visit, a drawn-out pause followed.

Finally the clinical director uttered, 'I cannot help you. You must understand, surely, that I cannot disclose any of my patients' names.'

His meaty face, bedecked with a thin aperture of a mouth and a pair of gimlet eyes, looked dull and wintery.

'Okay, no worries, in that case can I have a word with his therapist, please?'

'I'm afraid, that would be impossible,' Mr Globe said unemotionally.

It was like being stuck in a honey pot. To be in a fly skin, to become a fly caught in honey. Trapped and powerless.

'And why would that be?' Luke couldn't hide his sarcasm.

'Julia Bower is not working with us anymore.'

Luke waited for continuation in vain. It was a highly laborious conversation.

'Can you please tell me where she is now? I would really appreciate it.'

'I don't know,' said Mr Globe and added already on his own initiative, 'she went on holiday and has not come back.'

For a second Luke thought that this was a joke. Out of place, out of character for this robot in an expensive flashy suit, sitting motionlessly in front of him, like he was nailed to the chair. But still a joke…

His misunderstanding didn't last long. And it was then when he comprehended for the very first time that they were dealing with somebody very evil and merciless, and extremely clever.

A cold shiver ran up his spine when he was walking back to reception along the corridor. Luke Weir felt like he had been watched, watched for some time now and the watcher was not far away.

'That was quick,' the tall, muscular receptionist flashed a set of perfectly white teeth at him.

Luke was holding the door handle, ready to go.

'Unfortunately for me,' he shrugged his shoulders, 'it looks like I came here for nothing.'

'And you came here to…you don't mind me asking…to investigate what specifically?'

'Investigate?'

'You're a private detective are you not?'

Luke couldn't argue with such a blatant fact.

'Yeah…we are investigating a missing person case.'

'At last!' cried out the receptionist. And then added, darting quick glances around, 'do you know what? I am going for my lunch break now! It's a café just round the corner. We can have a chat there. Much more private. If you don't mind, of course. I am Susan by the way.'

The machine gun stopped for a moment and Luke seized the opportunity.

'Nice to meet you too, my name is…oh, you know it already, silly of me. Hm, sure, it's a great idea to have something to eat…to be honest with you, I am ravenous.'

Susan didn't waste much time. She was ready to go straight away, as she was, wearing a loose fit white blouse with a badge, clipped on to its lapel, and a pair of cropped black leggings.

'It's quite cold outside.' Luke warned.

'Oh, don't worry, the place is literally next door.'

Which truly it was. And that was the only good point in Luke's opinion about the vegie café with an idiotic name 'Good morning, guys!'. The furnishings were equally irritating. The plastic chairs of bright lime green and meaty pink were tough to sit on and hard to move, their heavy metal legs scratched the stone floor with menace. The walls were painted in a merry yellow colour and bore a few placards advertising the advantages of various healthy diets. The person who was responsible for assorting them together was obviously suffering from colour blindness.

But worse was still to come. Luke decided not to waste time going through the endless menu written in a tiny fancy font, almost undecipherable, but followed Susan's advice.

'So, what have you found out? Tell me please, please!' Susan started twirling her long locks of hair around her perfectly manicured fingers, her widely set eyes were burning agog, her too full to be natural lips were parted.

'Erm…you know what? We are actually looking into another case of a missing person.'

'What? What do you mean?'

'It was one of your patients who we are investigating, rather his disappearance…'

Luke felt nervous himself. He wasn't sure if showing his cards was a really great idea. He would have given a lot to have his eccentric boss by his side at that moment.

'Who? I cannot believe! Another missing person! Where are the police? As usual—nowhere! I am not surprised in the slightest that crime is soaring in our country!'

Their order arrived. The pinkish content of the drinks and acid-green matter on their plates matched the surrounding entourage grotesquely. Sometimes it's damn hard to be a sleuth, thought Luke grumpily and had a few careful sips of his drink.

'Oh, I forgot to warn you. Are you okay?' Susan asked nonchalantly when Luke started coughing spasmodically.

'Erm…what is *this*? Waiter! Waiter! Can I bother you for a glass of water! Just ordinary water, please! No, I don't want lemon, or lime, just plain water. Tap water will do.'

'Are you better? You gave me a fright. I thought you were having a fit or something. It's a nice drink, you know. Healthy. Good for your body.'

'It's…it's how can I put it?' Luke finished his second glass of water and found that he had not only survived such a terrible experience but was capable of speaking again. Five minutes ago he had not been so optimistic.

'Hm… I must admit, they've slightly overdone this today. They've put a little bit too much of that spicy stuff. Ginger and paprika. To clean up your chakras, you know.'

'What? It supposed to be a mix of cranberry and raspberry juices. At least I got that impression when I was looking at the menu. I was not aware that this café caters for fire-eaters.'

'And coconut milk.'

'Erm?'

'You've forgotten the coconut milk. In our drinks. It should give a cooling effect…soothing…you know.'

'Perhaps, it was not added after all. Now, can I ask you…'

'No, no! We must eat. It is not good for your astral body to talk while taking your food,' Susan smiled at him encouragingly and placed a forkful of green puree into her mouth.

Luke was not so brave. He toyed with his food for a while, poking at it with his fork, bringing a tiny piece to his mouth, smelling it, putting it back, looking around at other people who seemed to be accustomed to these fiery specialities.

'Just try! Please! And I will answer all your questions,' Susan finished her meal and was gazing at Luke.

'What is it? Why does it look so alarmingly green? Can you honestly tell me what ingredients are hidden in this concoction?'

'Ha-ha! Very funny! It's just some avocado and green beans mashed together, with a touch of lemongrass and green olives. That's all.'

'Lemongrass…I am not so sure. Okay, I will risk my life. Oh! It's not too bad. I am not in immediate danger just now. And I don't think I will be requiring the emergency service of the fire brigade yet.'

'Do you want anything else…dessert? They have very nice cakes here.'

'No, thank you very much,' answered Luke rapidly, 'can we talk now? I really want to ask you a few questions. Please?'

'Hm…sure, just give me a minute.'

She waved to the waitress and asked for two carrot cakes with pineapple mousse. Luke decided not to waste time arguing, there was also a tiny chance that both portions were meant for Susan herself.

'We are investigating the disappearance of Mr Aaron Statham. We've acknowledged that he'd been attending Pilates classes, together with some physiotherapy sessions, here, at your clinic. Strangely enough, he'd kept it a secret, at least from his fiancée.'

'Oh! But how did you find out about our Julia? There is a connection here, I can see it!'

'To be honest with you, we…we didn't know about Julia…'

'Bower!'

'Exactly! The reason I came down here was just to have a chat with people who had met Aaron. Maybe, some patients who attended the same group or, perhaps, his therapist…which appeared to be Miss Bower…'

'You think, they had run away together! Genius! That would explain everything!'

'Your cakes, guys!' the cheerful waitress confidently placed the second plate of carrot cake in front of him.

'I thought…' Luke started doubtfully.

'Dive in! It's very delicious and at the same time *extremely* low in calories!'

The cake resembled very sweet rubber with a strong carrot taste.

'Do you like it? I could eat tons of this!'

'Erm…' replied Luke evasively and quickly used the pause, caused by the fact that the gummy texture of the dessert made it impossible for his vis-à-vis to open her mouth for a while.

'When did Julia disappear? About a year ago?'

Susan vigorously shook her head. As soon as she managed to unglue her teeth, she shot out.

'No, no! A week ago. She went on a short break. To the Lake District. Canoeing or kayaking. One of them, I think. To be honest with you I don't see any great difference between them.'

Susan had to stop conversing in order to defeat her cake.

'What? Are you saying that she has been missing only for one week?'

'Yep.'

'How do you know that…' he stopped short. Ran his long fingers through his hair, causing them to resemble a porcupine hairdo even more than usual.

'Know what?'

'That she is missing. It was just a week, she easily could have decided to stay longer, canoeing. It's a brilliant place for canoeing…' answered Luke absentmindedly.

'And kayaking,' added Susan and giggled.

'Exactly!'

'If you knew her, you wouldn't have asked this. She had never ever missed a day off work! Would you believe? She is always on time, I mean that. You could set your watch by her. Even our *Lump of Ice* got it. That she is not coming

55

back. Only he thinks that she's found a better job. But I don't believe that! She would have told me.'

'An ice lump…I'm a little bit lost here.'

'Our boss! Mr Globe.'

'Ha! How stupid of me! But please continue!'

'I thought, you were not listening…'

'No, no, quite the contrary. So, you were close, you and Julia?'

'Not strictly speaking…' Susan hesitated, 'we had good workplace relations, as we say, but close…she was not close to anybody. In our place, I mean.'

Luke Weir stared at the window. A gloomy autumn afternoon stared back at him. The window spattered with cold rain. A narrow cobblestone street lined with terrace houses, their brick walls of bull's blood colour.

Facts started lining up in Luke's mind, one after another, like skewered cubes of raw meat.

2nd October. Their agreement to take the case of the missing marathoner.

3rd October. The text message on Lisa's phone. Ten months after the last one. At the same day of their first visit to the school.

4th October. Schoolgirls telling porkies. Any scintilla of truth in their weird stories? To be discovered yet or, more likely, not.

10th October, today. The physio clinic. Missing therapist. Julia Bower. She was expected to be at work on the 3rd of October. The same 3rd of October…

That was very interesting. Luke lightly massaged his temples with his long fingers. As he always did when he felt a thrill building up inside of him. They were on the right track. At least. After a frustrating week wasted on checking and rechecking all these endless and nonsensical gossips. Not to mention a meeting with Lisa's mother. That was certainly an experience which would be difficult to forget.

But he was missing something else. Some other facts managed to slip away from him. Maybe the crucial one which would give them a proper clue to this mystery. It was like a mosquito buzzing around, irritating and evasive. He sighed.

'Are you with me?'

Luke looked at the rosy cheeked girl, full of enthusiasm and energy, gaping at him in a sort of annoying way. His thoughts had wondered so far away that he couldn't even recollect her name at first.

'You're an extremely absentminded person for a detective, don't you think? We can offer you a mind concentration program to deal with your problem. Very popular, by the way. Tailored to suit everybody. Reduced prices until Christmas.'

'Thanks! But I don't have any concentration, more to the point, mind problems, as far as I am aware,' muttered Luke crossly.

'But you might be *not* aware, you see the difference!'

'Susan, would it be possible for you to stop seeing me as a potential client, just for a second? Please?' Luke produced, not without an effort, his most charming smile.

'Oh…sure…I was just trying to be helpful…'

'Very much appreciated, honestly, but perhaps we will leave this topic for the next time? Agreed? Smashing!'

'You asked me why I was so sure that something bad had happened to Julia? Know what? She was a maniac of routine. She would always go on her holiday the same time and the same places every year, would you believe that?'

'You are saying…'

'Yes! She would go on holiday three time a year. At Christmas for two weeks to Spain, to see her mother and stepdad. They live there permanently now. For another two weeks in June to visit her best school friend in Cornwall. And the end of September, for precisely one week, she would spend in the Lake District.'

'Was everybody else familiar with her habits?' asked Luke, but he could already predict the answer.

'Yes, of course, she didn't make a secret of this. Moreover, how could she even if she wanted to? In a place like ours? It would have been simply impossible! Not only all our staff would have known but all her patients as well.'

'Who did Julia go to the Lake District with?'

'Nobody,' Susan paused for a moment then continued, 'it was a sort of holiday for single people, you know…to meet other single people. For friendship and so on…'

'Dating holiday?' asked Luke quickly.

'I wouldn't call it as such…but there was certainly an element of romance there. You see, Julia was a workaholic, yes, workaholic. I mean, she still is…' Susan looked confused.

'I know exactly what you mean,' Luke came to rescue her, 'her life was strictly scheduled, right? But she wanted some fun, we all want fun time from time,' he smiled encouragingly.

'You're right. The problem was that Julia's private life was not very exciting…quite dull to be honest with you. I even felt sorry for her. She was not, as you say, a popular girl.'

'What do you mean?'

'Good looking, easy going…chatty…'

'Aha! I see, not like you, actually exactly the opposite, as I grasped it.'

Susan giggled and blushed slightly.

Diary 2

*I cannot believe how easy it was! To fool you guys! The hardest part for me was not to burst out laughing. You, silly billy Mr **Weiry**! You looked at me, through me, like I didn't exist, like I was transparent. But I was just three metres away from you. Did it not make you scared?*

But you know what? I think that even you began to sense something. Even you, a conceited buffoon, started to sense danger. At the clinic you positively looked spooked. And how right you were! You shouldn't have gone there, you shouldn't!

I was watching you. And I am watching you now. And I will be watching you…I will become your shadow…but unlike a real shadow you will not be able to get rid of me on a cloudy day.

If you and your batty old companion don't stop snooping around…then again, it doesn't matter, you will not find anything.

But I don't want to lie to myself, you are annoying me. I must admit, just a little—it's true. But annoying.

And I cannot stand people who are bothering me. People who are throwing sand in the wheels. So, my advice to you will be simple—leave the case alone.

Chapter 5

Luke was driving back to Lady Holroyd-Kugushev's house, a cheeky smile glued to his lips. He was really pleased with himself and looking forward to presenting all his findings to his picky boss. True, he hadn't managed to speak to anybody who knew Aaron personally, nor did he get the names of those people. Instead, he absorbed a lot of highly important and interesting information from his new acquaintance, who doubtless would be a valuable ally to their investigation.

Luke was moving at a snail's speed now, he was properly stuck in an endless traffic jam. Strangely, the delay didn't upset him much. His thoughts ran back to their meeting with Susan.

He agreed with her fully, that something sinister must have happened to Miss Bower. It had nothing to do with premonitions or visions, so much favoured by Arina, instead it had a logical basis underneath.

She was one of the most important links to Mr Statham's disappearance and now it was her who had disappeared. The next day after they had started their investigation, the same day when they had visited the school.

Coincidence? Luke shook his head in disbelief. You must be joking, old boy! That means...somebody...the killer (if it was, of course, a murder) was following them very closely.

Luke was drumming his fingers on the top of the steering wheel absentmindedly. He was thinking about Miss Bower. His information on her was scarce but it was something. What did he know for sure? Was she dead? Probably. Was she murdered? Probably. Did she know her murderer? Certainly yes. If she was murdered, she knew her murderer.

She might have died accidentally, however. Drowned for instance. But then it would be fair to suggest that the authorities would inform her relatives, work, friends if she had any, whatever...but definitely—work. Nobody had contacted

Physiotherapy & Pilates Practice "Better life" regarding Julia's accidental death so far.

The rain eased up, but the heavy slate clouds looked as depressing as ever.

If her body has been discovered…because it might not be. This now looked very probable, and we would never know how Julia Bower met her end. His thoughts were also heavy and dark. Luke had a sudden urge for fresh air. He lowered the side window but pulled it up almost immediately. Humidity made the pollution much worse.

At last the traffic started moving a little faster, changing from the snail gear to the tortoise one. Luke felt how exhaustion was crawling over his body, clinging to him. The lunch was a mistake, it left him thirsty, sleepy and gave him heartburn.

Luke put a couple of polos into his mouth and sucked them thoughtfully.

Miss Bower was not a spring chicken, even by modern standards forty-four would be regarded as middle aged, neither was she attractive. And she was single. Not a good combination, thought Luke. He'd seen her photo on her Facebook profile, which Susan had found for him. A square chin, a thin-lipped mouth, not accustomed to smile. Serious eyes, serious looking face, simple short haircut.

Strictly planned life, deadly tedious, Luke shuddered. That was why Julia Bower went on this holiday. For single people. To try to invite some light, some warmth into her dreary life. Maybe to meet someone, even for a short time to pretend to be happy.

Everything comes to an end, even the most boring, tiresome and, seemingly, endless situation. Eventually, Luke managed to turn into a side road and let his frosted cherry F-type Jaguar plough through the metres like a rocket. By four o'clock post meridiem he stopped in front of Lady Holroyd-Kugushev's house.

It struck him once again—how quiet, how tranquil it was here, away from busy roads, traffic congestion and crowded high streets. He left his car in a small parking area, squeezed between a large number of stones and weird looking plants, all miniature and twisted. It was obvious that the owner of this place didn't have a car and cared little about those who were burdened with one.

A crow cawed twice. Then again. A lonely and ominous caw. It looked like no other sounds could reach this place, this weird, withered garden. Bewitched garden. Among the whitened boulders, by the three-tier pagoda Luke noticed a very large lopsided jet-black bird washing itself awkwardly.

Luke winced. The creature looked unnatural and unhealthy. Then something really strange happened. A short hairy leg materialised from nowhere and positioned itself upright. Luke reached into his coat pocket for a handkerchief, took off his glasses and with shaking hands wiped its lenses. When he returned them to their usual place it didn't make any difference. The leg was still there. What is more, the other four black limbs joined its sibling.

'Five?' whiffed Luke and almost immediately uttered a nervous titter, 'Chernomor, seriously, you gave me a real fright, come on, come here, puss, puss!'

The black cat turned his round head and lazily observed the intruder with his yellow saucers. Then yawned widely, showing his white and very sharp teeth. Stood up on his feet, and, with his shaggy tail stuck high in the air, walked proudly away.

'Ungrateful brute forgot who was looking after him and the other two for many weeks in the absence of their noble owner', commented Luke to himself and rubbed his hands.

It was getting cold rapidly, the sky, still asphalt and grim, didn't give away any hope of a better evening. The chill was piercing through his fashionable camel jacket easily, like there was nothing in its way to Luke's shivering flesh.

Luke Weir came to the front door and stopped. The door was slightly ajar. That was very unusual, very unlike Lady Holroyd-Kugushev, who was well known for her fear of burglars.

He rang the doorbell anyway, and Mozart's Turkish March burst out. Luke jumped swearing under his breath. That was something new which she had forgotten to mention, thought Luke sulkily. As a long-standing cat-house-sitter he felt a pang of dissatisfaction. He also sympathised with the feline residents who were, surely, deeply shocked by this novelty.

'Erm…is anybody home? Hello! Arina, are you there?' Tired of waiting outside, Luke invited himself in.

No answer. That was getting really weird. Where, the hell, was she? Luke listened carefully. The mute house was unbalancing him even more than the new doorbell tune. Then he thought he could detect trickling water somewhere. More likely—in the kitchen.

An immense hall, cladded with family portraits of haughty looking ancestors entirely from Arina's side, was dimly lit and had a haunting atmosphere about itself. On the right hand there was the dark wooden door to their detective office.

In the middle, further on, a steep staircase leading to the first floor could be seen. And the door leading to the kitchen and the living room was on the left.

It was always kept open because of the cats, but now it was closed. Luke frowned. The front door was open and the kitchen door—closed. Strange. Very strange. Especially for a person like Lady Holroyd, who was devoted to her routine.

Luke knocked on the door, again without success. Waited a little. Not a sound, except the dripping water coming out of the kitchen. He pushed the door open, walked in and froze immediately.

****

It looked like there had been a massive explosion. All the floor was covered in shattered glass with a messy pool of something whitish and lumpy in the middle. The rack with carefully assorted herbs and spices was knocked over and the contents of the bottles bestrewed generously over the cooker. But the worst of it was yet to be discovered by the transfixed Luke. He was slowly making his way across the soiled floor when something else caught his attention.

He stood with his mouth wide open and his hands raised in despair, gawping at the sink with the dripping tap. Luke had a serious phobia, and this phobia was to do with blood. Anything, from a tiny ruby-coloured drop could put him in a stupor.

But what was smearing the usually pristine clean grey granite sink more resembled a brutal murder scene. Bandages and pieces of kitchen roll, scattering the sink in a great number, were soaking in blood, some dirty dishes and even the walls of the washbasin were also covered in its clotting substance.

'Aah! Ooh!' uttered Luke in a weakening voice. His head was spinning, and he lost the feeling of his legs. He was altogether turning into a pathetic jellyfish at the time when his boss, probably half-dead by now, needed him the most.

He propped himself against the wall and closed his eyes for few seconds. Then, trying not to look at the bloody debris, picked his way through the sticky floor aiming for the side door which led out to the back garden. Luke was shaking, he had a nasty taste in his mouth and was about to be sick.

He stretched his hand to push the handle down, when the door magically started opening itself.

'Incredible!' Luke exclaimed, then added carefully, 'is it you? Are you…what's happened?'

Lady Holroyd-Kugushev, who emerged on the doorstep, didn't say a word. She was very pale and her right hand was wrapped up in gauze dressings. She suddenly looked older, disillusioned, tired. Very tired. Like fatigue was consuming her wholly.

'We are not making much progress, are we?' her voice sounded listless.

'We are, actually! I brought your very interesting news!'

'Really?'

'Really! But, firstly, explain to me please what disaster took place here in my short absence?'

'Hm… it's not very important.'

'Not important! I cannot believe! I've almost collapsed in a heap, and you're saying it is not important! What tosh!'

'Oh, sorry, I've forgotten that you are allergic to blood. Hm…it's just a minor domestic disturbance…sort of…'

'Damned cats!' worked out Luke.

As a visual confirmation of his suspicion, the two cats followed their owner meekly, Chernomor and the creature-of-the-forest, Brahms. The latter looked even more cross than usual, which could be, perhaps, explained by his state. He looked like he had just undergone a long and refreshing shower.

'When I heard a massive bang, like a gas explosion or a bomb, or a car crashed into my house, or whatever, I thought my heart would leap out of my breast! I bolted downstairs, almost breaking my leg on the way! At first, I rushed to the front door…you know, I couldn't detect the source of this almighty blow…' Lady Holroyd was losing her breath, she had to stop in the middle of the sentence.

'Arina, you need to calm down yourself! Come on, please, sit down. I'll make some tea…'

'No! I don't want your blasted tea!'

'Martini, then?'

'No! Something stronger!'

'Whisky? I could do with one myself. Just go and find the comfiest chair among your vast collection of sitting contraptions. Leave the rest to me. Then you can tell me what really happened here, my lovely boss.'

'Don't be too cheeky, don't push the boundaries!' growled Arina but followed his command.

'This horrid creature! I will give him away!' Arina said some ten minutes later, after she had a few generous sips of the dark amber liquid. Then elucidated, 'Brahms! He tried to quench his thirst by boozing my precious kefir! Brute! Should be kept in a cell! Chained!'

'Oh no, surely not! He doesn't deserve *that*! Just, perhaps, a little bit more discipline,' said Luke casting a careful sight at the party at fault, who was cuddling by the fire.

'He not only destroyed my brew—now I have to start the laborious process from scratch! But also broke a very good jar...'

'What process, sorry?'

'Uh! Luke, don't interrupt me! Brewing kefir, *of course*! In this insular country one cannot freely enjoy the fruits of other civilisations.'

'Erm?'

'Kefir is very good for your health! Didn't you know? Never mind! Coming back to my story, if you are ready to perceive it, of course. What I was saying is that this wild beast was trying to open the jar's lid, which was fitted properly, by the way, and broke the whole jar in the process. You've seen the result, haven't you? When I dashed in, he was devouring the contents.'

'Awful!'

'Awful, indeed!'

'But why was he so wet? And this...blood...'

'Oh, I cut myself when was trying to clear up the mess. That's all.'

'Are you sure that it was him? I mean, I was under the impression that Brahms is not the one who is really clumsy in this house...'

A long pause followed. A heavy, strained pause, before Lady Holroyd opened her mouth again.

'I was so convinced...Brahms was right there...and I went mad with him. I took him outside and threw a bucket full of water over him! He was so filthy. And he looked *so guilty* as well. And now...when you mentioned that...I don't know, I'm not so sure anymore.'

'Have you seen Nero recently?' asked Luke casually.

Arina shook her head and helped herself to another mouthful of recuperative fluids.

64

'Nero, Nero! Where are you? Come here!' she called in vain. 'I'll not be angry with you!' promised Arina lamely.

'He will be hiding now?'

'Of course, he will. For hours! He is the worst of the whole lot! Poor Brahmsy, poor cat. How unfair is life!' with these lamentations Arina hurried to the sulking, wrongly accused forest creature.

His response was clear. He growled and hissed at his honourable owner.

'Sorry Luke, I have to spend some quality time with my precious beast. First, your mummy will dry you properly…then a nice treat…those fish coloured biscuits you like so much…'

'Be careful, he is going to scratch you!'

Ignoring his warning, Lady Holroyd went to the downstairs bathroom and took a large, soft and fluffy caramel towel from the airing cupboard. Then she carefully approached Brahms, who was sitting on the dinning-table with his tail lashing nervously. She cooed and fussed around him, gradually gaining his trust back, until she could dry him properly, wrapping the warm towel around his body and gently rubbing his gorgeous stripy coat.

'Do you want me to clear up in the kitchen?' asked Luke boldly.

Arina laughed and declined such a sacrifice.

'I'll do it myself. Don't you be worried—it won't take me more than ten minutes to make the kitchen presentable once again.'

'What about your wounded hand?'

'I'm much better, thank you! The bleeding has stopped, and I'll wear gloves. No, Luke, please, you're too valuable to be wasted on this trivial occasion, he-he. Moreover, I don't want to find you stretched across the kitchen floor for hours in a sort of catatonic state.'

'Oh, thanks, boss! That's really thoughtful of you! But I'm sure, I can manage…'

'Don't be so touchy! You better order something for us to eat!'

'I'm not really…' started Luke and didn't finish the sentence. He suddenly realised that he was not full anymore. What is more, he felt quite peckish himself. 'All right, what do you fancy tonight?'

'Italian. I've recently discovered a very nice little place nearby. Their Spaghetti Marinara is exceptional. And tomato salad with black olives is an absolute must!'

It was not too long before peace was fully restored in Lady Holroyd-Kugushev kingdom. Chernomor, partly hidden by the heavy velvet curtains, was sitting in the 'sphynx' pose with his front paws tucked underneath his body on the windowsill, meditating as usual. Brahms was wriggling on his back on the dining table, trying very hard to fool somebody into tickling his belly. And Nero, who eventually revealed himself from one of his numerous hiding dens and rubbed himself against the legs of his owner for a long enough time to be forgiven, was now purring loudly from one of the two most comfortable armchairs by the hearth.

The human part of the small group, assembled cosily in the living room, was still enjoying their meals and the second bottle of Puglia Rosso. The conversation was slow and ruminant. Luke's usual meticulous report, together with his boss's morning findings, left a lot for comprehending and discussion.

'We absolutely must talk to somebody there who knew Aaron, who did physiotherapy or Pilates or whatever in the same group with him. I cannot believe that you failed to get access to the list, to any list, actually! Where has your usual charm gone, eh?'

Luke threw up his hands in a way of great despair and adopted a corresponding facial expression.

'I've tried…but the staff are obviously terrified by this Lump of Ice, he is a sort of a workplace dictator.'

'Hm…' retorted Arina sceptically.

'Am I right that you've crossed out Lisa from the *prime suspect* position?' Luke changed the subject swiftly.

Arina placed the last forkful of spaghetti into her mouth. Chewed it with obvious pleasure. Put her fork and spoon neatly together in the middle of the empty plate. Had a large gulp of the wine. Wiped her mouth with a paper napkin.

Eventually she looked at Luke.

'You might be right, I admit that. At least, let's agree for now that she continues to be a suspect, but not the prime one.' And quickly added, 'it's possible that it was somebody else who did it. But, of course, it could be still her after all.'

Lady Holroyd didn't like to give up her theories, when she was forced to do this, she would come up with all possible obstacles and excuses. Luke was fully aware of this habit of hers.

'So, what do we do? Is it time for DCI Crawnshaw?' asked Luke reconcilably.

'I'm afraid so, it is the time for Supt Crawnshaw.'

'Supt? What do you mean? When did he manage to be promoted to Detective Superintendent?'

'Recently, couple weeks ago or so.'

'Isn't he too young for that? How old is your son-in-law?'

'Late son-in-law.'

'Oh, I keep forgetting that they divorced.'

'I'm surprised that he didn't scarper from my wonderful daughter before.'

'What a kind mother you are,' laughed Luke.

'Just being realistic, that's all. Going back to your question, my ex-son-in-law is in his early forties, forty-two actually. So, relatively speaking, he is quite young. But I don't think it goes against him, his age, I mean. Peter Crawnshaw is young, ambitious and energetic. He fits perfectly well into the modern society of fast-track career climbers.'

****

The fast-track career climber was already there, sitting in the depth of a murky, leather cladded bar, with his left hand supporting his cleft chin. Lady Holroyd-Kugushev hesitated for a second at the entrance of this grand, five-star hotel, giving herself a moment to study this enigmatic man. It was long enough, however, for him to register her appearance. He waved to her, stood up and welcomed her warmly, not missing out their usual cheek kissing, like nothing had happened in their family, like he was still her only son-in-law.

He looked older, more wrinkles clawed his forehead, his dark blue, almost black, indigo eyes stared at her without a single blink. She was always puzzled by this ability, it reminded her of a snake. Superintendent Peter Crawnshaw, she thought, you resemble a very handsome and equally unpredictable snake. And somehow I don't want to be among your enemies.

A polite cough brought her back to reality.

'What can I do for you, my Lady-in-law, this time?'

She smiled nonchalantly and he smiled back, but his smile was carefully measured, thin lips were strictly following their master's orders.

'It's the same case of the missing marathon runner...'

'Yes, of course, and, as far as I am aware, I've sent all available information to you.'

'It was very helpful, thank you very much Peter, but as you see, we need something else now. And, by the way, congratulations on your promotion.'

'Hm, thanks, Arina. Please, tell me how can I help? I am all ears.'

And she told him. It took her about a quarter of an hour to update him on their progress. He didn't interrupt once. When Arina finished, he took a sip of his iced mint tea, toyed with a pristine starched napkin, unfolding and folding it. Waved to a waiter to get the bill. Checked his stylish, brand-new iPhone.

Ten years ago he would have lit a cigarette, Arina thought, now he has to find different distractions, being creative. She laughed in her mind.

'I'll see what I can do for you,' he said after a long pause, 'give me a few minutes and I'll be back. I just need to have a word with someone. Do you want anything else, Arina? No, okay,' and he left her, already tapping something on his iPhone.

Peter Crawnshaw didn't go far, his sharp silhouette could have been seen in the hotel's foyer. He sauntered to and fro, careless to the rest of the world, his confident manners were of someone who had been in power for a long time.

How did he manage to be fooled by my dear daughter, wondered Arina once again. Lady Holroyd's eldest daughter Iris was a great disappointment to her mother. She was the cuckoo fledgling in their family; she was so different from all of them, that the idea of a baby-swap didn't sound too ridiculous.

From the age of five she had been spending most of her free time in front of the mirror. At the age of thirty-six Iris was still maniacally faithful to her old habit. She wouldn't have thought of leaving her house without looking perfect. Even going to a local shop for a pint of milk would've required Iris to spent at least an hour polishing her appearance. On one occasion, when Iris, eleven then, had broken her impeccable long nail, painted in a sky-blue varnish, she was so devastated that she preferred to cry for hours and be left behind, rather than going for a day out to the seaside with the rest of the family. Definitely an alien child.

On the other hand, Sasha, her thirty-three-year-old daughter, couldn't be more different. Named after her father, Alexandra or Sasha, was not, strictly speaking, a beauty queen, with her beaked nose and thin face ending with a sharp bony chin. But she had so much life about her, so much energy and magnetism, so she was always the centre of attention.

Sasha always wanted to be a scientist. In her early childhood years, she had been enchanted by everything to do with fossils. She would treat each piece of the most filthy, dusty and disgusting looking rock as Aladdin's cave, expecting to find in its depths fragments of the rarest and the most peculiar living creatures. Be like daddy, she would always say with a rascally grin.

But in her last year at school Sasha had managed to surprise everybody by her, at first glance Ill-considered decision to change her plans and become a marine biologist instead. She'd explained it, in her usual concise manner, that she didn't wish to stay in her famous father-palaeontologist's shadow forever. She would rather betray her first love, than be compared to the professor, Sir Alexander Holroyd, all the time.

If Holroyd Senior had been hurt, he didn't reveal it, instead he'd respected his daughter's resolution and gave her his full support in achieving her new goal. Sasha had submerged herself into the new endeavour with her usual enthusiasm and soon became truly passionate about it.

Arina was missing her younger daughter so much! Working for the WWF, Sasha had to go to the other side of the world, just off the North Island of New Zealand, to study Maui dolphins—the smallest and the rarest of all Cetaceans. She was trying to save this amazing creature from vanishing off the face of our planet. Alongside her, as always for the last two years, was the bearded giant Clive, a marine microbiologist and a profound scuba diver, her soul mate in all aspects. They had been planning to get married next spring. It would never happen now…

'You've being thinking about Sasha?'

The Superintendent's stealthy appearance startled Lady Holroyd.

'Bloody hell, Peter, do you do that deliberately?' she exclaimed haughtily.

He grinned, obviously pleased with himself, as she continued.

'You don't creep up behind somebody's back, especially if somebody is of advanced age. You might easily give a heart attack to that person. Don't they teach you on your police courses how to behave yourself?'

Demonstrating a good understanding of his relative-in-law, Crawnshaw just perched himself next to the fuming detective.

'Would you like anything to drink? I mean a proper drink?' he made an appropriate suggestion.

'Hm, yes, all right. I would like…'

'Martini Bianco with a slice of lemon and two pieces of ice? Correct?'

He waved to the waiter who materialised from nowhere.

Supt Crawnshaw made an order. For himself he asked for a large glass of the most expensive cognac the bar had on its list.

Arina only raised her eyebrows.

'The meeting with our new PCC has been cancelled… by above,' he pointed his index finger up to the celling. 'So, I'm a free man for tonight,' Peter answered her unasked question.

'I see. How did you guess that I was thinking about…hm… Sasha?' she asked quietly, trying to keep her voice steady and unemotional.

'It's just this special look in your eyes. I'm sorry, I didn't want to upset you. Please, forgive me. How are you…coping?'

'I'm coping, I don't know how, but I'm coping, thanks, Peter. Oh! What is it?' Arina was referring to a serving cart, wheeled in by a waiter. It was well-laden by all sorts of, looking extremely appetising, small dishes. Arina noticed shiny bullets of black and green stuffed olives scattered among white cubes of feta cheese; translucid slices of Parma ham coiled on the bed of a green salad; cast iron pan full of king prawns fried with garlic and parsley. There was also a thin pizza bread with cheese and tomato on the top and a bowl of small red sausages with shallots.

'Just a humble snack to go with our drinks,' clarified Peter, 'I hope that it will meet your satisfaction?'

'You shouldn't…I mean have gone to the trouble…it wasn't necessary…' she was eyeing the prawns.

'No trouble at all! I don't know about you, but I'm famished! And I'm sure you can be persuaded to have a speck of something! We can't really send it all back, can we?'

'I suppose not…okay then, I will have a piece of this thin bread…no, no, the small one! Yes, thank you! And something from this pot, and some olives, perhaps…'

'What is else troubling you, Arina?' asked Crawnshaw in a while.

In her heliotrope tunic and pale blue jeans, she looked sophisticated and, at the same time, unbelievably young. She was also very beautiful. She was wearing a thin silver bracelet on her right wrist and a matching long silver necklace with a malachite pendant.

'You're very observant today, Peter.'

'Only today?' he mocked her.

'Today especially,' Arina didn't pick up his facetious tone. She was dead serious. 'I think that somebody is following me.'

Crawnshaw killed his smile immediately.

'Tell me everything! Is it anything to do with this case of yours, by any chance?'

Arina hesitated for a moment.

'No, I don't think so. I know that it might sound strange…but…'

Lady Holroyd held a dramatic pause. She was always good at it. Her ex-son-in-law looked fairly concerned and it pleased her. Maybe he would not think that she had eventually lost all her marbles. Perhaps, one or two, but certainly not all of them!

'Something had happened in Austria. This general. Klaus. And his strange mature daughter. I think that they were up to no good,' she resumed.

'Who? What do you mean? What general?'

'Retired general, actually. I'd met this weird couple on my holiday. Which I had to interrupt because of the new case.'

'Fuck!' uttered Supt suddenly.

Arina was shocked. He had never sworn in her presence before. She was going to say something appropriate, but just one glance at his face changed her mind.

The Superintendent looked like he'd seen a ghost.

Chapter 6

A tall, emaciated figure in a coat of a freshly boiled carrot shade was approaching them. Her high heels were clicking aggressively, and her eyes were fixed on Peter's face. Her thin lips were firmly set and matched the coat colour.

'Iris, what are you doing here?' asked Lady Holroyd.

'Oh, hello mother! I didn't expect to meet you here.'

'And *who* did you expect to see here, if I may ask?' asked Peter coldly.

'Oh, never mind now,' she gave a husky snigger, 'can I join such a cosy family reunion?'

'It's nothing to do with family or with you. It's a business meeting.'

'With drink and food? *Really*?'

'What Peter said is true. I needed his help with our new case.'

'And our freshly minted Supt came tearing along right from Wakefield at your command, just to please you!'

'Don't make a scene here! I'm not your husband anymore, have you forgotten that?'

'Iris, calm down! What is the matter with you?'

'I didn't ask for your advice, mother! I'm speaking to my husband!'

'Ex-husband! Bloody, *ex*!' the Superintendent's face became very pale, and his nostrils started to flare up.

People in the bar, however few there were, began to look in their direction. Iris seemed to enjoy their attention and gave away a small smile. She was still standing by their table, resembling an eyesore beacon from a building site at night.

Only when a barmaid had been sent down by a senior member of staff to hover around them, did Iris slowly unbutton her coat and sit down.

'A glass of water, please,' she addressed to no one.

A glass tumbler of water half-filled with ice appeared almost immediately.

'Anything else?' enquired a polite voice.

'No, thank you very much, it will be more than enough,' she cut short.

Arina realised that she hadn't seen Iris for a few months and was shocked by the changes in her appearance. Iris was always slim but now her face was haggard, covered in thick layers of make-up, it looked dull and artificial. It grotesquely reminded her of a Pierrot mask. Her long, bleached hair had become thin and brittle.

'Have something to eat, Iris, please!'

'No, I don't want your food, thank you very much! It looks horrendous! It's so fatty!' the last words she almost spat out.

Arina glanced at Peter. He looked disgusted. Contempt was written all over his handsome features. When he noticed that he was being watched, he didn't bother to change his expression, instead he smirked at Lady Holroyd.

What an arrogant bastard, she thought, Iris did well to get out so easily. Then Arina turned to her daughter and was stunned by a look full of scalding hate.

'Why are you looking at each other like two conspirators?' Iris shrieked.

'I'm sorry, Arina, for all this, I truly am! I have no desire to plunge you in the middle of our domestic predicaments,' Peter said apologetically, which, of course, had the opposite effect on Iris, who fumed even more.

'Have you been talking about me? Don't bother to answer! You both are such pathetic liars!'

'Iris, calm down!' Arina had enough of this soap opera performance, 'as I said before, we met to discuss my case. That's all! And anyway, why would it matter so much for you now?'

'That's where you are wrong, my darling mother! It matters for me very much! I am still his wife, has he forgotten to mention to you this small detail, when he was pretending to be free? Yes, I can see! We are *not* divorced!'

'Is it true? Peter, is it true what she was saying?'

The Superintendent didn't answer at first. His demeanour became unreadable again, he was once more in control of his emotions.

'We don't live together anymore, we live separate lives now, not only in different houses but in different cities! We are basically divorced, just some formalities left, papers to sign, you know. That's all!'

Iris puffed scornfully.

'Explain to my naïve mother, who adores you by the way, why you're protracting? Because it's you, not me who is not signing papers!'

'It's ridiculous!'

'Fine, I'll do it for you. You know, it's everything to do with his bloody promotion, of course! So, strictly speaking we are *still* a wife and a husband! In that case I don't see anything wrong with me checking on my beloved half, do you?'

'You're ill, Iris! You behave like a spoiled little girl who has lost her expensive toy. I'm going now. Mind you, Peter, I'm not impressed with you either! Good-bye! No need to get up, I will see myself out.'

And, with her head high, Lady Holroyd-Kugushev sailed away.

****

The last leaves have fallen. They are under her feet now, their golden and crimson rustling mass is up to her ankles, it gives her a feel of decay. She looks up. The sharp, bare treetops are piercing the sky, and the sky is bleeding.

There is more rustling. This time it is behind her. She wants to look back but doesn't dare. Her heart is falling deep down, like leaves which are already dead.

Heavy breathing. Heavy footsteps. More rustling. She tries to run, but her feet are stuck, they are trapped. Leaves weigh a ton. Didn't they teach you at school? That the fallen leaves are as heavy as a concrete lump.

It is all quiet now. It's all over now. She is safe. Just her and autumn trees.

But why are they moving? They are supposed to be still, there is not a single waft of wind around. Perhaps, something wrong with her eyesight?

Oh, no!

One of the nearest trees, a squatty one, with widely spreading branches, a cherry tree, perhaps, is splitting in front of her eyes. And the left part—black as soot, moving towards her. It's getting bigger, it's taking a different shape. It's not a tree anymore!

A man in black is approaching her! He is not very steady on his feet. Is he drunk?

She wants to scream, but her throat is dry as a desert and her lungs are full of sandy dust.

He is not drunk. He is simply limping, his right leg doesn't work very well, it's unreliable.

He is so close now. But she still cannot see his face. It's hiding deep inside the hood of his coat. She knows that her death is coming. And she is useless. Her doughty body has betrayed her at the end.

Arina looks around. There is nobody except herself and the murderer. She tries to run away, but her legs are like barrels, they don't obey her! Even worse— they don't belong to her! Arina felt a sickening horror creeping over her. She raised her hands up, brought them close to her eyes—thick, ringless fingers resembling cocktail sausages, were not hers.

Who am I?

Why am I so scared?

Because he is going to kill me. The killer.

The figure in a black mackintosh is so close now, she can discern his breathing.

He is looking at her from out of his hood, watching her, deciding what to do. Or has he already decided everything? Why is he waiting?

She hears some rustling again. But it isn't the leaves which make this noise. It his right arm enveloped in waterproof material scratching against the pocket from where it's trying to come out. And there it is, what seems like an empty sleeve, holding something heavy. It comes to life now.

His motions are so quick. So precise.

A heavy rock crushes her skull.

Before the darkness comes around her, becomes her, she is able to see his face. Just a glimpse. But enough to utter a short cry of a deadly wounded bird. Or somebody who realised their blunder, only too late.

****

She stayed in bed for a while, fully awake, with eyes open and mouth as dry as the Gobi Desert. She could still feel the ferocious impact of the boulder. She could still feel the nausea of recognition.

You killed again. And you liked it. You're a little bit sad. But just a little. You're getting used to this. What is it that drives you to kill? There is a reason, surely, as always…we all kill for a reason…I just need to guess…to find out…to open your head…*to see.*

She shivered. She was so close…too close? There was a great danger there, she knew, she was stepping over an invisible barrier, where safety had been left behind.

Arina forced herself to get up. Went to the window and drew back the curtains. A black furry cat was enjoying the view of a foggy late morning, sitting

75

on the windowsill. He turned his large head and squinted at her a few times. Arina did the same out of courtesy.

An old lady with a dishevelled grey mane and her black cat were looking out of the window, she thought with bleakness.

Everything was wrong. The sky was not bleeding under the sharp treetops simply because the treetops were not sharp or bare, trees still had a lot of foliage around themselves. Especially if most of them were conifers—pine trees, larches and spruces.

A slight mist made the landscape resemble one of those Chinese ink and wash paintings. In black and white. Smudgy. Not real. Like somebody's dream.

Am I still dreaming?

The silence came with a fog. Which covered all clues. All bodies.

A phone call brought her back to reality.

'Hi! I hope I didn't wake you up?'

It was Luke, of course! Who else? Did she expect somebody else? If she was asked this question, she would have been lost for an answer. One thing she was sure about—it was not Luke she wanted to chat to right now. She felt sad and vexed at the same time.

'No!' she snapped.

'Oh! Have I caught you at a bad moment? If so, I can call later, but...'

'Better now! I don't want to ruin my day waiting in vain for your next call. Fire away!'

'I think it's important...erm...'

'Luke, I haven't got an eternity on my hands, say what you are going to say and make it quick. If you are capable of that, of course!'

'No need to be rude, boss. I was about to tell you...'

'Yes, I am all ears.'

'Hm, I don't know how to start...'

'Come on, I am really losing my patience. Will you deliver at last or not?'

'I have to confess...make a confession sort of...I hope you will not be cross with me, more cross than you already are, I mean...'

'Luke, I really have had enough of this babble of yours! I'm finishing this call!'

'Wait! I've forgotten something!'

'Nothing new about this! As long as I've known you, you are always forgetting something. No need to go far for examples, just recently you have been waiting for me at the wrong airport! You, fathead!'

'We had a call from the principal.'

'What?'

'From Ms Kale.'

'Yes, I know who you mean, I'm not suffering from Alzheimer's yet. Unlike somebody I might know.'

'She called on our agency contact number, and, because we were out of our office, the call has been transferred to my mobile.'

'When did she call?'

'Erm…a few days ago.'

'What!' barked Arina.

'At first, I didn't think that it was so important to interrupt you, and…then…frankly, completely forgot about it.'

'And now, what, you've changed your mind? Why to bother anyway?'

Arina's face turned scarlet and she was gripping her phone with all her power. She struggled hard with herself not to hurl it out of the window.

'I've tried to call her back. No answer. I called the school. Nobody has seen her for the last couple of days.'

'What?'

'Yeah, it seems that we've got the third missing person on our hands,' Luke tittered nervously.

'I don't think it's funny, Luke! Your giggling is simply inept. When did she call you?'

'Hm…I think…one day last week…'

'Check your phone. Do it now!'

After a long pause filled with hectic scrolling through his long list of unsaved numbers, he came to the right one.

'Ms Kale called us on fifth of October. Last Wednesday.'

'And when did you find the time to return her call?' asked Arina morosely.

'Yesterday,' Luke answered timidly.

'What about informing me first, eh?'

'I've just remembered and…you know…decided to check with her first what really was going on. What was troubling her. Because I thought at first it was, frankly speaking, a waste of time. It's coming back to me now. We were just about to interview that horrible Lisa's mother, that big-mouthed hag.'

'Oh, yes, I remember. And somebody called you when we were sitting in that crammed, stuffy, gaudy room of hers. I thought I would be sick any moment. And then you went out for a few minutes, and when you came back you had this boring expression with your eyes rolling up and eyebrows raised to the celling. Another of your numerous girlfriends who would not leave you in peace, I thought then. But I was wrong, was I?'

'Honestly Arina, I was going to mention it to you but…you know how it is. We had so much to do, so much to discuss…it slipped my mind. That's all. I'm really very sorry…honestly.'

'Stop saying "honestly" all the time! Is it your favourite word now? Just stop littering your language with those mundane common words. It's sickening! Such a highly educated young man like you should be ashamed of this habit.'

'Okay. Do you want to know what she had said, by the way?'

'Yes!'

'*I've seen him again. You know who. I'm old and old-fashioned and so on, but I'm not touched in my head. And I am worried. I didn't like what I'd seen. There's something wrong with him. When I tried to squeeze her for more information she just clammed up. Then* she asked me to forget all about it.'

'Just like that? Without any explanation?'

'Yeah, she didn't want to be laughed at, especially by you, *by your arrogant, pompous boss*, those were her own words, honest…hm…'

'Come to my place now, Luke! We have to go back to the school. It's more serious than you think. I'll tell you later about my dream last night. I think…no I am sure that something nasty happened to that silly old hen.'

****

All the way to the school they tried not to let increasing panic get over them. But it was difficult. The presence of ominousness was palpable.

Instead of going straight inside the school, Arina insisted on walking round the school's massive grounds first. After a quick check with the receptionist, who confirmed the absence of the Principal since Monday night, Luke joined the elder detective.

'They are actually not very worried, just a little bit concerned. She apparently is known for her short absences. She goes to Scarborough usually for a short break, when things are too hectic, or somebody upsets her. Just for a few days. Then she is back like nothing happened, refreshed and full of energy.'

'Does she warn anybody usually? For example, her personal secretary?'

'Yes, usually.'

'But not this time?'

'No,' Luke admitted reluctantly.

They walked in silence for a while. Arina didn't have a plan or any idea where to go. So, she decided to wonder around and count on something to click inside of her head. Like a sort of recognition or premonition.

Nothing! Her head was as empty as a perforated bucket. She just hoped that Luke wouldn't notice her bewilderment.

They passed a deserted playground, a tennis court, an open-air swimming pool, which was drained at this time of the year, the vast playing fields with an impeccable state of grass; they rounded a small lake with a dozen moored rowing boats, bobbing up and down carelessly. Still Lady Holroyd felt nothing.

'Are we coming back to the school?' asked Luke.

'No, not yet. I don't know…shall we go through this wooden gate?'

'Is it not closed? No! Strange…'

The single timber gate was so old and weathered, it was not clear how it was still in one piece. A rope which was used to tie it onto the fence had rotted away a long time ago. The gate couldn't be fully opened, as it stuck into the earth, but there was enough space to squeeze through.

'The school grounds are not so secure as it seemed at first glance. This school is not a fortress after all,' Arina said meditatively.

'Anybody could get in…'

'Or out.'

'Exactly,' Luke summarised.

'Is there any point to continue?' Arina asked.

'I don't know, maybe it would be better to come back to talk to her secretary…or other staff?' Luke tried to sound positive.

'Sorry for all of this, I don't know, I hope I am not turning gaga.'

'Ha, not yet! We can come back the other way, through this wood or park, or whatever it is.'

'Yes, all right,' Arina agreed listlessly.

Soon her mood improved. The park full of colourful small trees was so beautiful, so captivating. Their thin black branches decked with golden, crimson and purple leaves were in the shape of an umbrella. They were Japanese cherry trees, guessed Arina. Some of them had already lost a lot of their leaves and formed a multicoloured carpet underneath.

Soon they reached a clearing with a single old tree in the middle. This tree was completely free of any leaves, its soot-black sharp branches spread widely. The tree crouched itself ready to spring on them.

A large messy heap of leaves was raked by its side. There were some chopped twigs among the leaves, together with rolled up pieces of old newspaper on the top. An old-fashion rake with a thick wooden handle was left leaning against the heap.

'Somebody is going to make a bonfire shortly,' suggested Luke.

'Somebody, hm, a gardener more likely,' chuckled Arina and suddenly stopped. She was staring at the raked leaves.

'I shouldn't take my dream so literally,' she murmured.

Luke turned around and looked at her. His face became pale and serious, his eyes behind his rectangular glasses were wide and dismayed.

Arina couldn't stop herself, she continued walking, though, her steps were slow and unsteady. It was if she was dragging herself through layers of thick wet mud. She also couldn't stop gazing at something which resembled tree branches.

'There is no signal here, damn it!' Luke was tapping his phone vainly.

'Luke, go, go to the school and call from there! From their phone!'

'But you, are you going to…'

'Yes, I will stay here.'

'No, Arina, I cannot let you! You go and I will stay!'

'Stop arguing! You will be much faster than me. Make a call and be back straight away. I'll be absolutely fine! What can happen to me?'

'I suppose…but if the murderer…if he is still here and decides to attack you.'

'I've got my pepper spray with me. As usual, I'm well prepared. Plus, I don't think that he (or she) will do anything stupid.'

'You haven't forgotten to renew the licence for this highly offensive weapon of yours?'

'No! Go! Just go!'

The fog, which had just started to emerge early on, was in full flow by now. Luke's bright coat had been already swallowed up by the milky drizzle.

With colours rapidly draining away, the figure became more visible. There were no doubts—the body buried in the pile of autumn leaves and dried twigs belonged to Ms Kale, the Principal of 'Lombardy Poplar Grammar School'.

Her face with sagging cheeks was shining through the debris. Her forehead was stamped with a large carmine leaf; its fat, widely spread pimpled lobes resembled a starfish. It looked grotesque. It was a bizarre picture. You want to laugh and the same time you are fighting back sobs in your throat. Conflict as usual.

You didn't hide her, why? Arina asked herself. And almost immediately a guess, which made her blood curdled, came to her.

The first impression was correct. This pile was prepared to be burned. Only not by a gardener to clear up the garden rubbish, but by you—to get rid of your next victim.

It was getting so cold now, even in her long black coat and a thick scarf Arina was shivering. The light wind started to rustle fallen leaves behind her. It was so subtle, so weightless, that she could barely hear it. And she didn't feel it. Maybe because it was not a wind at all…

She stayed frozen to the place, she held her breath She became all ears. The rustling stopped. Then resumed. With each second it was getting closer and closer. Somebody was creeping up behind her. Somebody…a murderer…of course… was just behind her.

She was taken off guard. The fear was so immense, that her brain stopped dictating its rules. Her instincts took over for the best.

Arina ran as fast as she could. Her small, but heavy cowhide haversack was slapping painfully against her back. Her long coat was in the way. Her chic slim-fit knee-high boots were already hurting her feet, they were not meant for running across the countryside.

Soon she would be out of breath. Soon the killer would catch up with her. Death was just a hand distance away from her. What a silly and pathetic death it would be!

Arina was desperate to look back. Just to steal a quick glance.

But it would be too risky. He was much younger. The killer. Much fitter. Even if he was limping. He is probably just a few metres away from her.

The wet leaves under her feet were slippery. Treacherous. The disaster was waiting to happen. And it did happen.

Arina stumbled over some stones hidden under the thick, mushy, muddy mass and fell down. If it was not for her outstretched hands, Arina's fall wouldn't have been as harmless as it was. Only a rusty metal taste settling in the mouth…only fear devouring her guts…

She was breathing hard, and her pulse was throbbing at her temples. Arina slowly got up. At first, she thought that she went partly blind, then the darkness in front of her eyes subdued, leaving just a thickening milkiness which was shrouding her, trapping her in its embrace.

A dark silhouette emerged out of nothing, it was approaching her fast.

'Luke! Luke, come here! Quick!' she shouted with great relief.

'We're coming!' sounded distantly.

The figure darted sideways. And Lady Holroyd-Kugushev leaned against a slimy trunk of whatever tree it was, totally drained.

Diary 3

I'm still out of breath. And not because I'm unfit or… crippled.

No! Certainly not!

It's because I'm furious!

I would kill that old hag with my own hands. Getting at her wrinkled, thin throat would be such a pleasure!

Ohhh! How I hate her!

I must calm down. I must.

Nothing changed, really. It was close, I admit, but I'm safe now. One thing is bothering me though. It's—how? How on earth did she know?

I couldn't believe my eyes when I saw them messing about my…hm…nice little arrangement. If it was not down to my innate cautiousness, I would have walked straight into them. I would still escape. I am sure of it!

But it would be messy. Completely out of my style. And it's me here who dictates the next move. Not circumstances or those two.

Certainly not!

But how? It was not a coincidence. I could see that they were looking for something. For someone.

For this Kale.

Did she manage to contact them, to tell them? Even so, how would she predict where she would find her own end?

Impossible! Unless…no! I don't believe in all this psychic crap. It can all be logically explained.

I obviously underestimated that flabby toad. Otherwise, she would be alive, wouldn't she? It was all her fault. She was not supposed to die. She was supposed to be my secret weapon.

But it didn't work out! She appeared to be shrewder than I expected. Than anybody expected, I am sure of it. Who would suspect to find any speck of intellect in that gob of fat?

I must not be distracted by all this nonsense! Distraction is a failure. And I'm not a failure! Not anymore! I am not far from my final goal. The journey there was not an easy one. But I'm used to obstacles. They will not stop me. Not now, not when I'm so close…

I'll continue on my way whatever it takes!

Chapter 7

He was an old and not very nice man. His small face had a great resemblance to the grimace of a very ancient monkey. His washy eyes were red-rimmed and full of pain. And he himself was full to the brim with gnawing pain, shredding his decaying body to pieces.

He had been dying for a long time, for many years the most advanced medication kept his body alive. But for his soul, petty from the start, it didn't do any good. It was always vitriolic, and age didn't improve it, rather made it worse.

The dying man was sitting in a comfortable armchair, specially designed for his needs, in a glass veranda from where he could enjoy the wonderful view of one of the most attractive rocky beaches of Cornwall. However, his features bore an expression of somebody who had just been forced to down a glass of pure vinegar.

A thin woman of insignificant age, wearing an old-fashioned heavily starched nursing cap, silently appeared from the adjoining room and coughed politely. The old man jerked and hissed through his thin bluish lips.

'What do you want?'

'I just wanted to check how you are, sir. And if you're ready for something light to eat?'

'For pity's sake, I don't want anything, stupid woman! Did you get it? I am not hungry! Get out of here and only come back when you're called!'

He started coughing violently after this explosion, his arthritic fingers were pinching spasmodically a tartan plaid blanket, which was thrown over his knees. The nurse was watching him dispassionately. When the seizure subdued, she wiped his mouth and changed his cotton bib which was already covered in sputum, generously streaked with blood.

'I'll bring a clean one in a minute.'

The patient didn't reply, his eyes were partly closed and had an inane expression about them. He already looked half-dead.

As soon as Barbara, the nurse, left, the old man opened his eyes immediately. A strange cunning smile touched his smeared lips.

'They think I'm dying, that I'm practically dead. They don't have a clue how wrong they are!' he murmured with a passion of pure insanity.

With the same odd smile, he fumbled with some buttons on his automatic chair, rising its back so he could sit straight and turning it round to face the internal door.

'She won't catch me by surprise again, stupid cow!' he confided to himself.

Then he released the brakes and drove his chair inside the house. There, in the shadow of the thick floor length curtains, he waited patiently for his nurse to appear. His devious plan worked well—the poor woman jumped up as she almost collided with the invalid.

When Barbara had regained her usual composure, she bent over her patient and began to tuck a fresh napkin into his collar carefully. The old man was watching her every movement suspiciously. When she finished, he asked her in a husky, almost inaudible voice.

'Any letters today? From him…'

Barbara shook her head.

'Are you sure?'

'Yes, sir.'

'When did you check the last time?'

'Just now.'

'You're lying! Liar! You didn't have time!'

'I can check the mail again, if you wish.'

Barbara didn't seem to be bothered much by his unfair accusation, obviously, she was used to this. When she returned empty handed, the old man tried not to show his disappointment, he simply sent her away with a curt dismissive gesture. Alone, he started talking to himself again.

'It's been a few days, I think. I need to check…I'm sure…oh…only two days without a letter from you. Unless they are hiding them from me now. I don't trust them! Liars!'

Jabbering under his breath, the old man drove his chair through an enfilade of rooms one bigger than another, their palatial adornment could have made any decent stately home of England look mediocre in comparison. All the doors were wide open so the old man could glide through them effortlessly.

It was getting dark, the light in the house was dim, and the humped figure jammed in the silent, fast running chair, looked macabre.

In a few minutes he reached his destination without meeting a single soul. He already looked exhausted, but he couldn't allow himself even a moment of rest. He had to check. He wheeled himself into the study, furnished as opulently as the rest of his dwelling, straight up to his massive desk.

Before getting to the secret place where he kept the drawer keys, he looked around surreptitiously. It was even darker in the study, each cavernous corner of it could hide a villain. The old man was squinting and frowning, straining his poor sight to its limit. Satisfied at least, he proceeded with opening one of the countless secret compartments which the desk was teeming with.

The sought drawer was deep and almost empty, it contained only a few letters. The man's hand was shaking when he took a thin letter from the top and brought it up to his nose, then with a vexed grimace moved it away, trying to make sense of tiny scrawling, which was doubling in front of his eyes. Eventually, he had to use a magnifying glass to read the date on the letter.

'Damn it!' he exclaimed in desperation. 'It was only yesterday! I cannot believe! How the days are dragging! Sorely dragging! Abysmal sorrow fills my days now…I am becoming a poetic sort, how ridiculous! Me, who has never ever given a second thought to all that bookish rubbish. Who only read financial papers, never touched anything else since my schooldays. Am I dying for real? No! I have to be more patient, I have to…But I wish he sent me another letter today, it would make my pain abate for a while.'

****

Luke was worried about Arina. She didn't take the questioning by the police well. Not surprisingly, regarding the circumstances.

'I've lost him, do you understand, Luke? I've lost our murderer. I was so close,' she put her index finger and the thumb together, leaving about a millimetre between them. 'And I failed. I am a rubbish private detective,' she tried to laugh sarcastically but her laugh reminded more of a sob.

They had been waiting for almost an hour in the school sports hall to be summoned by the police. In the same hall where just eight days ago they were themselves interviewing the girls. The bench they were sitting on was hard and

86

uncomfortable, and the whole situation seemed bizarre and unreal, and had a bitter irony about it.

'Arina, please, stop torturing yourself! We are very lucky that nothing really bad has happened to you! And you were so right about the place and everything! Look at the positive side.'

Arina didn't answer. She pressed her lips together and was gloomily observing two approaching authoritative figures. Lady Holroyd didn't try to conceal her annoyance with these two young officers, both of whom looked like it was their first serious case.

'Hi, I'm DI Robins,' a thin young woman, with a very pale complexion and insignificant features, introduced herself, 'and this is DS Higgins,' she pointed at her male colleague, who easily could have been still in his teens.

They sat down on the opposite bench. The junior officer flipped nervously through his notebook before finding the page he was looking for. Then he cleared his throat and started checking their details. After they finished with the formalities, DI Robins took the initiative in her hands.

'So, you are private detectives, as we heard?'

Luke nodded affirmatively.

'Hm, how do you explain your discovery?'

'What do you mean?' asked Arina in her iciest voice.

'Coincidence, purely coincidence, officer,' quickly interrupted Luke.

The officer obviously didn't like their answers, as she knitted her thin brows and started biting her already quite chapped lips.

'What were you doing in the school grounds? I know for a fact that you came here to talk with Ms Kale, the deceased.'

'Walking!' answered Lady Holroyd haughtily.

'What do you mean?'

'We were walking. You know why people sometimes go for a walk? A stroll?'

Two red spots appeared on DI Robins' usually pasty cheeks.

'Ms Kale wanted to talk to us. We tried to contact her by phone but without any success. So, we came down here, to hm…to see her…' Luke's attempt to save the situation failed hopelessly. Even for this pair of cops, however inexperienced and not very bright they were, the discrepancy was obvious.

Luke turned red too, took off his glasses, breathed on their lenses and started cleaning them enthusiastically with his vivid silk handkerchief. DI Robins and

DS Higgins stared at his handkerchief, which was covered in vibrant pink, red, blue, yellow, green, purple and orange butterflies. They obviously had never come across such an accessory.

'I don't understand one thing,' said Arina abruptly, 'why we are wasting our time here, when you should start investigating immediately? Sorry, we cannot help you more. As my assistant tried to tell you, we had nothing to do with this tragic case.'

'Our colleagues are already dealing with this murder, I can assure you,' DI Robins said gloomily, 'just, please, answer our questions as clearly as possible. It won't take too long, I promise.'

'I have nothing to add!'

Luke looked at his boss. Her face was set iron hard. He knew this expression too well. It was his turn again to butter up the police. He tried not to divert from the truth too much, the same time missing out everything to do with Arina's visions and other, not so easily explained, events. After he finished his edited version of the matters, there was a momentary silence.

'It sounds a wee strange, if you don't mind me saying,' DI Robins said eventually. She didn't look at all at ease and was chewing her lips even more eagerly than before.

The younger office acquired an expression of one who had just met an alien alighting from a flying saucer. His mouth went wide open and his eyes stared from their sockets.

'It's extraordinary!' he exclaimed at last, 'you must be a real psychic! So, you were saying that you went for a walk, after unsuccessfully trying to locate the principal, and—hey presto—found a body. Do you know, you've got a gift! A paranormal power! We could certainly use it in our police work! It's just like in this film, 'Hideaway'. Where the guy is psychically connected to a serial killer, you know, gets all sort of horror visions.'

DI Robins turned red.

'Sorry for that,' she said angrily, 'I don't know what got into him! It's his first day in the field…'

'No worries, we understand,' said Luke trying very hard not to burst out laughing.

Even Arina couldn't conceal a discreet smile.

'I think we will call it a day now. If we have more questions we will be in touch. And again, I apologise for my junior colleague's inappropriate behaviour.'

****

Luke was sitting opposite his boss in an old, traditional countryside pub, deep in his sad thoughts. His face was pale and glum, he barely touched his beer.

'If I…if I only, just for once, didn't behave like a complete senile ass, she would have been alive. Oh no, I can't bear this!'

Arina looked at him with concern. She knew that she must find the right words to calm down the young man, to reassure him, but it proved to be immensely difficult for her. She was never good at this sort of thing.

The pub was unusually quiet. Only some muffled voices could be heard in the background, or occasionally the fireplace would give away some crackling sounds of the logs burning lively inside it.

Arina sipped her wine, then cleared her throat.

'This lad, you know, the DS, what's his name?'

'Higgins, I think,' Luke answered apathetically.

'Higgins, yes, thanks. He is not as stupid as he looks. His remark about the supernatural power…he didn't realise, of course, how close he was…I suppose…what do you think?'

'Yeah.'

'Mind you, I don't like to be called psychic, you know that, don't you?'

Luke nodded indifferently. His eyes behind the glasses were unreadable.

Arina took a deep breath. Had another gulp of wine.

'You were really good with the police. Me myself, I just couldn't cope. Actually, you were brilliant!'

'Arina, stop it! You are not able to comfort even the most optimistically spirited person in the world! You're incapable of showing any empathy, I'm afraid. I did what I had to, for a short time I'd actually forgotten that it was me who was responsible for this brutal murder. Poor woman!' Luke sniffled uneasily.

Lady Holroyd was lost for words. She didn't know how to react to this quite rude remark by her secretary. After a short pause Lady Holroyd-Kugushev continued, assuming her usual, down-to-business, reticent manner. 'Firstly, we need to concentrate on catching our evasive killer. You wonder how I feel about missing him like that? Like a silly, pathetic, old hen! Believe me—not good! But we must put our emotions aside! We simply must. We can have a good old moan later. We cannot allow ourselves to get sloppy right now. Drink up your pint and order another one, I pay. And then start thinking!'

The little speech had its effect, as Luke, after a few heavy sighs, finished his drink and went to the bar. He returned with a pint and a large glass of wine. Luke took off his colourful coat, which he had kept on the whole time they had been in the pub and hung it on the back of his chair.

'I'm ready, sorry for…'

'It's okay, Luke, no need to be sorry. What was your first thought about the incident? Just think!'

He adjusted the spectacles, rested his prominent chin on the crook of his hand and looked at his boss.

'You mean, what I…'

'Have you noticed anything strange…something which wasn't fitting in, perhaps?' Arina prompted him.

Luke squinted his eyes and lightly massaged his temples. Then his eyes popped open and full of life.

'We need to start from the start!' he suggested intelligently.

'That's a very good start!' agreed Arina.

'Let's see. We know "for a fact",' as he mocked DI Robins and succeeded in stealing a tiny smile from Arina, 'that Ms Kale was alive on Monday. As far as we know, she could have still been alive and well until Tuesday morning.'

'She was,' Arina said quietly.

'What? How do you know? The police didn't say anything about the time of her death. At least, to me. But they didn't see you in my absence, right? So, how…you didn't, did you?'

'Yes, I did a quick check. Don't worry, I used my gloves. And I didn't move or disturb anything.'

'Oh, Arina, you are not supposed to interfere in a crime scene. It's a rule, and maybe a law as well. If they find out, if they find your prints…'

'As I said, I was wearing gloves!'

'All the time?'

'Oh…yes, I'm sure. Stop making me nervous at once! Anyway, how else would I have learned the time when this poor woman was murdered? Approximately, of course, but approximately enough to realise that she met her killer on Tuesday morning. Early morning, I think.'

'Rigor mortis?'

'Rigor mortis, or more precisely, receding rigor. It will be gone soon, only mortis will be left.'

'That means that the time of her death would be within twenty-four hours, plus another twelve hours needed for the process to be reversed?'

'Around thirty to thirty-two more likely, she still had her legs pretty rigid. And don't forget that she was kept outside. As far as we know, of course.'

'Oh, so you've examined her properly,' Luke shook his head in disbelief.

Arina completely ignored his remark and continued, just as if nothing had happened.

'Let us see…we arrived at the school in the early afternoon, we'll say about one o'clock?'

'Later, half-past one?'

'Yes, I agree. Then, how long did it take for us to find the body…another half-an-hour, forty minutes?'

'Say, two o'clock. Which means she was killed on Tuesday…at six in the morning, plus or minus a few hours…'

'I would say it was around six o'clock. Look, it would be dark earlier and later… people would begin to get up, there would be a risk of being witnessed by some "early bird".'

'Do you mean, that he'd planned it?'

'Of course, he planned it.'

Luke felt his blood turning to ice. It was so quiet. The fireplace stopped uttering hissing and crackling noises, the logs were burning out rapidly. The pub suddenly looked totally empty. Even the barman had abandoned his post.

'But…'

Luke didn't recognise his own voice, husky and frightening.

'Yes?' eagerly asked Arina.

The jerky flames were playing tricks on her face, aging it, grooving its already existing wrinkles deeper, making her eye sockets fathomless. The sight was so infernal, it was almost unbearable.

The last order bell made Luke jump. Fortunately, it also had broken the spell.

'Phew! Do you want another drink?' Luke asked smiling nervously.

'No, thanks! We need to keep our heads clear. We've come across a very dangerous foe. We must be on our guard all the time.'

'I agree. What I was going to ask you, I mean it didn't seem strange to you…why to wait until Wednesday?'

'Because,' Arina snapped her fingers, 'he knew.'

'He knew what?'

'He simply couldn't get rid of her body before. That is elementary, Luke!'

'You've lost me, boss.'

'This Tuesday, the day of the murder, it was outdoor activities day at the school. You see? He killed her all right, because it was very early in the morning, but then…he had a dilemma, to take the body somewhere and bury her there or wait. As we know he chose the latter.'

'How did you know about this?'

'We were sitting in the school sports hall for a long time, waiting to be questioned, and I was looking around and saw this colourful poster. About these fresh air benefits or outdoor goodness or whatever they call it nowadays, with a big date in the middle.'

'The eleventh,' said Luke softly.

'The eleventh,' Arina echoed.

'Do you think that he arranged their meeting beforehand, lured her outside under a false pretence?'

'Guys, time to leave, we are closing now!'

They both were startled by the barman's voice.

'We're going, already gone,' Arina smiled charmingly, then turned to Luke quickly and said very quietly, 'no, in my opinion, he was waiting for an opportunity. He was waiting for his victim to come to him.'

Luke got up and started arranging his long burgundy scarf around his neck, his hands suddenly felt clumsy, unsteady.

'As I understood you rightly, he, our murderer, is familiar with the school premises, is that what you're trying to tell me?'

'Of course, he is,' Arina answered lightly, stood up herself, put her long coat on and then added, 'he knows everything that is going on in this bloody school.'

Chapter 8

Luke didn't sleep well that night. He nodded off for an hour or so, the rest of the night he mostly spent tossing and turning in bed. Tantalising thoughts would not leave him alone. At seven o'clock he admitted his defeat and got up.

When Luke met his reflection in the bathroom mirror, he recoiled in disgust. His usually pale face looked now even more morbid, with a nasty greenish shade added to it. There were noticeable black circles under his blood-shot eyes. And his carroty hair stood up more inappropriately than ever.

'I look like a real serial killer,' Luke said self-critically before stepping under the scalding shower jet.

After that he felt a little bit better, but still was full of dark thoughts and decided to clad himself accordingly. Luke took his time going through his vast wardrobe, before deciding on a pair of Chino dark grey trousers and a black skinny shirt which went inside. Then he went to the kitchen. A bean-to-cup coffee machine Jura S8—a long-desired purchase, which actually came as a birthday present from his parents, warmed his heart immediately.

He refilled the water tank and poured some milk into the milk container which was already connected to the machine. After a short hesitation he chose his drink for this morning—a latte with a touch of almond syrup and extra foam. Luke brought the clever machine to life and took two croissants out of the fridge, when the doorbell rang.

'What the hell!' Luke exclaimed annoyed, 'it's not even eight o'clock yet!'

He didn't have to go far as the front door was just a few metres away from the kitchen in his minuscule semi.

'Hi!' saluted a girl with a shoulder length mint hair and heavy makeup. She was wearing a very short (almost non-existent) black leather skirt and fashionably ripped fishnet tights. She also had heavy black boots, up to her ankles, and a red loose sweater which was almost falling from her shoulders. A taxi was reversing on the street, opposite Luke's house.

'Ah!'

'It's Luke, right? I'm from the Supt. My name is Roxanne,' she held out her cold narrow hand mutilated by enormously long false nails, which colour matched her hair.

'From whom?'

'Superintendent Peter Crawnshaw,' Roxanne smiled showing her beautifully white teeth.

'Ah?'

'Can I come in?' asked the girl politely.

'Oh, sorry, of course! Silly of me…I…erm…just…it's a little bit early for me. I mean I am not entirely switched on yet. But please, come through!'

'Thank you!'

Roxanne had a sweet soft voice and pleasant manners, which were very much in contradiction with her appearance. She carefully wiped her feet on the door mat and graciously bent over her voluminous drawstring leather bag, from which she produced an official looking envelope.

'This is for you,' she said giving it to Luke, 'it's consent to disclose all membership personal data in this Physiotherapy Practice…'

'"Better life", the place is called the "Better life".'

'What a pretentious name that is!'

'I totally agree with you! And you've not seen it inside! Erm…thanks a lot for the document! But…I don't understand—do you work for the police?' Luke asked incredulously.

'Ha-ha, yes, you could say so,' the girl smiled, 'I'm working undercover right now, if you mean my flashy outfit.'

'Of course, not! It was not on my mind at all, I assure you!' said red faced Luke.

'It's okay, I don't mind! I was actually thinking of changing…can I use your bathroom for a minute, please?'

'Sure! By the way, would you like some coffee? I was just making some latte…'

'Sounds great, thank you very much! I can smell your coffee already, it smells delicious! I'll be back in a sec!' and Roxanne, swooping her bag, disappeared in the shown direction.

'Wow!' said Luke to himself and went to the kitchen to finish preparations for breakfast.

He took out of the fridge two more croissants, added them to the other two, which were waiting patiently on the tray, opened the already preheated oven and slid the loaded tray inside. Then Luke wiped the bar table briskly and started serving the coffee drinks.

'Oh, it's really a stylish little kitchen you've got here!'

Totally transformed Roxanne was standing at the doorway. She was wearing an unassuming pair of khaki cargo trousers. A beige scarf was wrapped around her neck and shoulders. Her face was clean and free of any traces of make-up. And also, was very beautiful, as Luke had chance to observe.

The girl was obviously starving. Her two croissants had disappeared rapidly, and it didn't take long for her to be persuaded to have the third one. As well as an extra-large mug of latte with whipped cream.

Luke was pleased to notice that Roxanne's healthy appetite didn't have any effect on her figure, which was dainty and, altogether, extremely attractive.

'Now I'm ready for the day,' Roxanne heralded after she licked off the last wisps of the cream from the brim of her mug.

'I'm glad that you're satisfied with my humble bachelor breakfast,' Luke said so primly that Roxanne laughed.

'Are you going to this place today?'

'Oh, yeah, I'll just give my boss a quick call, she must be up by now…erm…I hope…'

'My regards to Ms Sherlock H.,' purred Roxanne and squinted her green cat eyes.

'I beg your pardon! Oh! I see! It's funny… but I wouldn't call her that…especially in her presence.'

'Any chance I can meet this legendary lady?' asked Roxanne casually.

'Why do you want to meet her, if you don't mind me asking?'

'I've heard so much about her! She has aroused my curiosity.'

'From this pompous Supt of yours?'

'You guessed correctly,' Roxanne smiled lightly, 'the Superintendent has a very high opinion of Lady Holroyd-Kugushev.'

'I bet he has!'

Roxanne started at Luke.

'Sorry if I hurt your feelings,' Luke went on, 'but this guy, who happens to be her son-in-law, erm…ex-son-in-law, but it doesn't matter in the slightest! He is just forty something, by the way, and being the husband of her eldest daughter—it's just unspeakable!'

'Are you not jealous yourself, by any chance?'

'No, of course, not!'

Luke didn't know what came over him, why he suddenly became so angry. Not because of the possibility of something going on between Roxanne and Peter Crawnshaw? Certainly, not, he dismissed this thought eagerly. Even if they were having an affair, it's not his business.

'Luke!'

'Yeah…'

'Are you here? It looks like you're miles away. Thanks again for everything, but I really need to go.'

'Where do you need to go? I can give you a lift.'

'Oh, thank you very much! I was going home, you know, I really could do with a few hours of work on my dissertation…'

****

On the way to the clinic Luke decided to test the waters. Arina seemed to be in high spirits, her eyes were sparkling with energy and a smile of satisfaction was playing on her lips.

'It was nice from Roxanne to bring this consent to us rather than me going to the police station.'

'Hm…yes, I suppose, it saved us some time. Roxanne? Luke, who is Roxanne?'

'Oh, she is a criminal psychologist, liaising with the police. She is working undercover, mixing with all sorts of underworld criminals.'

'Why?'

'Because, firstly, she is helping the police, you know, fishing out some important information about drug dealings and drug dealers, and so on.'

'Sounds like a story from one of the numerous criminal serials you watch non-stop. Not a very original story, either.'

'I can dispute every single point you make, Arina, but I don't want to waste my time on it.'

'Hm.'

'You can 'hms' as much as you want, I'm not into an argumentative mood. But maybe you would like to know the second reason why Roxanne put herself forward for this very dangerous work?'

'Go on, Luke. You, obviously, will not let it go.'

'Because she is gathering material for her PhD dissertation,' Luke said proudly.

'Oh, she is a girl with brains. I see. It does make a difference.'

'You are impossible, you know that? You are the most spiteful, the most sarcastic person I have ever come across in the thirty-five years of my life.'

'In that case you haven't seen much in your life, my dear boy!'

'We are almost there,' Luke announced coldly.

'Stop sulking!'

'I'm not sulking! And…we are actually here!' Luke announced with relief.

It was strange to go to the same place with Arina. He knew that she was very alert, she was darting quick but attentive glances around, she would not miss anything. Like a hound who picked up the trail or was about to do so.

Susan, the receptionist, met them by her desk with a wide and uncandid smile glued to her plump lips.

'Hi, this is Lady Holroyd-Kugushev, meet Susan. Susan, may I introduce you to my boss and a senior partner of our "H&W Private Investigation Agency".'

It was almost too much for Susan, her cheeks blushed fiercely, and the smile got even wider. The poor girl even produced a poorly performed, awkward curtsy.

'Very…hm…excuse me,' she nervously cleared her throat, 'it's very nice…hm…to meet you, I'm…very honoured.'

'Good morning,' Arina said formally, 'we brought a court order compelling the disclosure of your members' personal details.'

'Oh, thank you very much…sorry for your troubles, but, you know, we have strict rules here, very strict. I could have lost my job if I…'

'It's fine, my dear, no need to apologise, you were doing your job, we understand it. Now, can we proceed with our enquiry, please?'

Susan took the consent form, which Arina held out to her, looking more unsure than before.

'Susan, if you want to take this paper to your clinical director first, we can wait here,' Luke said reassuringly.

'No, no! That won't be necessary, I can do it later! Please, come over to my office. I'll show you around.'

They went behind the reception desk and only then they saw a door leading to another room. The door was painted the same shade of pastel blue as the surrounding walls, and apart from a thin plastic handle of the same colour, which was very difficult to notice anyway, the door was practically invisible.

'Well-hidden nook where you can escape bothering you patients,' joked Luke and receive a more human smile from Susan.

The office was just a small square room with two desks positioned at right angles to each other, with a swivel chair between them. There were two computers on both of them, a phone, a printer and some stationary. The wall on the left had shelves stacked with folders, and the right one had a large canvas print with a pink magnolia. A window was in front of the main desk and the door was behind it. Three chairs stood in line by the window.

'I've opened our archive records for you. There is a spreadsheet with different activities for the last year and names of participants,' Susan said pointing at one of the computers, 'I can also provide you with hard copies if you wish.'

'No, thanks, we're fine!' Luke said.

'Yes, please!' Arina said at the same time.

Susan nodded and reached for a yellow folder clearly marked with some numbers and letters.

'You're well organised here,' complimented Arina and said addressing Luke, 'you had better plunge into the computer stuff, while I'll have a look at the folder. Can we use your photocopier?'

'Yes, of course! Let me show you…'

'No need, thank you!' Luke grinned.

'He is good at this,' said Arina generously, but quickly added, 'modern technology, I mean.'

'Okay, I'll leave you to it. If you need anything, I'll be next door. I'm just going to Mr Globe and then I will be at reception. Do you want something to drink, coffee or tea?'

'No, thank you very much, we're fine,' replied Luke already ensconcing himself by the computer.

Arina settled by the window. She put on her ultra-slim rimless reading spectacles, opened the folder and laid it out across her knees. Then she got a notebook and a pen out of her bag and placed them on one of the chairs next to her.

****

The two and half hours they spent in Susan's office proved to be very productive. They found out that Aaron Statham had his physio sessions every Tuesday afternoon, from four until half past five. On Thursdays, at the same time, between four and half five, he attended the Pilates classes. The groups were surprisingly small, including Aaron there were eight people in the physio class and six in the Pilates, all men, as these classes were divided not only by fitness level but also by gender.

The final list of people of interest contained just ten names because two of them (together with Aaron) participated in both classes. It also included their age and brief information.

For physio:

1. (Aaron Statham—27 y/o, a PE schoolteacher, former long-distance runner, a spine trauma caused by a fall from the roof, Leeds.)
2. David Pearson—38 y/o, a bank official, cross-country bike-rider, trauma connected with a bike fall, Harrogate.
3. Derek Turnbull—48 y/o, a software developer, cervical herniated disc due to many hours of sitting, Ripon.
4. George Hunt—43 y/o, a gardener, tree-surgeon, work-related injuries, Boston Spa.
5. Jan Cribble—59 y/o, an antiques shopkeeper, ex-rugby player, head/neck injury, Harrogate.
6. Keith Small—32 y/o—a bookmaker, retired jockey, spine trauma due to many falls, Wetherby.
7. Todd Fisher—39 y/o, an ex-soldier, retired due to injuries, freelance cyber security analyst, Harrogate.
8. Marek Lubieckii—46 y/o, a builder, work-related injuries, Harrogate.

For Pilates:

1. (Aaron Statham—as above.)
2. David Pearson—as above.
3. John Broad—41 y/o, Pharmacy assistant store manager, car crash injuries of the spine, Otley.
4. Keith Small—as above.
5. Owen Gould—24 y/o, a bodybuilder (is it a profession now or what?) and a part-time model, for improving posture, some spine injuries in the past connected with lifting heavy weights, Leeds.
6. Roger Grainger—50 y/o, a radiologist, used to play cricket for many years, neck/shoulder trauma, Knaresborough.

'It's short and clear, and has got what we need for a start,' Lady Holroyd waved the two pieces of paper to Luke proudly.

'Are we finished here?'

'I think so. Have you saved all these files?'

Luke chortled.

'Yes, of course, all have been saved onto my laptop and, additionally, to a memory stick.'

'Good! And have you printed everything that I asked you to?'

'Of course, boss!'

'Very good! So, we can start from people who live in Harrogate now. Oh! Bother! Look at the time! It's already almost three o'clock!'

Luke thought for a minute.

'Do you know what? Why not to contact those from the list who live further from Harrogate? Say, let me see…hm… this chap, a computer nerd, Derek Turnbull. He lives in Ripon. We can try him.'

'Or…Roger Grainger,' said Arina going through the names.

'Who? Oh, I see—the radiologist from Knaresborough.'

At this moment Susan came in, a smile on her face, her white teeth shining.

'How are you doing, guys?'

Arina screwed up her face at this inappropriate address.

'We are good, we've just finished, thanks a lot for your cooperation,' Luke replied quickly.

'My pleasure. Is there anything else I can help you with?'

'Actually, yes. Is there any way to find out who from these ten people are still with you?' Arian asked showing the names to Susan.

'No problem! If they are in a bold font, they are our current clients. Let me have a little look on our current database. Thanks Luke, no need to move you chair, I can easily squeeze through. I'm not *so* fat!'

Arina rolled her eyes up and turned away. After a few swift clicks Susan delivered the goods.

'Funnily enough, there are two, no, actually three who are still our patients.'

Lady Holroyd didn't see anything funny about this, but wisely decided to keep her thoughts to herself for now.

Instead she asked, 'Who is covering Julia's sessions? I presume that they are still going ahead?'

'Yes of course, we never cancel therapy sessions during our staff holidays. In this instance there are two therapists who have taken Julia's classes. You see, she was…quite unique in a sense…'

'What do you mean?'

Susan licked her full lips. Twirled her long blonde hair.

'I can't believe that I will never see her again'.

She shook her head. Rolled her round bulging eyes up. Sighed tardily, like an actress who did not learn her role well. After a long theatrical pause Susan fired off in her usual, machine gun manner.

'What I was going to say was that she ran both sessions, physiotherapy and Pilates classes. Usually, we have different therapists to do them. But Julia, she designed the sessions herself. Both, physio and Pilates exercises were aimed at men with similar types of injuries. She was really proud of her achievements. It will be difficult to find anybody to replace her.'

'Thank you, Susan, now we understand.'

'Would it be any use for us to have a word with the two therapists who are running Julia's classes?' asked Luke.

Susan thought for a moment, then shook her head.

'No, I don't think so. Your guy, Aaron, he was with us…let me check…since last January, January 2015. And he stopped in September.'

'In September?' exclaimed Arina and Luke together.

Susan looked again on the computer screen in front of her.

'Yeah, it was his wedding coming up, and he decided to stop for a while. I'm reading Julia's notes here—not quitting, just having a short break due to personal circumstances, in brackets—wedding & honeymoon.'

'In total—almost nine months, hm, in that case he must have met at least one other therapist,' Luke said thoughtfully. 'Do you remember, you've mentioned to me before that Julia was a person of habit, that she would have a holiday three times a year? At Christmas—but that's not of interest to us as Aaron Statham joined your clinic in January. In June for two weeks and the end of September, which is also irrelevant. Can you please tell us who replaced Julia Bower in June 2015?'

'You've got an exceptional memory!' Susan exclaimed. 'And also, you happened to pay more attention to my words than it seemed to me then.'

'His appearance is deceptive, I agree. He looks like he hasn't got a clue most of the time,' contributed Lady Holroyd with a sardonic smile.

'Oh, thank you very much, boss!'

'I said—that you look like—I didn't mean that you're actually clueless,' then giving a sharp look to Susan, Arina slowly repeated Luke's question.

'He is not working for us anymore. We've lost touch with him,' Susan replied reluctantly.

'Shall we start from the beginning,' Arina suggested still fixing her eyes on her, 'who is he and what happened here in June last year?'

Susan licked her lips again. She tried very hard to avoid their eyes. Her blushing face assumed an expression of someone sucking a sour lemon.

'I honestly don't know where he is now. He was…a temporary member of our team,' Susan sighed heavily, 'it was actually me who brought him in. Damn, if I only knew!'

'Knew what?' Arina asked after waiting in vain for continuation of the story.

Susan's mouth was quivering and her wide set, bulging eyes were staring into space.

'He was so charming, you know, very attractive, sexy, his chiselled abs were just perfect!'

Arina's face didn't give away any emotions, but inside her there was a tempest of impatience brewed together with roaring frustration.

'Can we have his name and address?' Arina asked, trying very hard to control her temper.

'Oh, you see, here we've got a problem!' Susan announced with an idiotic smile. 'Kevin, that's not his real name of course, but I got used to it, ha-ha, silly me! He was the best dancer I've ever met! And, mind you, we were really desperate! So, you can finish the picture yourself. How would I know that he was a con-man?'

'Susan, hold on, please! Can you go through your story again but this time a little bit slower,' pleaded Luke.

'It's really embarrassing for me, but okay, if you insist…We were short of staff last year, like the year before, like always to be frank with you. It's all to do with our clinical director, Mr Globe. He cannot deal with people, he is too demanding, too unfriendly, too arrogant… Anyway, he lied to me from the first minute we met…'

'Who? Who lied to you? Mr Globe?' Arina asked in the way an irritated teacher would speak to a half-baked pupil.

'Of course not! Kevin! I meant Kevin. We met at a night-club and he caught my attention straight away. How he moved, like a wild gracious animal, you know, who lives in jungles. Wild and free. We had a few drinks together, we talked. He was a very good listener. I thought he liked me. And…and it was so easy to talk to him, like I had known him for ages…So, I told him about problems at work, how we were struggling, how we were desperate for more experienced staff. And would you believe it! I really cannot forget it! Purple and blue and red strobe lights. Rhythmic loud music, bum-bum-bum…and we were sitting very close to each other. His handsome stubbled face leaning closer and closer to me. Because of the music it's difficult to hear. Our cocktails, mine was bright yellow, his was lime green, the whole atmosphere was electric, pulsing…Who would not believe him? Who would not fall under his charm?'

Susan stopped for a moment, then went on, 'Cutting a long story short. Kevin said, what a coincidence, it's your lucky day and so on. I'm the right man, I'm between jobs and would very much like to help you out. Just for a while, before you find somebody else. The next day he arrived here, dressed in expensive sportswear, bringing a very impressive CV and all sorts of certificates and diplomas with him. When he flaunted a few names of local celebrities, golf goers, members of those posh golf clubs, like Rudding Park Golf Course in Harrogate or Alwoodley Golf Club in Leeds and so on, whom he knew both professionally and socially. Naturally, our director couldn't resist and hired him immediately.'

'You're saying that Mr Globe is a keen golfer and that was a reason why Kevin has been given a job. But what about references?' Arina asked.

'Oh yeah, Mr Globe is a very keen golfer, he is a golf maniac. If he was capable of having a passion, it would be everything to do with this game. Regarding references, ha, checking references was a joke. He gave us two names, supposedly his patients. It was me who contacted them, they couldn't praise him highly enough.'

'How did you know that they were not genuine?'

'We didn't know then. It all became clear after he had run away.'

'What? Has he disappeared also?' Luke exclaimed and pushed back up the slowly sliding down glasses.

Susan smiled sarcastically.

'Yeah, he disappeared all right. But there was no mystery about his disappearance. All our cash, together with the most expensive exercise machines have gone with him.'

'Oh, it must have been a tough time! You have probably lost a lot of your patients?' Arina said.

'Of course! It was especially tough for me! Mr Globe took a decision to punish the guiltiest person of all—meaning me! He has come up with the genius idea of a twenty percent pay cut. Which has lasted three months! For three months I've been getting peanuts!'

Luke and Arina exchanged quick meaningful glances. Another line of inquiry? Possible...

'We are truly sorry to hear how you've been mistreated,' said Luke in his best soothing voice.

Arina used the pause in Susan's lamentation wisely, squeezing her next retort.

'Susan, we want to thank you very much for your help, it was really invaluable for our investigation. And just before we leave you in peace, one last request. We're going to start with these three men who are still with you. Can you say anything about them, anything at all that comes to your mind? It doesn't have to be long, just an impression.'

'Oh, I'll try...let me see...they will be David, Owen and Roger. Owen is easy! Everybody knows Owen Gould. Our exemplary patient, would never miss a single session. He is a harmless enough guy, a little bit obsessed with his body, his looks, you know.'

'Is this you, Susan, saying this?' said Luke with a broad smile.

'Yeah, I know what you mean. But if a bloke can only think of his muscles and how they look on a screen or in a photo, and never gives a single compliment or a friendly smile to a girl, who, mind you, works her socks off, helping him to achieve the dream of his life...'

'We've got the picture, thank you,' Arina interrupted, 'how can we reach him, is he at work now or at home?'

'He's here! As always! If he is not with us, you can bet that he is at this swanky gym in Leeds, pumping up his muscles. I have my big doubts about his work, by the way! He put it as a part-time modelling job, yeah right, when does he find time for that?'

'We will try to find out,' Arina said with a thin smile. 'Just before we talk to him, can we check the other two? Is there any chance of finding them here as well?'

Susan looked at the list and shook her head.

'No more luck, I'm afraid. It's too early for their Pilates session, which has been moved to seven pm now.'

'It's okay, Susan, we'll just have to catch up with them later. Can we talk to Owen, please?' Luke said, disconnecting his laptop and putting it away into its suede bag.

'I wouldn't keep your hopes up too much, if I were you,' Susan noted with an ironic grin, 'he is not exactly a talkative guy.'

Chapter 9

How right Susan was, thought Luke drearily. They had been conversing with Owen Gould, or at least trying to do so, for almost fifteen minutes and achieved nothing. The three of them were sitting in a small private lounge, comfortable and quiet, where everything seemed predisposed to a pleasant, relaxed atmosphere, for an easy, informal chat. Unfortunately, it didn't work for Owen Gould.

Despite an impressive muscle mass which was wrapped around his, otherwise, thin body, like an oversized puffer jacket, he didn't strike one as a powerful or confident man. Quite the opposite. Owen looked jumpy and unsure of himself. His small, deeply set eyes were not still for a single moment, they were darting from side to side, successfully avoiding any eye contact with Arina or Luke. Above all, his communication skills proved to be far below average.

'What do you remember about Aaron?' Luke asked, after explaining in a few words the reason for their interview.

'Say it again?' retorted Owen in a husky voice, immediately giving away his broad Yorkshire accent.

Luke repeated his question.

Owen crossed his legs, scratched his closely shaved head, them mumbled, 'Dunno, mate.'

'Owen, please, it is very important for our investigation, can you recall anything to do with Aaron Statham? Anything, every single detail, however small and insignificant it might look, is important for us,' Arina said in her clear impeccable English.

Owen looked even more puzzled.

'What she's saying, man?'

Luke sighed and tried again.

Owen thought for a moment, then shrugged his shoulders.

'Photographs,' Arina said to Luke sotto voce.

Luke nodded and shook out of the A4 envelope a couple of the best pictures of Aaron they had. He laid them out on the coffee table in front of Owen.

'Do you remember him?'

Owen squinted and cocked his head to the side. Then took one photograph and brought it closer to his eyes.

'Yeah, haven't seen him for a while.'

'That's right, as we were saying before, he, Aaron Statham, disappeared about a year ago, yes?' Luke tried very hard to stay calm.

'So you say,' replied Owen Gould noncommittedly and put the photograph back.

'Good that you remembered him. What can you tell us about him?'

'Not much. He had Pilates classes the same time.'

Luke thought that soon he would not be able to control himself anymore and would commit a brutal murder in front of his boss, who, as he noticed, had similar thoughts passing through her mind.

'Yes, thank you, we already know that. Did you talk at all?'

'Yeah, we must have. But it's not a social club, if you know what I mean. We go there, we work out, we get checked by our trainer, we have personal goals to achieve...'

'We get the point, thank you, Owen,' interrupted Arina, 'can you remember anything you talked about?'

Owen snapped his fingers.

'You've got me there! I remember now! Yes, of course, this bloke was going to marry some chick from work! Cannot remember her name, though...That was the point!'

'What do you mean?' Arina asked.

'He was working on his injured leg, of course! To impress his girl. To turn up to their big day without crutches or stick. You can imagine, one day he limps like a cripple, the next day he is all there!'

'It was a surprise then?' Arina couldn't hide her excitement, 'so, what you are saying is that Aaron could actually walk without a stick? Could he possibly run again?'

'I dunno about running, but he could certainly walk.'

After Owen hurried back to his massage session, Arina turned to Luke and exclaimed, raising her index finger, 'My vision was correct! As I thought! He went for his last ever run, just before his wedding, from which he has never returned. Because he was murdered.'

If there were any doubts in Luke's mind, he didn't have time to express them because at this exact moment with a triumphant broad smile appeared Susan.

'It's your lucky day, guys! Mr David Pearson himself will be with you shortly!'

'How? How did you do it?' Luke asked.

'Magic! Ha! I just decided to give him a call and check with him if it's possible for him to come here slightly earlier?'

'Slightly? You must be kidding! It's almost two and half hours earlier!'

'I made him an offer he couldn't possibly resist. A half price session with our yoga guru, just before his Pilates class.'

'Oh, Susan, thanks a lot, really, but would you not be in trouble again because of this?'

'No worries! I'm working hard on promoting our new important member of staff—Mr Ladhari, that's all,' she gave out a mischievous grin.

'And this, what's his name, David Pearson, he just agreed to do this? Is he not working or busy or what?' Arina wondered.

'Firstly, David works nearby. His bank is just literally five minutes away. And secondly, knowing him, I can guarantee that he would find plenty of excuses to wriggle his way out of there to get a cheap bargain with us, or anybody else as a matter of fact.'

'Oh, is that so?' Arina noted incredulously.

'That must be him!' Susan suddenly announced, and, holding her mobile up, added, 'It's a door buzzer, we fitted a silent system which sends an alert signal on my phone. We don't want to disturb our patients unnecessarily.'

'She's not as stupid as she looks,' Arina admitted when their hostess went out.

****

David Pearson was a stumpy, serious looking man, who looked older than his age of thirty-eight. After Susan introduced them and excused herself, he shook their hands in a confident, self-assured manner, at the same time scrutinising them through his heavy eyelids. Then he lowered himself comfortably into an armchair, leaned back and clasped his hands together.

Unlike with Owen Gould, it didn't take ages for David Pearson to remember Aaron. Straight away he knew who they were talking about. But that was almost all. He was very much concise in expressing himself, trying to get away with as few uncommitted interjections as possible for his answers.

Yes, he knew that Aaron Statham was a marathon runner, a famous one, but it was all in the past, he was struggling even with walking. No, he was not aware that Aaron could walk fairly normally. Yes, he was trying to get better, why otherwise he would come to this, between you and me, dubious and madly expensive place. About the wedding? Yes, now it came back to him, all those sessions had something to do with Mr Statham's approaching wedding, perhaps to be able to walk down the aisle without making a fool of himself? It was a joke, by the way.

Only at the end of their chat did David Pearson become more talkative and reveal something which left them stunned.

'I don't think that Aaron kept a secret of coming here, at least not from his fiancée.'

'What? Why do you think so?' Arina asked, the two vertical lines between her eyebrows as deep as ever.

'I don't think, I know. I saw them together here,' he gestured towards the front door, 'with my own eyes, after one of our sessions together, I think it was a physio one, so it must have been Tuesday. I cannot give you the exact day, but it was in August, towards the end, when we had this mad hot spell at the end of the summer. I remember it well because the girl looked beautiful in her tiny sky-blue summer dress, I mean tiny, I could almost see her knickers.'

'Are you sure that it was his fiancée?' Arina asked and gave a rapid look to equally baffled Luke.

'What do you mean? Okay, strictly speaking, I don't know—we'd never been officially introduced, but putting two and two together, who else would give Aaron a lift home just a few weeks before the wedding if not his future wife?'

'Can you describe the girl, apart from her *tiny* frock? As detailed as possible, please' Arina inquired in a heavy, sombre voice.

David Pearson suddenly seemed to realise the significance of all these questions. He goggled his usually small round eyes, so they popped out of their blanketing lids like two shiny black olives. His mask of superior confidence began to slide away, revealing more human qualities such as nervousness, diffidence and wariness.

'Hm…it was a long time ago…I will try, though. Certainly she was a very attractive young lady, with beautiful long blond hair. Slim as well, like a girl from those fashion magazines, like a model. Oh, there is another thing, I got the impression that she was very young, you know? *Too* young even for Aaron.'

'Oh, my God!' whispered Luke.

'Did you by any chance overhear her name?'

'No, I am sorry.'

'Have you seen her again?' Arina continued.

'No, no, just once.'

'And she was giving him a lift?'

'I honestly cannot swear on it. She met him outside of our place, and then they walked away together. I assumed she would drive him home or wherever they were going, because Aaron didn't drive.'

'How did he travel home usually?'

'Oh, I'm not so sure what was happening on Thursdays, our Pilates day. Vaguely remember that it might have been his colleague, you know, one of the teachers, or a friend. Sometimes Aaron would take a bus to Leeds. I can help you with Tuesdays, however. It was one of us, from the physio class, sort of mate of his. Todd was his name.'

'Aha, Todd Fisher,' Luke said checking the name against their list,' Todd from Harrogate. We're in luck again, we might have a chance to talk to him tonight, Arina.'

'I'm afraid you won't,' Dave noted gravely, 'he passed away last year.'

'What?' Luke jumped.

Arina was also astonished but managed to conceal it better.

'Do you know what happened?' she asked.

'Not exactly. There were rumours that he took his own life. But you know, if it is true, I would not be too much surprised. This guy, Todd, he was a moody bloke, grumpy sort. As I heard he had been depressed for some time. We didn't see him the last few months anyway.'

'Did he quit the class?' Arina asked.

'No, he was still a member of our group, and he would turn up occasionally, but we saw him less and less. And, if my memory is not playing tricks with me, I reckon I have not seen him since the end of July 2015.'

****

'Damn! Damn me!' Arina was furious, 'Everybody, everybody who could be of any help for us—just...' she snapped her fingers in frustration, 'bloody dead. I should never have taken this wretched case. I should have stayed in the Tyrol and enjoyed my vacation there.'

'Hm...'

'What do you mean, Luke, by saying "hm"?'

'It's just happened that I've recalled something.'

'And?'

'That a certain retired general had got on your nerves, and you were not too upset to cut your holiday short.'

'Oh! Never mind! What are we going to do now?'

They were sitting inside Luke's Jag, parked about a hundred metres away from "Better Life", and the relentless rain was whipping their front window.

'It's unfortunate that we failed to meet Mr Grainger, the radiologist, tonight but it was otherwise a very productive day, boss.'

'We have so much to do! And we have to hurry, I feel it! And it just drives me mad! We need to see those girls again, particularly one. With long blond hair. To talk to her seriously. Enough childish lies!'

'Angel? You think it was her?'

'Who else, my boy, who else? She practically told us herself, only we didn't believe her then, did we? And why? Because it didn't fit his image of an ideal innocent young man, which was cleverly concocted and presented to us by Lisa. Lisa again.'

Luke nodded meekly.

Lady Holroyd-Kugushev stared gloomily at the poorly lit cobbled street, which was quickly flooding.

'Also we need to check all the details of this unfortunate soldier's death.'

'Yes,' Luke agreed again.

'Not mentioning the other seven patients we need to see.'

'You're absolutely right!'

Arina looked at her companion suspiciously, but his blissful face revealed nothing to her. Luke started the engine and drove carefully, avoiding deep puddles, with which this place was replete.

'I've got an idea,' he started gingerly when they were back to the A61.

'Go on.'

'I know who can help us with Angel. Roxanne! She is a highly qualified criminal psychologist, she will find ways around Angel's twisted adolescent mind. I'm sure of it!'

'Not her again!' protested Arina but without fire, just following the habit not to trust a new person. She felt tired. Confused. Powerless. The case was flowing out of her amateur hands like a dirty, contaminated liquid.

'Can I ask her to come round to go over the case, tonight perhaps? Will it be okay with you, Arina?'

'You mean—to my place? Tonight?'

'Yeah, if you don't mind. Just to save us some time. Some precious time, hm?'

'Oh, whatever, Luke. Will she be willing to come at such short notice?'

'I'm sure she will, especially if it will be you who invites her. I'm driving, you see.'

'Insolent boy,' Arina said under her breath but loud enough for Luke to be able to hear this.

After a short, slightly awkward conversation, which took place on Luke's phone between Lady Holroyd-Kugushev and Roxanne, the former admitted reluctantly, 'Yes, she seems pretty enthusiastic to be involved in our investigation, if she is prepared to go out on such a foul night. Presumably, she knows that she will not be paid. Does she, Luke?'

'Of course! It's nothing to do with money. Roxanne is very keen to get some new experience in dealing with more unusual cases, and, particularly, working alongside such a shrewd and talented private detective like you, boss.'

'Oh Luke, cut the crap! I don't feel the need for cheap flattery!' Arina exclaimed, but Luke could see that she was pleased.

At eight o'clock sharp, Mozart's Turkish March doorbell chime filled Arina's house.

'It must be Roxanne,' Luke said happily, 'dead on time!'

And of course, he was right. It was Roxanne, but a very different Roxanne. This time her hair was jet black, styled in a short bob. She had a beautiful emerald ring on her right hand, which matched her green cat eyes, elongated even more by an eyeliner. She was wearing a long raincoat over a slim-fit floral tunic and a pair of black leggings. She had a big umbrella in one hand and a bottle of red wine in the other. Her voluminous leather bag was slung over her shoulder. She also had a wonderful smile on her lips.

Luke took her wet coat to hang in the downstairs bathroom, Arina got a bottle of wine. Roxanne was combing her sleek hair in front of the hall mirror and felt herself at ease almost immediately.

'Luke, bring Roxanne up to date with our case and I will order some food, Chinese?'

Luke didn't have to be asked twice. He took Roxanne to the living room, showed her to the most comfortable chair near the live fire and gave her a brief introduction to their case. Roxanne was simply transfixed, she didn't interrupt him once, just listened to what he had to say with her full attention.

When he finished, she said, 'I need a smoke to digest this lot.'

Luke thought the same, but his best side won over and he fended off the temptation. When, a few minutes later, Roxanne returned from the back garden where she had indulged herself under the porch, her black hair was glistening with rain drops, like they were diamond speckles. She smelt of expensive cigarettes, floral perfume and the freshness of the night.

The meal arrived, they ate straight out from their takeout boxes at the large dining table, not wasting time on small talk, almost in silence, the three of them deep in their own thoughts, in their own world. They didn't have a need to fill the space with empty words, they were comfortable with a lull.

Pleased, Luke spotted several approving looks from Arina. But the best followed. When they finished eating, they went back to their more comfortable armchairs near the fire, and as soon as Roxanne sat down, she was joined by the forest creature, Brahms.

'Oh, please, be careful,' Luke warned her, 'he is not a timid cat, he is a wild beast. Quite a dangerous one, I would say. He doesn't like to be hobnobbed by strangers.'

Roxanne smiled and tousled his thick shaggy mane, instead. Surprisingly, Brahms let her do this without skinning her alive. He even uttered a deep, hoarse rumbling.

'Unbelievable!' exclaimed Luke, 'this animal has never honoured me with even a hint of a purr, me, who has looked after him and the other two so many times! And look at you! He accepted you straightaway! Unbelievable!'

'Yes, it is unusual, I must admit,' Arina agreed with her secretary, 'perhaps, you are used to cats, Roxanne? Have you got any yourself?'

Roxanne nodded and showed them a series of photos on her phone, picturing a pretty Siamese cat called Linda. Then the ladies spent the next quarter of an hour talking about cats. Luke sipped his wine, admiring Roxanne. She herself reminded him of a graceful cat, with her long eyes and smooth, elegant manners.

The funny thing was that nobody was rushing to talk shop. It looked like they all were enjoying this short period of peace and easy chat, pushing away the dreariness and gravity of this case. At least for a while.

Later on, they decided on the following: Roxanne would go to the school and see the girls under the pretext of providing counselling services, such as emotional support and reassurance in the light of recent tragic events. Of course, she would try to deliver such services but her main purpose would be to get more sense from Angel and Fairuza, if possible. Angel was to be her main object.

'Are you sure you can do it? Have you worked with young people before?' asked Arina.

'I'm sure and no—I have not dealt with teenage girls before. But I've got the right papers and right attitude.'

'Hm…if you think it will be enough…' Arina didn't sound at all convinced.

'How are you going to do this, Roxanne? We don't want to force you into some unknown territory,' Luke was not sure either.

Roxanne laughed airily.

'Please, don't be worried! I'm very resourceful, I can assure you. As I said, I've never counselled adolescents before. To be totally frank with you, I've not counselled adults either.'

'What?' cried Luke.

'I am astonished,' simply added Arina.

'But!' Roxanne continued in the manner of a teacher explaining some elementary stuff to not too bright pupils, 'it's not really as difficult as you might imagine. Really one thing you have to do well, it's listening. That's all. That is the key to success, psychological or any other—the ability to listen.'

'Yes, thank you, Roxanne, we get the picture,' jumped in Arina who didn't like to be preached to. 'It's late now and we have a busy day ahead of us, so I suggest we finish for today.'

'Roxanne, I can give you a lift,' Luke offered without delay.

'Oh, thank you very much Luke, that's very kind,' Roxanne smiled in her enigmatic manner and squinted her eyes.

'And, Roxanne, we will pick you up tomorrow. It would be better if we introduce you. We are lucky that the acting head, principal I mean, is a nice guy who we got along well with—a maths teacher, Mr Baxter.'

'I don't know how long he will last in this position, though,' Luke remarked with a sardonic smile, 'in this *feminist* establishment.'

'Not long, I think. Until they sort themselves out and stop running around like headless chickens,' Arina agreed, 'until then we've got an ally there.'

Chapter 10

'I hope she will bring us luck, which we desperately need,' Arina welcomed Luke next morning.

'Who?' Luke was even more dishevelled than usual, his spiky hair was sticking out in all possible directions.

'Wake up, Luke!' Arina snapped. 'I meant your protégé—Roxanne, of course!' Then she locked the front door and buttoned her long black coat up, as it was another cold, windy day with the grey rainy sky.

Luke yawned loudly and shook his head like a sodden dog.

'Good morning to you too, boss!' he said and yawned again.

'How can you drive? You're half awake!'

'I can drive in my sleep,' Luke boasted and yawned the third time.

'It's ten already! We need to rush!' Arina said peevishly fastening her seatbelt.

'Did you have another bad night, Arina?'

Arina sighed and nodded.

'We're almost there, Roxanne lives in one of these little streets off Roundhay Park.'

'I just know that we have to hurry. That the murderer is after another victim…I don't know…the dream I had…it was a weird dream. But I know that we cannot waste any time. And also, we have to be very careful. I won't say anymore.'

'You're frightening me,' Luke tried to speak lightly but his arms had been covered in goose bumps already.

Arina closed her eyes tightly. She tried hard to push away last night's dream. If it was a dream? She began to get confused in distinguishing between *just* dreams and visions.

Arina took ten deep breaths. It was her usual technique to bring calmness and light inside her soul. It didn't work this time, however.

She hadn't gone to sleep easily last night. There was too much on her mind. She tried to read but couldn't concentrate. Eventually, she closed the book, switched off the bed light and tried to relax. With age there comes along insomnia, she thought bitterly and prepared herself for a long, restless, frustrating night. Two cats, Nero and Chernomor were sandwiching her from both sides, and Brahms made himself comfortable on the top of her legs.

'You are lucky bastards,' she commented enviously and started counting sheep.

Somehow, on the second hundred ewes she began to drift away. She was still aware of Chernomor's soft snore and Brahms's loud purr, but she already felt a weightless cocoon of so much desired sleep wrapping her protectively.

For some time she was in and out of this dreamless light sleep. Then, suddenly, out of nowhere the fear came. Arina found herself walking nervously through the net of night streets. They were deserted, these narrow passages, cramped by tall dark buildings without windows. She knew she had to run from this dead city, but she couldn't find the way out. The more she ran, the more she was getting lost. But the worst was still to come.

It was a barely recognisable whisper, more like a waft of wind. But it was burning her neck like the flames of inferno. And it was saying very nasty, very dangerous things in her ear. The language was not familiar, but the meaning was. She turned back but there was nobody. She tried to run but the voice was still there. She would look right and left but see nobody. Still the whisper was filling her ears. Her heart was limping madly. Her thoughts were meddling into an unknown zone.

Then the whisper turned to a laugh. Malicious, jeering laugh, which she couldn't escape. It was following her everywhere like a pestilent botfly. Arina was getting tired of her endless run. There was no exit out of this urban labyrinth, she understood now. That was what the unbodied voice was telling her. Portending her ill fortune.

'We're here!' Luke announced and brought Arina back to reality.

Arina rubbed her frozen fingers together and looked out of the car window.

A slender figure in black detached itself from the stone wall surrounding a Victorian mansion and its grounds, an impressive grand building now converted to flats, and walked swiftly in their direction. This time Roxanne chose to look prim and plain. She was wearing a very ordinary trouser suit and had a pair of ugly old-fashioned glasses balanced on the tip of her nose. Under her arm she was holding a large, official looking folder.

'You seem well prepared,' Luke noted with a wide grin.

On the way to "Lombardy Poplar Grammar School" they went through some particular points of interest on which Roxanne was going to concentrate. She still looked relaxed and didn't show any signs of agitation or nervousness prior to the unusual task looming ahead of her.

Mr Baxter, the acting principal, was very happy to see them back and welcomed the idea of counselling with open hands.

'I don't know why we haven't thought about it ourselves, probably because we all were, and still are, in such shock,' he shuddered.

He didn't look great. During these couple of days, he had aged a lot, his haggard face was showing all the signs of stress and his livid blue under-eye bags were huge.

'The police are still on site, half the school premises are cordoned off and we live as if under siege most of the time. And it's half term approaching,' Tom Baxter threw up his hands in a helpless way.

'Is it the last day of term today?' asked Roxanne, first time showing a shade of concern.

'No, no! Don't worry! We're breaking up next Friday, so you have the whole week, plus today,' he gave her a friendly wink and smiled reassuringly.

Roxanne's charm had already done its work, Arina and Luke could leave her there with light hearts.

****

They had a busy agenda for the rest of the day. They were going to meet three people from their list. Two—from Harrogate and one—who they had failed to see yesterday—from Knaresborough—Roger Grainger, the radiologist.

He had missed his Thursday session due to a *very* important meeting at the hospital. Today was his day off, not the whole day of course, just the morning. His job was *very* demanding, and no way could he allow himself extra free time. The detectives had to be satisfied with whatever was on offer.

Luke pulled over by an impressive looking cottage, towering on the side of the Castle Bank, with its bevelled leaded glass windows facing the river Nidd.

'Must have cost a fortune,' Arina noted meditatively.

'Yeah, arrogant so-and-so! *I can spare you just twenty minutes of my highly valuable time,*' Luke mimicked the radiologist's voice very well.

'Hush Luke, he might hear you,' Arina warned him but couldn't hide a roguish grin.

Arina's words appeared to be not too far from the truth. They were heard, but not by Dr Grainger. Two Yorkshire Terriers, absolutely identical at first glance, as well as at the second, bolted out of the house towards the gates, welcoming them with heart-rending barks.

'Hi! You must be those private detectives interested in Aaron,' the dogs' owner had to almost shout to outvoice his noisy pets.

Luke and Arina just simply nodded.

'You can come in now,' Grainger addressed them in his usual patronising manner and then, changing his tone completely, cooed to the still furiously yapping terriers, 'boys, boys, calm down, these people won't harm you, will they? They won't delay our nice morning walk for long, will they?'

Dr Roger Grainger bent down and patted both dogs gently. It had an immediate effect. They stopped barking and started jumping up and down like matching hairy tennis balls, uttering shrieking yelps at the same time.

'Baby-boys, baby-boys,' he continued cooing, 'want their little biscuits, come on, come on! Let the detectives come through. It will not take long, I promise, little rascals!'

Arina felt like throwing up if this ridiculous show continued any longer. Fortunately for her, Grainger walked his dogs to the house and waved to the guests to follow. It is bad to feel so negative towards a potentially valuable source of information, she rebuked herself in vain, because it was difficult to find anything amiable about this man.

He was a not particularly big guy, but he seemed bulky, out of place. He gave the impression of someone best to give a wide berth to. He took up the whole space around him, there was no room for anybody else. He suffocated people. With his round belly, round shoulders and dome-like bald head, he saw himself as the centre of the Universe and behaved accordingly.

Dr Grainger showed them into a sparsely furnished living room, he didn't offer them anything to drink, which was quite agreeable to them as they didn't want to stay any minute longer than was necessary.

It was clear from the start that he wasn't an admirer of Aaron Statham.

'I really don't understand what it's all about?' he said testily, 'Much Ado about Nothing, that is all it is, *I* say. This ex-runner, a marathon runner of the past, you know, he might have been famous once, many moons ago, but everybody around him treated him like he was still some sort of a celebrity.'

'So, you don't think that anything bad happened to him?' asked Luke lightly.

'Don't misinterpret my words, young man! Don't accuse me just because I cannot help you. It's not my fault!'

'Of course not!' Arina said in her calm controlled voice, 'we just need you to help us to get know this man a little bit better. To build up a picture, or a small fragment of this picture, like in a jigsaw, in order to understand what has happened to him. You've already given us something new.'

'Really? Such as?' asked the radiologist with his round face slowly turning red.

'That Aaron was well liked, a popular guy. And that not everybody approved of this.'

'Approved what?'

'His popularity,' Arina answered quietly.

'I've had enough of this! That's it! Our interview is over!' Roger Grainger jumped up out of his chair, followed by his two little dogs who jumped up after him yapping their heads off.

'Just before we go, please, can you tell us if you have ever seen Aaron's fiancée?' Arina asked bringing into play her disarming smile.

Grainger grunted, folded his thick arms across his chest and measured her up and down with his arrogant look.

'No! I've never seen his fiancée. Now, I don't want to be rude, but, as you can guess, my time is extremely precious and I'm afraid I have to go now. I'll show you the way out.'

Luke and Arina got up and walked to the front door, which Grainger opened wide.

'Thank you very much! We really appreciate this,' Arina tried to sound sincere, 'we will not bother you again, I promise. What nice dogs you have here! Aren't they so cute and so beautiful!'

'Hm, do you really like dogs? I thought for a moment…never mind… yes, they are! They're just like my babies. And I spend all my free time (which I don't have much of at all) with them.'

'I totally understand you! I myself have got a couple of little dogs,' lied Arina shamelessly.

'Really? What kind of dogs are they?'

'Oh…they are…pugs!'

'Oh, they're extremely intelligent I heard, I would love to meet them! You could have brought them with you today! Anyway, I'm really sorry but I promised these two boys to take them for a long stroll.'

'Good-bye! And thank you very much again,' Arina said and started walking to their car.

Luke who was tailing her obediently, suddenly stopped and looked back.

'By the way, do you know who gave Aaron lifts home,' asked he out of the blue.

Grainger frowned and thought for a moment.

'There was his colleague from school, I think he lives not far from Leeds. They would go to a pub afterwards occasionally. I know this because they asked me a few times to join them.'

'Did you?'

'Twice. As I mentioned already, I am very short with time. There was nothing special about these evenings, nothing worth mentioning in case you wonder. A few times actually it was me. I dropped him near his place on my way to the hospital, late meetings, you see.'

'And other days?'

'He went by bus, I guess. And again, it's what I think. I might be wrong.'

****

'That was really good, Arina,' Luke laughed heartily, 'about your two pugs. Ha-ha! Absolutely ingenious!'

'Thank you Luke,' Arina said modestly, but Luke noticed that she was pleased.

'What do you want to do now, boss? Do you fancy a quick lunch somewhere here, in one of these historic pubs before heading off to Harrogate?'

'What time is it now? Twenty to twelve. Plenty of time. Do you know, Luke, how strange?'

'What is strange?'

'That I have never been to Mother Shipton's Cave.'

'Erm?' sometimes Luke found it difficult to make logical links between Arina's statements.

'The weather has improved, I can even make out some blue patches above us,' Arina jerked her head up.

'Do you mean that you want to go there *now*?' Luke asked in bewilderment.

'Correct! It won't take long. Plus it should be reasonably empty, kids are still at school.'

'But why on earth—now?'

'Because…because I feel it will help our investigation!'

'In what way?' Luke asked with a flippant smile.

'In a way of me getting closer to…oh, doesn't matter Luke, you wouldn't understand anyway! But I need to go to this cave. You can wait outside if you wish, you are not obliged to follow me everywhere.'

'Of course, I will go too. I will not let you go there on your own, it will be slippery down there, and I don't want you to lose your footing there, fall and break you neck, your ladyship!'

'Oh, how thoughtful of you,' Arina said in a stern voice, but deep inside she was glad that she wouldn't be alone. She couldn't explain even to herself why she felt so vulnerable, so exposed. It was very unlike her.

They bought tickets and walked along Sir Henry Slingsby's woody pathway in silence. Arina was right, and there was almost nobody in the park. Just a small group of Japanese tourists was descending mossy steps to see the famous well.

'Do you know where the cave is?' asked Arina.

'Over there,' Luke showed her the way.

'I didn't know that you had been here before, you could have easily stayed in the car.'

'No, it's fine, Arina. I was here a long time ago, before I knew you.'

'With one of your girls?' asked Arina indifferently.

'Yeah, with a Czech lass, her name was Madlenka, I think, or it was Petra…I was working on my Czech language then and…'

'This is all very interesting but, perhaps, you can save the story for another time. I would like to go to Mother Shipton's Cave now.'

'But the Petrifying Well, you don't want to stop there?'

'Yes, all right, if you insist,' Arina agreed without enthusiasm.

After a few minutes of staring at the hanging petrified objects, she moved away. The cave was slimy and frigid, and menacing shadows were filling its corners and crevices. The crooked figure of an old woman was almost invisible.

Arina came closer to the statue and stretched her arm out to touch it. She felt nothing. Just a freezing emptiness slowly shrouding her. And the fear from last night coming back to her, catching up with her, like an old rheumatic pain.

Arina heard approaching steps. She quietly wished good-bye to the figure and left the cave. Luke was waiting patiently outside, he decided to give this place of public attraction a miss for today.

'Did you sense anything?' he asked her on the way back to Harrogate.

'I'm not sure. Maybe. I don't want to talk about it, maybe later.'

They didn't stop for lunch, they just grabbed some sandwiches from a coffee-shop and ate them in the car, mainly by Luke, because Arina barely touched them. She slipped into her sleuth shoes once again. Like a hound who was about to pick up the scent, she became totally focused on the case. And nothing else existed for her at those times.

Their next stop was planned to be an antique shop in Harrogate, which belonged to a certain Jan Cribble, fifty-nine, an ex-rugby player and a former member of the physio class. Arina decided against arranging a meeting beforehand this time. No need to give him time to prepare himself, to cook up a plausible story. So, they arrived unannounced.

The shop bore the unassuming name of Cribble's Antiques and had a classic heron figurine, a silver pitcher and some vintage homeware displayed in its window. It was approaching two p.m. and the shop was open.

No sooner had they alighted from the car, than the owner popped his head out of the door and gave them a fleeting assessment with his sharp dark-blue eyes. Apparently, he was satisfied with the result as he opened the door wider and smiled affably.

Arina went in first. Luke followed her, he was frowning and looked confused.

'Mr Cribble, I assume?' she said in her well-modulated voice.

'Yes, that would be me.'

'Good. We are private detectives investigating the disappearance of Mr Statham. Mr Statham? Aaron? Do you remember him? You went to the same physio classes at Physiotherapy & Pilates Practice "Better Life" last year.'

'No, I didn't.' his smile was fading away.

'Arina,' Luke tried to say something but Lady Holroyd-Kugushev ignored him and addressed Mr Cribble more forcefully.

'Your name and address have been given to us by the practice and we really need to talk to you. We believe that a very dangerous man, a murderer, is on the loose, so we really haven't got time to play games. If you want to see our papers...'

Mr Cribble shook his head heatedly. He looked scared now.

'Mr Cribble have you ever played rugby?' Luke used the pause wisely.

The thin as a rake man gave him a wild look and shook his head even more vigorously, risking breaking his scrawny neck.

'Are you Jan Cribble?' asked Arina enlightened.

'No! Of course, not!' he answered, and a weak smile sneaked back onto his face. 'I'm Gordon! Gordon Cribble. It's my brother who is Jan, you see.'

A ceramic monkey in the corner of the shop was showing its yellow teeth in silent laughter. Arina ignored the impudent animal and proceeded with the next question.

'Can we meet your brother, please?'

'I'm afraid you cannot,' Gordon Cribble answered merrily. 'He, my brother and his wifey, they moved to Australia about five months ago. Nicer climate for his sport injuries, nicer and friendlier people as well. He is doing alright there, got himself another little shop, antiques are antiques everywhere, even in Down Under,' he giggled.

The monkey was choking with laughter now, its glassy eyes were full of menace.

I'm going mad, this place is driving me mad, thought Arina.

'Would it be possible to speak to your brother on the phone, or perhaps on Skype?' Luke came to life once more.

'Hm...I'm not really sure...another reason he emigrated there was (can I speak frankly with you?) that he wanted to start a new life, cut off old connections sort of...he wouldn't be pleased with me if we started stirring up the past. No, I don't think that I can do that.'

'You think we are joking here? You think we have nothing better to do than to play riddles with you?' Arina lost her temper finally, her face didn't get red, it turned ashy white instead, her eyes were burning through the little man, her lips were twitching involuntarily.

Even Luke felt threatened, let alone Gordon Cribble, not the bravest man at the best of times, who seemed to dwindle under this fierce attack, becoming even thinner. Like a needlefish he was silently opening and closing his mouth.

'Luke, be so kind and show this gentleman the court disclosure order!' commanded Arina.

Gordon Cribble looked sideways as if seeking support from his inanimate friends: the sneering monkey, the melancholic heron, a brass Tibetan Buddha and an ill-assorted group of German garden gnomes. Then he shrugged his shoulders helplessly and gave in.

No need for the disclosure order. He understood the situation and would try his best to persuade Jan to contact them. No, no other way. It will be his big bro who will make the first move.

'Now we have to wait until this asshole of an antique dealer will take pains to call us. Damn it! What a frustrating day!' Lady Holroyd-Kugushev didn't bother to hide her bad mood.

'Maybe we will strike lucky with the Polish chap, Marek?'

'Maybe you will!' Arina snapped, 'you are always over the moon when you get a chance to practice your silly languages.'

Luke didn't reply, just chuckled casually and checked his Sat Nav.

'We are almost there, aha, I think that must be Marek himself!' Luke said, pointing towards a tall, healthy-looking man in worn jeans and big heavy boots.

This time Luke insisted on calling their witness beforehand and arranging their meeting. Arina didn't like the idea but didn't stop him calling Marek Lubieckii and chatting to him in a funny mixture of the two languages.

Marek was waiting for the private detectives in the car park of a small local pub, leaning against the side of an open white van full of builder's tools, smoking. He had a pleasant honest face fringed with a short wheat colour beard. He shook both their hands cordially.

'We go inside? In the pub?' he asked in a heavy accent.

The pub was called "The Green Witch" and had on its signboard an evil looking hag with the face of a shamrock shade, naturally.

When they settled and ordered their drinks, Marek looked at Arina, then at Luke with the impression of a young dog eager to obey its master's orders.

'Ask anything. Please! I like to help!'

They started with the usual questions. Arina asked, Luke helped with the language, switching time from time into Polish, but not often as Marek seemed to understand English very well. He had, however, some difficulties with expressing himself, but they were steadily easing off. The more he relaxed the easier he could speak.

Apparently, he liked Aaron very much and was very sorry when he had quit their physio sessions so suddenly.

'We became friends, you know,' Marek confessed sadly, 'he was really, really nice to me. Didn't mind that I am a Pole. Not like others…'

'So, others didn't like you,' Arina said quietly, 'can you give us some names, please?'

'Names?' Marek suddenly looked alert, 'I don't give names, no, no. I don't want troubles.'

Luke glanced at Arina and she nodded discreetly.

He turned to Marek and spoke to him in Polish, in a soothing and confiding way. Marek finished his beer and wiped his mouth with the sleeve of his checked shirt.

'Okay, but I will not say nothing in court. Okay?'

Both detectives nodded.

'His name—Jan. Big man. Strong. Played rugby many years ago. Aaron had words with him. He protected me. We were pals, you know.'

'You are saying that Aaron and Jan were enemies?' Arina asked carefully. It was like walking through a minefield, one wrong step and it would be the end of the story.

'Yeah, Jan didn't like when Aaron spoke up for me. Aaron was good. Kind. He said he will pay for this.'

'Who said? Jan Cribble said it to Aaron?'

'*Tak*,' Marek affirmed in Polish.

Arina nodded thoughtfully.

'Who else upset you?' asked Luke.

Marek looked confused. He thanked Luke for the second pint profusely. Took the glass to his lips, then put it back on the table without tasting it.

'It was strange,' he said eventually.

Arina and Luke waited patiently for the continuation.

'It was very strange,' he went on, 'this ex-soldier. He was nasty to me. But friends with Aaron. So, then he was very nice to me. Pretended. I didn't like him.'

Luke undertook his interpreter role once again. Arina was sipping her grapefruit juice, waiting.

After a short, quite animated discussion, Luke summarised:

'What Marek was saying is that Todd Fisher, you remember Arina, the ex-soldier who killed himself?'

'Yes. Yes of course, I remember.'

'Who was a good friend of Aaron, and that is according to almost everybody we have spoken to so far, he was not so nice to other people. Specifically, to our Marek. He used to play nasty jokes on him, mainly making fun of his English. But when Aaron was around, he was a totally different man, nice and friendly, and butter wouldn't melt in his mouth.'

'Did he…did you, Marek, talk about this with Aaron?' asked Arina.

'No! I didn't. Not good to grass on other man!' he answered seriously.

'We understand. Now Marek, have you ever seen Aaron's fiancée? You knew that he was going to get married, right?'

'Yes, of course! I was invited by the way!'

'Did you go to the ceremony?'

'No, no! It was good that Aaron invited me! Very good! But, no, I had to go to Poland! My *matka*…she was very, very ill…' Marek suddenly sobbed, 'she died.'

'His mother,' quietly explained Luke to Arina, who hissed back: 'I guessed!'

'We are very sorry to hear this,' she said aloud.

There was an uneasy pause.

'I need to smoke,' Marek announced after he calmed down a little bit, 'then we talk. About wedding. It was strange. Secret. But Aaron told me something. I didn't like their plan. But it's complicated, I'll tell you more when I'm back…in a sec.'

But Marek Lubieckii never came back.

They waited for ages before Luke decided to go outside to check on Marek. They wanted to give him some space, some time to sort himself out. Unfortunately, it appeared to be a bad decision.

Chapter 11

Barbara, a private nurse, was watching the old man humped in his electric wheelchair, which was as usual positioned to have the best view of the sea from his vast glass veranda.

The old man seemed to be asleep. His eyes were closed, his cheeks sagged and a thin dribble of saliva was running from his weak mouth down to his sunken chest covered with a cotton bib.

He might as well be dead.

Barbara smiled discreetly. The invalid uttered an unhealthy wheeze and drooled even more. Barbara frowned.

Not yet. But definitely soon. Her nursing experience of many years suggested so.

Under the starched nursing cap required by her employer, her thin pale face was unreadable and looked ageless. She could be anything from thirty to sixty. Barbara was actually fifty to the day. It was her birthday today. Out of these years she had worked thirty-two in total, which was surely enough for anybody.

Barbara had spent all her life looking after other people, usually very old and very ill people. She was unmarried and childless, the latter she didn't regret much. The former she regretted a bit. But soon everything will change. Her life will change.

This time she smiled openly. She wanted it to happen right now, she was so fed up with waiting. How easy it would be to strangle this wreck right now. She licked her lips carnivorously. He was half-dead anyway. More than half to tell you the truth.

She looked down at the letter she was holding. Her hands covered in bulging veins were shaking slightly. Barbara didn't want to give him this letter that he was so desperate for. It would feel good to make him suffer a little bit longer. She sighed.

A standard DL envelope with the far from standard letter inside. Barbara wanted to burn it. She imagined herself burning this thin letter in front of the paralysed with anger old man. She chuckled. The old man's eyelids started twitching. He was dreaming.

Barbara turned away, she couldn't tolerate the look of this pathetic cripple any longer. The sea view was as ever magnificent. If there was one thing she was going to miss, it would be these wild rocks, and the smell of the sea, and the sky so volatile, so unpredictable, so magnetic. It would be so easy to disappear there, between the clouds, to enwrap oneself in their thick weightless layers, to be absorbed to the last atom by them.

Suddenly Barbara sensed something, like a sharp icicle screwed into her heart. The old man was still jammed in his electric chair, motionless as before, but his eyes were slightly open now. And they were following her, spying on her. Barbara shivered.

'Are you plotting something, Barbara? Are you? I can read your mind like an open book, silly cow.'

'It's a letter for you, sir,' she said in the neutral formal voice she had employed for many years. I could be an excellent actress, she said to herself with a bitter satisfaction.

He swore under his breath and snatched the letter from her with unexpected dexterity.

'I need my glasses! Can't anybody open this bloody envelope? I need light, I can't see a damn thing! Have you turned into a Pillar of salt? I was not aware that I'd employed Lot's wife.'

'Your glasses are on the top of your head, sir. If you give me the letter back, I will open it for you. And with light...'

'No way you're going to open my letter! For you to poke your long nose into it, no thank you very much! Give me my letter opener, the one with the ivory handle. It should be somewhere around! And bring me my magnifying glass, these glasses are absolutely useless! Come on! Chop-chop!'

He was jerkily clenching and unclenching his parchment-like, small fists, speckled with liver spots. The unopened letter was waiting lonely on the old man's knees swathed in the tartan plaid.

The efficient nurse came back in no time, carrying with her a portable lamp, which she clipped promptly to the wheelchair armrest, and a quite remarkable vintage letter opener, which she handed carefully to her patient.

The old man slid the blade through the folded edge of the envelope and shook out a single-page letter. There were just a few lines of typed text there. Barbara, who was watching her patient closely, leaned over and placed the required magnifying glass on a small table adjusted to the multifunctional invalid chair, at the same time she ran her eyes over the contents. Then she left bearing a subtle smile of satisfaction.

Not too long to wait! Please, don't lose hope! We are so close now. Be patient however difficult it might be. Cordially yours, A.

The letters were dancing in front of the old man's eyes like looneys. Even with the assistance of the magnifying glass he struggled to make sense of the tiny signs.

When he had grasped the meaning of the message, a wave of bitter disappointment engulfed him. By now he expected more. Much more. The old man felt powerless, useless. It was a new feeling in his long selfish life. It was like finding oneself in an empty dark room with no windows or doors. And no hope.

It was ridiculous from Aaron to ask him to be patient and not lose hope. How impudent young men are nowadays! Lord Mount-Hubert screwed up his face in his usual fastidious manner.

But of course, he shouldn't be too tough on his nephew, he reproached himself almost immediately. Aaron, the old man had to admit, succeeded in impressing him, which happened extremely rarely.

He's got my blood in his veins, certainly, he has, thought Lord Mount-Hubert curling his lips. Much more than of his weak mother—my stupid late sister who managed to find the biggest ass in the whole world to be wedded to! A pilot! How ridiculous! No surprise that he crashed one day. The only problem was that he crashed together with his wife, leaving his teenage son to be an orphan. And what was much worse—literally without a penny.

Even now, many years after, the old man's face flushed with annoyance and anger. He had been in the middle of a very important business affair then, and the last thing he wanted to be bothered with was his estranged nephew. Fortunately, he was not a long-term burden, the boy appeared to be a very talented athlete. Unfortunately, his career there didn't last long.

The old man rubbed his itching eyes. He suddenly felt uneasy. He didn't delude himself. He was far from the typical avuncular figure from children's stories. He was cold and distant with his nephew, he was also quite greedy towards him. He didn't let him starve or anything like that of course, but he was not generous either.

Why would he want to help his uncle now?

Why did Aaron contact him in the first place?

Because he did something bad (not too bad in his opinion, just a few naughty things)? Or because his nephew had suddenly felt lonely in this world and wanted to be close to the only living member of his family?

Or, more likely, to be close to a very rich uncle, to be sure that the inheritance would go in the right direction. This was a decent enough reason for the old man. He would have done the same.

There were so many questions swarming inside his head; the more he thought about this, the more questions appeared. And it was not good. During his long career as a very successful entrepreneur he had learnt many important things, one of which was not to wander down the path of doubt for long. It would lead you nowhere. It would destroy you and all your best intentions, like an apple maggot destroying the fruit from inside, causing it early decay.

Make a decision and follow your instincts, that was his motto, and he was not going to betray it now.

****

Roxanne was at home at last. She stripped herself off the ugly outfit she had carefully put together earlier on to mingle into the school environment. She was not sure if it helped actually.

Roxanne took a long shower and washed her short ash-blonde hair (the black bob, alongside the mint mane, was one of her numerous wigs, which she used imaginatively to match her different personalities).

Then she wrapped herself into a long velour bathrobe and dried her hair in front of the long oval mirror, which occupied almost the whole height of one of her bedroom walls. The bedroom was not big, but cosy, it had a gable end window overlooking an overgrown communal garden, full of trees and bushes. One of the trees, a huge larch had spread out so much that its branches reached the Victorian house itself. In windy days they would knock and scratch at the window, demanding to be let in.

Roxanne was very tired. She could see all the traces of fatigue on her face. Without any makeup it looked pale and insignificant.

It was almost eight o'clock in the evening. The day had proved to be long and challenging, which was predictable though. She had forgotten, or didn't realise, that dealing with young people in large numbers could be very wearing.

She felt knackered. Empty. Dissatisfied. What had she achieved? Nothing! Boasted like a stupid teenager. Didn't deliver anything. Shame! Shame…

She felt almost real pain. Mental torture could be really tangible.

Boom!

Roxanne jumped.

Boom! Boom! Boom!

A dry bough of the larch tree was making its presence felt.

The girl shivered. She was taken by surprise, off her guard. It was not good. It was worse—it was unprofessional.

How did she get into this?

She poured herself a large glass of red wine. She lit her long thin cigarette. She tried hard to escape. Too hard, perhaps?

Instead of starting to think at last.

What bothered you? Why did you become so upset? What unbalanced you?

Roxanne took out her notebook and a pen. She wrote down these questions.

An answer had been born already. It had matured inside her head like a good cheddar cheese.

The school. The girls. The atmosphere.

It all was breathing lies. It all was a big, fat lie.

Roxanne finished her cigarette. She had already changed to her favourite loungewear, a cotton flannel 2-piece pyjamas set of an apricot shade. She was sitting in her bed upright, knees bent, with a large comfortable cushion propped behind her back. Her laptop was by her side, on the right. Her notebook, open, full of scribbles laid upon her flat belly. An ashtray and the wine glass were sat on the bedside table. A wall lamp was casting a soft light from under its olive-green shade.

She liked to work here, to think. In her bedroom, staring at the stars on a clear night through the uncurtained window. Or listening to the rustle of the trees. Of course she had a perfectly equipped study, but in the evenings she preferred to stay here.

Roxanne lit another cigarette. She mustn't let herself be intimidated by these rich, arrogant and so overconfident girls. She mustn't. She was herself a beautiful, young and successful woman. Or at least that was what she wanted other people to see her as. She was a master of disguise, she was a natural chameleon. It was so easy to pretend to be someone else than to be yourself.

Her mobile phone beeped. It was the third message from Luke. She shook her head, not now, I'm not ready, I need more time, pleeeese! Roxanne stubbed out the cigarette and typed a short polite reply. Then switched her phone off.

As had been arranged beforehand, Roxanne started her counselling with the youngest, year seven, girls. That was, of course, a total waste of time. But it gave her the advantage of gaining better trust from the older ones. She didn't sound desperate to squeeze any information regarding their missing ex-teacher. It all came out quite naturally.

I understand how upset you are. I am so sorry for your loss. You are **such** *brave girls. Especially after what happened last year…as I heard…about your favourite teacher…you all were looking forward so much to his training…I am not at all surprised, you were making such progress…everybody told me this…*and so on and so on.

Sometimes Roxanne wondered, if in order to become a good psychologist one has to learn how to lie plausibly.

Her main object of interest, Angel, was one of the last she talked to. The girl was strikingly attractive. That part was true, but the rest…Angel was withdrawn, taciturn, she didn't give away anything. Not a single hint of her presumed love affair with her PE teacher, nothing. When Roxanne a few times mentioned his name, Angel froze, but didn't say anything. She sat with her eyes down, mumbling some meaningless phrases just for the sake of saying something.

It was obvious to Roxanne that Angel didn't behave normally. Whether she was lying or not was another problem, she just built an impenetrable wall around herself, which was totally out of her character.

Something really significant must have happened to Angel to change her so much since Luke and Lady Holroyd-Kugushev had spoken to her. Was she so attached to her headmistress, Ms Kale? In Roxanne's opinion it was most unlikely.

Leaves were falling heavily outside the window. Roxanne was surprised how quickly for the last couple of days the yellow rustling mass covered the ground. They were like dead birds. Or birds who had suddenly lost their gift to fly and slowly and inevitably were coming down.

Unfortunately, Roxanne failed to meet Fairuza, another claimant for Mr Statham's loving heart, as she was off sick that day. That will be a job for next week.

Linda, a petite lithe Siamese cat, jumped silently onto the windowsill. She was not in the best of moods as she started whipping her tail nervously at once.

'What is it? Linda, what is bothering you my darling?'

Linda turned her head and looked at Roxanne with her magnetic blue eyes for a moment, then turned back to face the window with the darkness behind it.

But Roxanne didn't come back from the school entirely empty-handed. Clare. The girl who had slipped under the private detectives' radar. Clare was in the same year as Angel and Fairuza. She was also a member of their running class. Only the difference was that she had quit it at the end of the summer term of the previous year.

When Roxanne mentioned, almost automatically, the name of Aaron Statham the girl reacted.

Clare had a clever thin face with deep-set eyes of a greenish-grey colour. Her brown-chestnut hair was tightened up in a thick ponytail. Unlike other girls from the running class, she was quite short, but had a slim, sinewy figure, with a pair of long strong legs.

She told Roxanne how shocked she was when Mr Statham had disappeared, and that was when she mentioned about her involvement with the running group. When she was asked the reason for stopping the class, she said it was to do with too much studying and not enough time for other activities. She lied. And she lied ineptly.

It didn't take a long time for Roxanne to drag the truth out.

Linda uttered a low growl full of annoyance. Then she hissed angrily.

'What is that? Who is bothering you? Is it another cat? A fox?' Roxanne tried to calm the cat down.

She got up and walked to the window. The nearest streetlamp, partly shaded by the trees, was casting an uneven dim light, which was jerking under strong gusts of wind. Roxanne squinted her eyes, without contact lenses she couldn't make out much of what was so disturbing her beloved Linda.

Roxanne slid the old windowpane up and leaned out of the sash window. The larch's branch brushed against her brow. She nervously pushed it away with one hand, with the other hand she was already holding Linda back.

Roxanne's heart was biting hard.

She thought that she heard some noise in the garden, directly underneath her window. The howling wind was in the way, muffling everything else of course, but by now Roxanne managed to distinguish something black and big moving slowly on the ground.

The scream died in her throat, she quickly withdrew her hand from the outside and lowered the window frame. It went down with a sickening thump. Linda jumped down from the windowsill and darted away, frightened to death.

Roxanne was shaking now. She was not sure who did she see down there, prowling about.

Was it a man? Or an animal? In that case, it surely was a *very* large animal. Like…who? A wolf? Don't be stupid, she told herself. A fox? No, it was *much bigger* than fox. A badger? That was more likely. Let it be a badger.

But she went back to the window and bolted it properly. A thing she had never done since she moved there.

Then came another loud bang. Roxanne swore under her breath. Next morning she promised herself to saw that bloody branch off.

She went to bed. She inserted her earplugs inside both of ears. She pulled her sleep mask on. She was ready for the night's sleep. Only she couldn't sleep. The bright horrible images were flashing in front of her closed eyes. She found it difficult to breath. She wanted to scream. Scream and scream out. To reach somebody. A murder? That was laughable. More—pathetic.

Roxanne started the mantra. I'm successful, very successful woman. I'm also beautiful and young. I'm going to be married soon. My fiancée is a very handsome and very successful businessman. We are both extremely successful people, we were born for each other. I'm going to deliver extremely important information for this investigation. Probably the crucial piece. Without me they would never find the truth.

Roxanne sighed, more like moaned. Like a wounded animal. A doomed animal which is ready to be slaughtered.

I'm losing myself, she said to herself, I'm getting more and more lost. I'm a lost child. Why is nobody going to rescue me? Even Luke, why? Why?

She fell asleep eventually. At dawn. When all monsters and foes were swept away.

It was so hot like in the middle of the summer. She couldn't sleep anymore. Roxanne got out of bed and almost blinded by her mask walked unsteadily to the window. Surprisingly, it had already been opened but not wide enough. She couldn't remember opening it, perhaps she did it when she was still half-asleep.

She stretched her hands out to fight the old wooden frame, trying to push it up more.

But her hands failed to obey her. She couldn't move them. They were paralysed. No! Something was holding them. Or somebody. Somebody who was outside the window, who had caught her, trapped her in its bone-crushing grasp.

****

It was the next day, Saturday the 15th, late morning. Arina and Luke were on their way to Ripon, to see Derek Turnbull, a self-employed software developer, former member of the Physio class.

'He sounded cross on the phone, I don't think we will get anything worthwhile,' Luke dropped a remark.

'Don't be prejudiced, he might be just suffering. Have you seen what his condition is, a medical condition? A cervical herniated disc! It's very, very painful. It happens to people who spend all their time glued to the computer, Luke!'

'Is that a hint?'

'Not at all, my dear, not at all. Keep concentrating on driving, that's right. Mr Turnbull, hm…what a horrid name…never mind, he might turn out to be a very pleasant amiable man full of helpful clues. Luke, what is the matter? Have you got something in your throat or what?'

Luke snorted and shook his head.

'Now, changing the subject. What is going on with our precious Pole? Did you manage to locate him, Luke, wake up!'

'Erm…I'm not sure about this.'

'About what? Luke! I am talking to you! What the hell is going on?'

'I've just realised…'

'Yes? I'm your patient audience. Go on if it's not too much trouble for you.'

'Roxanne, she hasn't contacted you today, by any chance?'

'No. Leave the poor girl in peace. She will report in full next week.'

'I know Arina, you're right but I still cannot stop worrying about her. As you said many times, we are dealing with an extremely ruthless killer.'

'Call her if you want.'

'I did. Several times. Her phone is off, going to voice mail straight away.'

'She might just want to be left alone, you know. She has got her own life to live, her private life. Better tell me about Marek, any news? Has he been kidnapped by aliens?'

'Oh yes, I forgot to tell you. He sent me a text message last night, a short one. Apologising a lot, saying that he had to rush out to one of his clients, some sort of an extreme emergency. He is a plumber, isn't he?'

'I thought he was a builder, but I suppose that could mean anything. Hopefully, we shall see him today, on our way back from Ripon. Did he confirm?'

'Not yet. He stopped answering his phone. Not surprising if he is in the middle of the *colossal catastrophe*. You remember his colourful language, sounds like the end of the world.'

'Most inconvenient. Anyway, let us hope that he will reply later today.'

They arrived in Ripon by half past one, left the car in a small parking area and walked to the Market Place where, by the Obelisk, they were supposed to meet Mr Turnbull.

There were a few, well wrapped up tourists wandering around the tall stone monument, taking photos and looking at their guidebooks.

'It's the earliest surviving obelisk in Britain, 24 metres, erected in 1702, it's capped with a weathervane bearing a representation of the wakeman's horn. Did you know that Luke?'

'No Arina, sorry, I've missed out on this particular important piece in my education.'

'I think it's him!' Arina pointed at the heavily overweight man with his hands in his pockets and a hard look on his fat face.

'I hope it's not,' Luke tried to joke but the joke had died out on his lips.

The man turned towards them with the swiftness of a Diplodocus and gave them a stern look.

'Hi! Are you Derek Turnbull?' asked Arina and smiled encouragingly.

'Yeah, that would be me, and you are…these detectives who wanted to talk to me? Is that right?' he said and burped loudly.

Derek Turnbull was a huge size, more like a gigantic lump of lard with his trunk arms, from top to bottom covered in tattoos. He had heavy mean brows and his long greasy hair, receding on the top, was plaited into a thin mousy braid. He was obviously still in the summer mode as he was wearing a t-shirt with some goth symbols and a pair of shapeless breeches. Altogether he looked totally miserable and permanently at war with the rest of the world.

'What do you want to know?' asked Derek Turnbull gruffly as he scratched his grotesquely protruding potbelly.

'Shall we go inside somewhere, it's getting quite chilly,' suggested Arina and then looking at him added, 'probably not for you.'

'No, I'm cool. You said on the phone it wouldn't take long, so I'm ready— go ahead. The sooner we finish the better by me.'

It was a cold day, with grey heavy clouds waiting to burst and a nasty, consistently blowing wind.

Luke started to ask the usual questions, Arina buttoned her coat fully and turned up its collar. She gave the man one of her heaviest looks to which he demonstrated total ignorance.

Very soon it became crystal clear that Derek not only looked at first glance unsociable but actually was. He didn't mix with anybody at the physio. He didn't have to, as he didn't go there to socialise, as he put it bluntly.

'We finished now? Can I go back to my work? I'm pretty busy you know,' Derek demanded after approximately ten minutes of noncommittal replies on every single question.

'Before you go, just one more question. What do *you* think happened to Aaron?' Arina made her presence felt at least.

Derek sniffed loudly, then gave her an appraising, surprisingly intelligent, look.

'He was asking for it,' Derek said after a long pause, 'Aaron was too trustful. Trusted everybody. And that is dangerous.'

You are certainly not guilty of such a fault, Arina thought but said nothing.

Derek kept another long pause before continuing.

'You asked me what I think, and I'm telling you that I didn't like some people who were hanging around him. Particularly, one,' said Derek before falling into another of his silent lapses.

'Do you mean—Jan Cribble?' Arina asked quickly.

'No, though he is a nasty piece of shit too. I was talking about Todd.'

'Todd Fisher? An ex-soldier?'

'Yeah, ex-whatever...I wouldn't trust a word he said. And he stuck to this lad like, you know, his best mate.'

'But he wasn't? How do you know if you didn't socialise with anybody, those were your own words,' Luke intervened.

'I watch people with these two eyes,' Derek pointed his two V-sign fingers at his eyes to illustrate his idea. 'I don't need to socialise to do this.'

'We understand,' Arina said trying to mellow him, 'but how, I mean, why did you come to this conclusion?'

'Ah, in addition to these two peepers one has to have something up there,' he tapped the top of his head vigorously and then suddenly grinned.

'Was Todd sexually interested in Aaron?' asked Arina directly.

'I don't know if Todd was a gay or not, hm…now that you ask me it makes me think…maybe he was, but not the obvious one, you know, more discreet type. What I am certain is that there was nothing homosexual going on between Todd and Aaron.'

'So, *what* was going between them? What was strange about their friendship?'

'Ha! If I only knew! They were so different! They didn't have anything in common! But then again, it was Todd who tried to be close to Aaron, to make Aaron be interested in him…to depend on him. For example, he was always giving him lifts home to Leeds after the classes. But he lived in Harrogate. It would take him ages to come back thanks to the horrendous traffic. But on the other hand…it seems to me that there was a lot of nasty old stinking jealousy about, from Todd's side.'

'Jealousy, why?' Luke asked baffled.

'There were plenty of reasons. Aaron—a young attractive guy, always at the centre of attention, popular with everybody. Even his injury didn't make him bitter. Mind you, he had lost a lot due to it, not many people would recover from such a blow. And he was always cheerful, supporting others. He was like a magnet to people. Hm, funnily enough, I liked him too.'

'Do you think Todd was jealous enough to kill Aaron?' Arina asked quietly.

Derek shrugged his massive shoulders.

'Theoretically? I'm not sure, I think Todd was capable of a lot of things, but to kill Aaron…what would be the reason? He wanted to be his friend, to be accepted in his circle, to be more liked by other people, you know, if Aaron is so popular maybe some of his popularity will come my way, that sort of thing. And, practically, didn't he knock himself off before Aaron disappeared?'

'We don't know. He was not in a good shape when he was found. So, again, theoretically, he could have done something to Aaron and then committed suicide.'

'Oh no, that is a definite no! No way would Todd kill himself out of a guilty conscience. In my opinion, he didn't have a conscience at all. No, it would be a different reason.'

Chapter 12

'He knew a lot about their friendship, didn't he? You know, for somebody who is not mixing with people it was quite a thorough psychological analysis, don't you think?' Luke said after they parted with Derek.

'Yes and no. He might be just an exceptional observer, as well as an excellent analyser. Two for the price of one.'

'Ha!'

'Just as well we got a copy of the death certificate in time. For a change, we've got some solid evidence in our hands. Still nothing from Marek?'

'Nope, boss. Oh, got a text from Roxanne, at last!'

'I told you that nothing had happened to her, what is she up to?'

'Erm…she is having lunch with Tom Baxter right now.'

'What a good move! She is a quite remarkable little thing, this protégé of yours. She will come back to us loaded with goods, I'm sure! Now, shall we drive to Marek?'

'Do you mean to his home?'

'Yes, why not? Come on, Luke, you've got his address?'

'Yeah, it's on my phone. It's not far from this pub we went to with him, "The Green Witch".'

'The Green Witch,' Arina repeated musingly.

'Nasty looking hag it was, indeed,' agreed Luke and for some time drove the car in silence.

'Luke, what is the matter?' Arina asked.

'What?'

'What is the matter with you? You look damn serious which is highly unusual for you.'

'Erm…you don't think that anything might have happened to her?'

'To whom? Ah, to Roxanne? Why should it? She is a very capable young lady who can look after herself perfectly well.'

'But we are dealing with a very dangerous and ruthless murderer,' Luke said weakly.

'Calm down, Luke. She is meeting our quiet, harmless Mr Baxter in a public place, so nothing to be worried about,' said Arina confidently but to herself thought, surely I'm right, Roxanne should be perfectly safe, but under one condition…if Mr Baxter is not our foe.

Luke switched off the engine.

'We're here.'

Arina looked around. They were not in a nice area. It was somewhere north of Harrogate and signs of deprivation were evident here. Long rows of terraced houses on both sides of the dirty and bumpy road were sparsely occupied. Their tiny gardens, or rather patches of land, were littered with all possible sort of rubbish. Those still occupied were not in much better condition.

A huge brown rat just crossed the road in front of them. It didn't seem in any hurry, it was walking with confidence and royalty, as if this place belonged to it.

'What a misery!' Arina murmured.

'You stay in the car, I can go on my own,' Luke said opening the car door.

'Thank you for the offer, but I'll be fine. I'm not afraid of rats,' Arina said getting out of the car, 'I just don't like them.'

Marek lived in the end house which looked much better than its neighbours. It had clean windows and a freshly painted door, and was provided with a bigger garden, kept in order.

Luke knocked at the door. And knocked again. Nobody answered. The whole place looked deserted, it looked dead. Arina quivered.

'He is probably still working,' suggested Luke.

'Who are you trying to convince? Yourself? I don't…' Arina didn't finish the sentence.

There was some movement next door. A miniature Asian woman with a baby in her arms and two little children clung to her long tunic came out of the neighbouring house. The woman immediately looked alarmed when she saw them. She turned back and was about to return to the safety of her house but the children were desperate for their walk. They started freaking out, pulling her in another direction. Arina took her chance.

'Oh, hello! What nice children we've got here!' she smiled and waved to them. Luke smiled too and started pulling funny faces, which he was a master of, to the children.

'Hello!' the mother still looked unsure but at least stopped going inside.

'Do you know where Marek is? We are his friends!' Arina said slowly and clearly.

The woman thought for a moment, trying to put the few English words she knew into use.

'No, he went,' she made a goodbye gesture with her free hand. 'Home.'

'Did he go to Poland?' asked Arina carefully.

'Yes, yes! Poland!' she pointed her finger at herself and then at her baby, 'mother! His mother!'

'You're saying that Marek went home to see his mother?' Arina asked in an unsteady voice.

'Yes! Yes!' the woman was very pleased that they understood her.

'How do you know this?'

The woman frowned, then smiled with relief, 'Friend! His friend said,' she nodded affirmatively, smiled again showing her small white teeth.

The private detectives didn't know what to say, they found themselves up a blind alley once again.

'I go now, good-bye!' the little lady said and started walking towards a small area with a sandpit, which didn't look particularly hygienic, an old, battered couple of swings and a slide.

Luke rubbed his temples nervously, 'I don't know what to say, I don't understand. I believed him, you know, that he'd lost his mother... Why would he lie about that? It's really weird.'

'I don't think he lied to us, Luke,' Arina said gravely.

'What? What do you mean? You don't think that he's just run away?'

'No, I disagree with you,' she said and added very quietly, 'and I believe that he's joined his mother. Dead mother.'

'What? Are you saying that he's dead too?'

'Yes, very likely he's been murdered. I don't think he's been kept imprisoned. Maybe at first, the first few hours... but not longer.'

'But how? You saw him, he is a big, strong guy. How could he be overpowered? Just outside the crowded pub? No way!'

'It's elementary, Luke! He was outwitted. And, by the way, the parking area itself was not crowded. There was nobody, do you remember? When you went out to look for Marek? You didn't see a soul.'

'Hm... okay, and then what?'

'Shall we get into the car? It's so cold here…so forlorn.'

Luke looked at Arina. Her fine-featured face was very still, her cheeks seemed more sunken than usual, but her sapphire eyes were burning with anger.

'He must have been quite upset yesterday, genuinely upset. He came out for a fag. And somewhere there, outside the pub, he met the killer. Marek was taken by surprise, unarmed, unprepared. Somehow he was fooled, lured perhaps, to his own van. Because we didn't find it, right?'

'I don't understand!' Luke slapped the steering wheel with the palms of his hands in frustration, 'he is all the time ahead of us! How could it be possible?'

'He is following us, that is one possibility.'

Luke turned sharply to face Arina. It was raining properly now, steady cold raindrops were falling down with a miserable destiny. The Asian lady with her baby was hiding under a big umbrella. Her two other children, oblivious to the weather, were still swinging merrily.

'And the other one?' Luke's voice suddenly sounded high pitched.

'I think you know yourself by now, but don't want to believe the obvious.'

'He's been tracking us. Yes?'

'I think so, Luke. No, now I'm convinced that—yes—he knows where we go, and he knows it instantly. So, how is it possible, if not by using a sort of smart tracking system?'

'GPS tracking device, for example. Which is so easy to hide…oh, shit! I have to take my Jag to be properly searched at once!'

'I'm afraid so. Do you know somebody skilful enough to do this?'

'Yeah, I know somebody,' Luke took off his steamed-up glasses and started to rub their lenses with his colourful handkerchief. His face was flushed with frustration.

****

Roxanne was walking home, the late lunch with Mr Baxter, Tom, as he insisted to be called, was over. She ate too much, she drank too much, and her inevitable headache was creeping over. It was altogether tiresome.

It was only four but darkening quickly already. Soon the clocks would go back, and it would be dark almost all day, she was not looking forward to it. Roxanne couldn't stand to be in the darkness, it made her powerless and vulnerable. The wind picked up now and was throwing handfuls of drizzle into her face, blinding her. She didn't anticipate such a rapid deterioration of the weather. Perhaps it was a bad decision after all, immature and childish. Perhaps she should have accepted a lift.

Tom offered to drive her home, of course, but she politely declined. She said that she wanted some fresh air and some exercise after such a hearty meal, which was partially true. But the main reason was slightly different—she was filled to the brim with Mr Baxter himself.

Roxanne still couldn't recover properly after her horrible nightmare. It was so real, so frightening, and it was so unlike her, because usually Roxanne slept without any dreams. A terrifying thought suddenly crossed her mind. Could it be contagious? Those mental visions of the great detective, called Lady Holroyd-Kugushev? What a ridiculous idea! She uttered a nervous giggle. No way! She was the one who was sane in their small assembly.

It was not the first time when Roxanne regretted her hasty venture. Why did she always want to prove herself? To get herself ensnared up to her ears, where there was no other way out except to be sucked in even deeper.

Roxanne lost her footing and slipped into a muddy puddle, partly disguised by soggy leaves. Her right foot enclosed in a smart lace-up ankle boot became wet instantly. It appeared that the high price didn't protect it against the elements. Roxanne swore loudly when, on top of all, she discovered that the floral pink prints, which adorned her boots, were ruined by brownish-yellow ugly smudges.

She took out of her bag a pack of dry tissues, pulled out several of them and attempted to rub the dirt off. Unfortunately, she made it worse. Even in this dim light she could see how badly damaged her footwear was.

In her distress she became totally oblivious to her surroundings. Roxanne was not too far away from her flat, but she chose to walk through a small park which was deserted at this time. Just a lonely dogwalker in a long black mackintosh could be seen in the far distance by the bushes, his wet little dog was stuck in the overgrown grass, sniffing for something presumably.

Roxanne started picking up the soiled balls of tissues, she would have to do proper washing at home. Or take the boot somewhere to be cleaned. Would they do it at a dry cleaners? She sighed and looked for a rubbish bin.

She noticed that the dogwalker appeared to be a little bit closer to her than before. He and his little companion started walking roughly in her direction. Roxanne bent down to gather up the last two pellets, which had been blown by the wind further away.

When Roxanne stood up, she noticed with a sinking heart that the man was striding now directly towards her. It was unnerving. Because of the deep hood his coat had it was difficult to distinguish the face, but Roxanne was convinced that it was a man.

The distance between them was dwindling. Not too fast but steadily. She felt ridiculous with her wet filthy feet (by this time her other boot had also leaked) and all these paper bits she held.

She forced a weak smile. She decided to ask the man where the nearest bin was. Surely, he ought to know. But at first she should say something nice about his dog perhaps. The man was very near now. She still couldn't see his face.

She looked nervously at his dog and froze with her mouth open. The little black thing was hanging in the air. It was not walking, it was suspended by its lead, which looked very much like an ordinary rope.

Roxanne dropped all her rubbish. The paper balls scattered away in all directions. Roxanne cried and pressed her hands to her chest hard. The man was tugging along an old fluffy toy, not a real animal. Realising that it had served its purpose, the false dogwalker calmly pulled up the rope and put the toy away into his coat pocket. After this he looked at Roxanne. He was smiling, she was sure of it, even faceless he couldn't conceal his crooked smile.

Roxanne's heart fell. She realised with a sudden clarity that she had met her end. She quickly looked around, there was nobody. Nobody, except the murderer and herself. The latter slowed down now, he knew very well that there was no escape for her and enjoyed every moment of this, like a cat playing with its prey.

Somehow, Roxanne broke the spell and ran as fast as she could. Of course she hadn't run far before he seized her. He grabbed her hair and pulled hard. The black bob slipped off her head. The attacker almost fell back losing his balance. He was squeezing the wig.

Roxanne felt like the icy cold rain was dropping onto her unprotected head. She was free again. She darted away like a hare chased by a pack of hounds.

This time she was lucky. She managed to get away. As soon as she left the park she saw a group of lively teenagers, they were smoking and laughing loudly. Normally Roxanne would give them a wide berth, but not today. She sensed their insolent looks, she was fully aware how awful she looked. They probably would have plenty to say about her behind her back, plenty obscene jokes would be made at her expense. She couldn't care less. One day, perhaps, she herself would be able to laugh it off. One day...but she didn't know when this day would come.

****

Next morning Arina and Luke went to see Roxanne. They were let into the flat by her fiancée Tom—a successful entrepreneur and very ill-mannered man. He was abrupt with them, almost rude. He looked sulky and bad tempered. It was not entirely clear if he was so cross because of his concern for Roxanne's safety or because he had to change his plans for this Sunday at the last minute.

The private detectives were shocked to see how different the girl looked. It was the first time they saw Roxanne without a wig. And the impression was ghastly. She must have suffered some sort of a skin disease, because through her thin blond hair could be seen a reddish scalp with scaly patches.

'I've got psoriasis,' she explained wearily, 'it gets worse when I'm under a lot of stress.'

Roxanne was sitting up in bed, with ashy gaunt face and eyes full of sadness and disillusion. She showed them where to sit: a comfortable looking black bean bag in the cocoon shape for Lady Holroyd and a velvet stool of bright colours, which resembled a miniature advertising pillar by her dressing table for Luke.

Arina had already said all that had to be said, millions of thanks and sorries and now nobody knew what else to say. The pause seemed endless and awkward. Luke was fidgeting in his seat which was too small for him, tangling and untangling his long legs like a heron who had landed in a robin's nest by mistake.

'I didn't see his face unfortunately,' Roxanne started at last.

'But are you sure it was a man?' Arina asked.

'Yes…and…no, I'm not sure anymore. When I saw him there, walking with his little horrible toy,' she shivered, 'I assumed that it was a man. But now, when I'm trying to think…it is possible that it could have been a woman. A big, strong woman. I'm really sorry, I cannot help you much. It was so stupid of me…'

'Not at all! You were very brave!' Luke exclaimed passionately.

'It was very stupid…' Roxanne shook her head not listening, she continued not addressing anybody, it was more like a monolog, 'I was not prepared…I should have anticipated something like this. He was waiting for me, or more likely, he was following me from the pub. In that case it could be possible…oh no, I don't believe it!'

'You don't believe, Roxanne, that it might have been Mr Baxter, that's what you are saying?' asked Arina who was listening to these lamentations attentively.

Roxanne shivered again and looked at Arina with wide eyes like she had just been woken up. She looked tiny and defenceless in her king-size bed, surrounded by all sorts of pillows and cushions. Her hands were trembling as she was lighting her long thin cigarette.

'Are you smoking in bed again? How many times have I told you…' Tom announced his presence. His fit, well-toned body in a sleek suit was impressively outlined in the door frame. He was not a particularly unattractive guy, in certain light he even reminded one of Daniel Craig. But his facial expression was fastidious and aloof, and his eyes had a cold, contemptuous air about them. Also, he had a habit of speaking in a mocking, dominant manner.

Luke felt a strong desire to strangle this smartarse. On the other hand, Roxanne did not seem to be disturbed by his behaviour. She simply waved her hand with the cigarette to him dismissively.

'Okay, I'm going now. Because I *have to*, not that I want to! Hoping very much that you will not burn the house down, and that…your guests will be understanding and tactful enough not to take up too much of your time, as you need so desperately to get over this horrendous event,' he smiled wryly and left.

'Are you sure that you want us to stay?' asked Arina diplomatically and, receiving an affirmative nod from Roxanne, went on, 'we will be as quick as possible, I promise! And if at any stage you feel tired and want to be left alone in peace, just simply tell us, is that all right?'

'Deal! But now I'm dying for a drink! Luke, would you be so kind to fetch me the bottle from the kitchen rack. Any bottle will do, and some glasses. There are plenty around. I hope you will join me?' Roxanne was almost herself now, her apathy had gone without a trace, the sleeping beauty role had been successfully played off and forgotten for good.

Luke untangled himself and glanced at Arina meaningfully. It was not even twelve o'clock yet, and it was against all Arina's principals not to start drinking too early, but there were times of sacrifice, and now was one of them.

Luke returned with two full glasses which he handled to Roxanne and Arina, then disappeared to the kitchen again, coming back with the open bottle and half a glass of wine for himself.

Roxanne almost finished her glass in one gulp. Arina gave her a reproachful look and had a mouthful of hers. Luke sighed and halved his drink, then refilled Roxanne's glass and sat down on his perch carefully.

'He is not a fit man, nor did he have time to change,' said Roxanne out of the blue, as if they had not been interrupted at all.

'Who?' Luke asked taken by surprise.

'Mr Baxter, Luke,' Arina answered instead, 'is that right, Roxanne?'

'Yes of course, sorry if I confused you but I've been thinking all this time about the personality of the murderer, you know,' she smiled apologetically, 'trying to create an offender profile, in other words, profiling our murderer. And Tom, I mean, Mr Baxter doesn't fit it at all. And another thing I was going to mention…again according to my profiling, the killer should be a man. But of course I could be absolutely wrong. I am just a beginner…'

'Hm, that's interesting and funnily enough, your views on the murderer's personality, so far, are matching mine,' Arina confessed and did justice to her glass of wine.

Luke, who didn't have to be asked, went to get another bottle. Their discussion was getting more and more interesting.

'Are you not driving, Luke?' Roxanne enquired after Luke finished his half-glass and the next full glass, and was on the way with the third one.

'I was going to ask you the same question, are you not collecting your car later today and driving us home?' added Arina.

'Collecting your car? Is anything wrong with it?' Roxanne asked.

Only then Luke remembered that Roxanne didn't know anything about their suspicions. When he explained her the reason why his chic Jag had to be serviced prematurely, she exclaimed, 'What about me? How did he anticipate where to find me? It doesn't make sense, does it? Unless…'

'Exactly! Unless the attacker was following you from the pub. In that case how did he anticipate that you would be having lunch there in the first place? And there we are—back to square one,' Luke said.

'Luke, ask your mechanic to look for a listening device as well…' prompted Arina.

'No, it's too far-fetched, he must be a genius technician in that case,' Roxanne replied.

'Not necessarily,' Luke said after he had sent a message to the garage, 'it's not very difficult, technically I mean, to set up these *taps*. the Internet is full of all sorts of advice and tutorials. But of course one would need quite a lot of money. And, supporting your theory ladies, I agree, its more in a man's character to come up with all these tricks.'

'Assuming that your car is tapped, which we don't know for sure yet,' Roxanne said and finished her wine.

'I think we all need something to eat,' Arina suggested, and looked at Luke meaningfully.

'I can order some pizza, how about you Roxanne, what would you like?'

'Sorry, I am an awful hostess! Let me call my local pizza place, I'm their regular customer. And please, don't mention about money, I don't want to hear about it. Everything here, I mean *everything,* is paid by Tom.'

'Will he be joining us? Or...' asked Arina carefully.

Roxanne laughed melodiously and shook her head, 'No worries, he will be very late. I know he is not the most charming man, but his heart is made of gold.'

The pizzas had been ordered, delivered and successfully eaten. During this time, the mechanic called to tell Luke that he was right; that there were a few *suspicious* devices found inside his car, which was not ready for collection yet. It would need another thorough check up before officially being declared safe for use. The mechanic was famously overcautious, which probably was not too bad for a man of his trade.

It was getting late. Roxanne began to look tired and sleepy, it was time to leave her in peace.

Luke started clearing up, he filled a black rubbish bag with empty carton boxes, loaded the dishwasher, he even swept the floor in the bedroom, removing all traces of their feast.

Arina stayed with Roxanne. They talked a little about the case again. Roxanne briefly reported her day at school, emphasising the changes in Angel's behaviour. She also for the first time mentioned the new girl Clare.

'So, what do you think was the real reason behind her decision to quit the running class?' Arina asked.

'I guess she didn't want to disappoint her favourite teacher. She was not good enough for the standards the other girls were achieving. And Aaron...he was too soft to tell her this. He didn't want to hurt her feelings. And here I'm coming to the quite important point, in my opinion. He couldn't bring himself to hurt other people's feelings, particularly young girls. You see?'

'I'm with you now,' Arina cried, 'Luke where are you? Come here and listen! I think we cracked one puzzle, Aaron's presumed romantic involvements with his students. It is highly possible that he was not having an affair with Angel at all! I even don't want to take into account our *oil heiress*, we never took her revelation seriously, did we, Luke? No! But anyway, it would not hurt anybody to talk to her again. Is she back tomorrow, Roxanne, do you know?'

Roxanne didn't answer at first. She suddenly looked like a mischievous cat, who had done some naughty things but didn't feel guilty and was sure of getting away easily. She averted her eyes and smiled enigmatically.

'Honestly, the last thing I want is to disappoint you, but I'm afraid I won't see Fairuza tomorrow or any other girl. Sorry.'

'Yes of course, and don't be sorry, we should have thought about this before. It's *us* who should be apologising. Stay at home as long as you want, have plenty of rest. Luke will call the school tomorrow morning and rearrange the sessions for you. Probably after half term? What do you think?'

Roxanne looked up, with her long green eyes tracing a pathway of an imaginary spider on the ceiling. It became very quiet. Luke stood in exactly the same spot where Tom had been a few hours ago, in the doorway, with a wet tea-towel over his shoulder. His rectangular spectacles misted up and he had a bit of a silly look. Arina was frowning, and the two vertical lines between her eyebrows appeared distinct and sharp. Something was not right and they both felt it.

Roxanne touched her scarred head lightly and winced. Then she leaned over from her bed and fetched from the bottom drawer of her bedside table a platinum wig, which she promptly pulled down onto her head. It had a long straight fringe and totally changed Roxanne's appearance. She looked now like a bored rich diva.

'You know, we are going away,' she said as a matter of fact.

'Away? When?' asked Luke in a strained voice.

'Sometime next week,' she yawned discreetly.

'That's a very good idea,' said Arina agreeably, 'I'm sure you will be much better when you come back in a few days or…you don't mind me asking, for how long are you going?'

'No, I don't mind, don't mind at all. I thought I had told you early on, no? Oh, I'm just going, I'm not intending to come back at all.'

'What?' Luke exclaimed.

This time Roxanne looked down and met his eyes.

'I'm moving in with Tom. It's time for me to stop playing silly games and begin living the life of an adult. I'm twenty-nine already! So, we have decided enough is enough! I've almost lost my life.'

Arina absentmindedly put her right hand deep into her thick grey mane and messed it up with passion.

'Yes, of course, you had a tttruly horrible experience yesterday, I'm…am…we're ssso sssorry for what happened,' red-faced Luke was stuttering.

Roxanne nodded pensively.

'Is it not a too hasty decision, I dare to ask?' Arina said carefully.

'It seems so, doesn't it? It's not really. We're getting married in a few months, so it is the right time after all.'

'Thank you Roxanne, for what you did for us, for our investigation, and now…it's time for us to go, to leave you to rest. I hope Tom won't be too late,' Arina got up with some difficulties, the bean bag was not prepared to let her go without a struggle.

'You're welcome,' answered Roxanne and yawned again.

'Let's go, Luke,' said Arina pulling him by his hand as he stood glued to the spot, transfixed as if under the spell.

'Good-bye, and thank you Luke, for tidying up. I think I'm going to sleep now,' with these words Roxanne lowered herself on the pillows to a recumbent position and closed her eyes. She started breathing serenely. She could have been easily already asleep.

Chapter 13

As she expected, Lord Mount-Hubert was hunched in his state-of-the-art electric armchair in the drawing room. It was adjoined to the veranda where he usually spent all day. But today the weather was so depressing that he preferred to stay inside the main building. The fact that she had anticipated this filled her with pleasure.

He was not asleep, however. He was aware of her silent appearance, watching her with his ill watery eyes closely.

'They came, sir. Can I bring them here?' Barbara asked.

'I wish you didn't, for pity's sake! But I suppose, I've got no other choice. Yes, you can bring them here now,' he said grumpily.

Barbara bowed her head topped with a stiffly starched nursing cap and left the room. She came back followed by the two private detectives.

When she introduced them, the old man screwed up his face in a contemptuous grimace. Being a lord by birth, he didn't consider people with non-hereditary titles as equals.

'Lady who?' he questioned Arina in a husky cracked voice.

'Holroyd-Kugushev,' answered the latter composedly.

'Holroyd? Never heard of such a family!'

'My late husband, Alexander Holroyd, an eminent palaeontologist who had been awarded the peerage for his achievements in science.'

'Hm, and the second one of your double-barrelled, this Kug…I cannot even pronounce it. Is it Polish? Are you a descendant of Polish immigrants or what?'

Arina fixed her amazing turquoise eyes on the old audacious man, holding a pause. Sitting on the high back Jacobean style oak chair, like on a throne, she looked even more grand and noble than usual.

'I'm a descendant of Russian immigrants,' she said eventually.

He chuckled.

'You haven't got any accent, why?'

'I was born here,' she answered.

He thought for a moment, calculating her age. Then continued the interrogation in his usual fastidious manner.

'So, what did they not like in Russia? Why did they decide to emigrate?'

'The Bolsheviks!'

'What?' asked Lord Mount-Hubert.

'And it was not them then. It was my father on his own who escaped the Bolsheviks in 1920, when he was fifteen years old. His parents didn't go with him. They had been killed before. Their deadly sin was that they were of noble birth,' Arina continued in a calm detached voice, 'the only treasure my father managed to smuggle from Russia was his name—Prince Kugushev. So, if it suits you better, feel free to address me as Princess Kugushev'.

Lord Mount-Hubert was pinned to his armchair, dumbstruck.

Barbara, who heard all of this, couldn't help herself liking this extraordinary woman. She was laughing loudly in her mind, watching her abhorrent employer being taken down a peg or two.

'Now can we go back to the main purpose of our visit and ask you a few questions about your missing nephew? Is that a yes? Good, thank you,' Arina finished with a conceited smile.

'What do you want to know?'

'We know that the police had already questioned you about Aaron last year. But there has been a new development in the case recently.' Since there was no reaction from the old man, Arina went on, 'That is why it is so important for us to speak to you again. Have you received any sort of communication from your nephew at all?'

'He sent me a few words then, in October last year I think, if I remember correctly,' Lord Mount-Hubert glanced at Barbara who nodded to him discreetly.

'You didn't say anything about this to the police, did you?' asked Luke who had done his homework well and knew the interview by heart.

'No, I didn't, because I received the letter from Aaron later in the month. He was explaining in it why he had to go away. Do you want to know? I assume so,' the old man chuckled, but his eyes glared with animosity, 'he had to run away because of his involvement with an underage girl, his student by the way. She was threatening him to go public with this, unless he cancelled the wedding. He chose neither.'

'What was her name?' asked Luke and at the same time Arina said, 'So you knew about the wedding?'

The old man rubbed his deformed fingers together and grinned widely, turning his wrinkled face towards Arina, then—Luke and back to Arina.

'One at a time, one at a time! I cannot deal with you both simultaneously. Who should I answer first? The lady of course, the Princess, hm…why does it matter now if I knew or I didn't know about the wedding, which never happened anyway? It's irrelevant, it's not important! Why should I be bothered every time when a woman wants to shackle my trusting nephew? Pff! Eventually, he came to terms, like all of them do, and acted appropriately. Aaron wrote me a letter where he explained everything and admitted how immature and silly he was to be drawn into this inadequate marriage, naughty boy!' Lord Mount-Hubert pretended to be ashamed of his nephew but didn't do it very convincingly.

'And the girl's name?' reminded Luke.

'Don't have a clue.'

'In other words, you don't believe that something bad could have happened to Aaron?' Arina asked.

'No! Why are you asking?'

'Because there have been very bad things happening in connection with your nephew's missing person case,' Arina said, 'because he is missing, he didn't go away voluntarily,' she looked directly at the old man, and her eyes were burning with anger, 'more likely—he has been murdered.'

'I don't believe you, I don't believe you! Where is your proof? No! No! He is alive!' the old man rattled on, clenching and unclenching his fists patched with liver spots.

'My proof is based on your nephew's character. I don't think that even you would believe that Aaron became a cold-blooded murderer, just like that,' Arina snapped her fingers.

'Murderer? How…What are you talking about? I don't know anything! Who was murdered?' his voice was hardly audible, his face turning to a pallid mask of horror.

'There are a few people who went missing, probably murdered but their bodies have not been found yet. The principal of the school where Aaron used to teach, she has been brutally murdered. And somebody else, a woman who was assisting us in our investigation was attacked just a few days ago. Fortunately, she managed to escape.'

The old man was sitting with his mouth half-open, his eyes glazed but his fists were still frantically working, clasping and unclasping.

Barbara thought, he won't last long, this Lady Holroyd will crack him like an old useless nut. She must act without delay.

She coughed politely attracting attention.

'Excuse me please, but I'm afraid it is too much for his Lordship. He is not a well man and he is very weak. So, please, can we stop for now? He *must* rest or he will have one of his coughing fits, which can be very dangerous for him, is that okay?'

The private detectives were on their way out, they apologised of course, but Barbara could see that they were confused and disappointed, and they still had many unanswered questions on their minds. They looked defeated. And this pleased Barbara immensely.

When they left, Barbara met the old man's eyes streaked with blood vessels, fear was written all over them. Her lips were set in a straight red line, any traces of her smile were gone, as if they were wiped off by a wet sponge leaving only a thin stroke of the carmine lipstick.

The nurse went to her room and closed the door behind her tightly. She felt suddenly free, it was like the toxic spell she had been under for so many years was magically removed. She deserted Lord Mount-Hubert in his opulent, tastelessly furnished drawing room without a word. And he didn't say anything either. He is afraid of me, she thought getting her tiny, old-fashioned mobile phone out of her uniform pocket.

She knew he would not be pleased but still decided to call. She was right, he was furious. He didn't shout but his words were so venomous and spiteful that they sounded even more menacing than if they had been cried out. She shivered.

Did she do the right thing? Did she betray this old, deadly sick man for nothing? These detectives were not stupid. Quite the opposite. They were on the right track. It would not take long for them to run him down.

And then what? What would happen to her? Could she still escape from his trap?

She listened to what he was saying, and her blood froze in her veins. It was too late to change sides now, of course. She had missed all her chances. She started crying. Silently and bitterly. Her face was distorted, but her voice sounded normal, even and dull, not giving her away even a bit.

****

The wind rose out of nowhere. A minute ago, it had been all quiet and motionless. Arina was out in her back garden, bundled up in an old thick cardigan of an indefinite colour and a gorgeous copper beech shawl with a complicated maze of gold patterns. She liked to come here with a mug of tea, sitting on a weatherworn bench inside of the wooden arbour encircled with the vine jasmine.

Admiring the view of the vast valley in front of her and the water reservoir behind, partially obscured by all these trees, which were mostly conifers, with bright flakes of birches and aspens in between. She knew well that it was the best place for her to think, to meditate. She felt tranquil, in full harmony with surrounding nature. This place always helped her to rebalance her energy.

The tall trees were swaying like long unkept grass. And they were creating a real leaf-storm, leaves dancing a saraband in the air.

A crow cawed from the gigantic spruce—a centenary sentinel of the house. Arina turned back and, behind her at the back door, she saw Sasha. She looked like she was still eleven or ten and was wearing a well-worn, sun-bleached blue dress, her favourite of this time. She was smiling unsurely, and her eyes were large and unreadable. Then she disappeared.

With a sudden impact Arina remembered her last night dream. She dreamed of Sasha, and in her dream Sasha was alive.

And still, she couldn't cry. Not able to spend a single tear to mourn her lost child. Arina froze in this uncomfortable position, with her head painfully screwed back and eyes burning of unshed tears, trying to recreate the image of her dead daughter.

It will be two years soon. 1st of March 2014, when the devastating news reached her. Sasha and Clive had gone scuba diving two days before and had never come back. Their small motorboat, which they used for leisure trips, was found later, capsized. Probably, they were caught up, while under the water, in a quick passing but severe local storm, lost their boat and were too far away from any land. The other option, which involved a shark attack, had not been suggested to Arina, but she herself had been free to follow up this scenario. She opted not to.

Enough whining, she ordered herself. She would go back to Sasha later, after the case is solved. She didn't have any doubts that she might fail or let the murderer get away unpunished.

157

'The game is afoot', she said aloud and then corrected herself, 'for two weeks had been already afoot, and there is no other way for me but to crack this mystery.'

Arina drank more of her tepid tea. Driven by their shepherd—wind, the flocky clouds were racing across the high, watery-blue sky. The three cats came to their owner, joining her one by one.

Chernomor was first, he came out of the house and sat next to her, sheltering from the piercing wind. He formed a large black furry ball and was watching her with his meditative yellow saucers.

Nero loudly announced his arrival by dropping an empty watering-can, against which he was rubbing his cheeks. Startled by the bang, he crouched for a second, then ran to Arina and started rubbing not only his head but the whole glossy body against her legs, purring loudly and drooling at the same time.

As usual it was Brahms who came last. He appeared from nowhere, silently and swiftly moving his hairy thick paws, with his fan-like enormous tail proudly upright. In one huge jump he landed himself on his owner's knees and secured position with those deadly claws of his, not painfully but tangibly enough for Arina to freeze under his substantial weight.

Now, when her small family was assembled, she could think clearly again. Poor Luke. He was almost in tears when Roxanne detonated the bomb. But for herself...Arina didn't regret that Roxanne decided to defect. Actually the opposite, she felt secretly relieved.

She had learned to work with Luke, and that was quite enough for her. Three was too many, the third person wouldn't fit in their well-established team. She tried not to be too personal. Roxanne was not bad, but only in terms of being an occasional ally. Even before Roxanne's decision Arina couldn't imagine how their trio would survive longer than one case. Anyway, it hadn't.

It's been almost a week since Roxanne's revelation. Time runs. And they hadn't caught the murderer yet.

She shook her head with annoyance. She had been so looking forward to questioning the old lord yesterday. And what a disaster! To be honest, the whole week was a total disaster! From last Sunday till today, Saturday the 22nd.

Arina put down her capacious mug with blurry cat patterns worn-out by numerous washings. There was some tea left but icy cold and totally undrinkable. The sharp squalls of wind started getting through the fissured arbour's walls more persistently. She knew that it was time for her to go inside the warmth of her house, but still she lingered. She liked these moments when exposed to severe weather conditions she could easily get away, escape into the safety of her house at any time, but, instead, she preferred to wait longer, to feel the harshness of the elements and imagining herself somewhere far away from home, not able to find shelter for a long time.

She liked to dare herself and at the same time to feel that at any point she could return to safety. Only it didn't work every time as she planned, sometimes she would cross the point-of-no-return without noticing it until too late.

****

On 17th of October, which was Monday, she was woken up by a loud knock on her bedroom door. Brought out of her deep sleep so brutally, Arina groaned and covered her splitting head with a pillow, trying to ignore what was going outside of her room. Luke, of course, damn Luke who had stayed the night in her place, was making all these almighty noises.

'Leave me alone,' she murmured and tried to return to the Land of Nod, though, without success as Luke's ginger spiky head was already peering out of the door, which was slowly opening.

'It's Jan Cribble,' he said in a conspiratorial way, 'he will be calling in five minutes. Oh, boss, you don't look your best, if I may say, hm!'

'Oh, Luke, shut up! I don't only not look my best, but what is more important—I don't feel my best either! Leave me alone, I'm asking you nicely!'

'I'm bringing my laptop here, you will need to do something with your hair, do you want a brush or what?'

Arina looked at him grimly. It was clear that he would not give up easily.

'Now, tell me what's going on, but be brief and coherent,' she said closing her eyes again.

'It was his brother, do you remember, the antique dealer from Harrogate, yes? As you know I keep my phone always switched on, so he called, Jan's brother, at this early hour and I answered. Eventually. I was basically still asleep. When I realised what it was about, I thought on my feet. I gave us ten minutes. There's only five left now.'

'Jan from Australia?' cried out Arina after a few minutes of arduous brainwork.

'Exactly! From Melbourne. Eleven hours difference, you know!'

Not wasting any more time, Lady Holroyd-Kugushev showed a remarkable outburst of activity. Firstly, she cast the pillow away. Secondly, she shouted to Luke to run and fetch her colourful shawl from downstairs. Thirdly, she got out of her bed and did a few energetic jumps to shake off the last traces of alcohol left from yesterday's long session of wine consumption. After this, Arina dug both of her hands into her lively hair and ruffled them properly. Then she powdered her face rapidly in front of the triple vanity mirror, trying not to look too closely at her sleepy, sluggish face.

When Luke returned with the shawl, he found his boss fully awake and freshened up with a delicately scented perfume. She had also significantly improved her appearance with a pair of sunglasses, which concealed yellowish bags under the eyes, and a dash of the pale pink blush to the cheekbones. With the copper beech and gold shawl wrapped around her shoulders she was fully ready to meet elusive Jan Cribble.

Mr Antiquarian from Melbourne appeared to show some resemblance to his younger brother but in a queer way. It was as if his thinner version—Gordon—had been blown and blown up, like a gigantic balloon. He had a very large face, absolutely wrinkle-free, like a baby's bottom, with a very wide nose, at least three times the size of the one which belonged to his younger *bro*. His neck was simply an oak trunk, and his dark-blue eyes looked like they might wheel out of their corresponding eye-sockets at any time, so disproportionally big and round they were. He had a lot of similarity with a petulant toad.

After they accomplished the questioning of Jan Cribble and turned off Skype, the private detectives looked at each other, astonished. That was a revelation. What this rugby player of the past had just told them. It was an enormous breakthrough in their up to now rather sluggish investigation.

'We will have to calculate our every move ever so carefully from now on,' Arina said seriously.

Luke just nodded.

'We also need your car ASAP,' she continued, 'will you call the garage and ask your genius mechanic to speed up just a little bit?'

Luke looked at his watch and smiled wryly, 'As soon as they open, which will not be for another hour and half at least.'

'Oh, it's not a civilised hour yet? Okay, so we have some time on our hands and I'm not going to let it be wasted,' Arina announced decisively.

'But we're going to have some breakfast first, I hope?' Luke pleaded.

'You can go to the kitchen and indulge yourself when I'm having a quick shower. Don't forget the cats! You're welcome to use your superfluous energy usefully.'

And that was it. That was Monday.

Luke's car was ready in the evening and they managed to get through to Aaron's only living relative—the noble uncle. They didn't speak directly with him, of course, it was Barbara, his nurse and personal carer who dealt with them. Not without obstacles the private detectives had got permission to visit the old gentleman, but not before Thursday.

Tuesday brought them the waste of a journey to Wetherby where they met another member of both Physio and Pilates classes—a retired jockey and a current bookmaker. His name was Keith Small, and he indeed lived up to his name. Not only because of his tiny and thin frame, but because of his contribution, which was so small, there was nothing worth taking note of.

Keith bore a sour expression on his jackdaw's face with a long, sharply protruding nose and vigilant dark eyes. His feelings towards any representative of the law were transparently negative. He didn't want to have anything to do with the investigation and apparently didn't give a toss as to what could have happened to Aaron or, more to the point, anybody else from that money-sucking place.

On Wednesday afternoon Arina and Luke paid a call to Boston Spa where they met a gardener and a tree-surgeon, which was proudly stated on his freshly painted smart truck. George Hunt was his name and for a change he turned out to be a nice, affable sort of a bloke. He was a tall and muscular man, with a wide smile on a well-tanned handsome face and a fair, fashionably trimmed beard.

George Hunt was easy to talk to, he was open and chatty. He was not too shy to show his straight large teeth, which looked even whiter in comparison to his dark face. He told them that he had recently come back from holiday in Greece. He usually went there at this time of the year. In winter he preferred to ski in the Alps, of course. In summer he would travel somewhere exotic for a few weeks. Clearly, he was an exceptionally successful gardener.

He was unmarried but had a girlfriend. They were thinking to settle down in a year or two. To start a family. Forty-three was just the perfect age for this, he thought. His girlfriend was ten years younger than him, however. Everything seemed to be planned nicely in his life.

This was the time to move the conversation into the desirable direction.

'Aaron was going to get married too, you knew about that?' prompted Arina.

This supposedly rhetorical question brought a shadow of incomprehension onto George's face.

'Aaron? Hm…I'm not sure…I think he was already married.'

Luke took the photograph out of his coat pocket and showed it to George Hunt.

'Is it Aaron? Ha-ha! I thought you meant the other guy, what's his name…' George stroked his beard thoughtfully, then gave out a nonchalant smile and shrugged his shoulders, 'no, sorry, I can't remember. It was ages ago!'

'Who did you mean, Mr Hunt?' asked Arina patiently.

'Oh, please, call me George! Mr Hunt sounds so official. And it adds on years to you, you know, makes you feel older. Ha-ha! Sorry, can you repeat you question?'

'When we spoke on the phone, you assured us that you knew Aaron pretty well, so who exactly did you mean, *George*?'

'Ah sorry, if I confused you a bit,' he caressed his sun-bleached beard, 'I thought that you were interested in this tough looking military sort of character…'

'Todd Fisher?' Arina asked hastily.

'Yes, yes, of course! That's him!' exclaimed George happily, beaming with excitement.

'So, what did you want to tell us about him?'

'About whom? You are confusing me again. Just a minute ago you were very keen to find out about Aaron, now it's Todd, my simple brain has stalled,' he grinned.

'What about telling us what you remember about erm…the person you thought to be Aaron,' Luke nipped in.

'The funny thing is, I cannot see them apart now! That's weird, isn't it? When I try to look back, I don't know who did what. I used to mix them up in the past, you know, even if they didn't look alike. Todd is the ex-soldier, right? He was not a nice guy I think, but again I'm not sure. He didn't do anything wrong to me.'

'So, you're saying that they looked alike?'

'No, not at all! But, you see, they were always together, inseparable. One gets confused easily. I knew that they were from my physio class, but who was who exactly…I was not getting too close to the other participants. I just went there to help my back, not to socialise.'

George spread his hands apologetically.

'Sorry for wasting your time,' Arina said coldly.

'Not at all, sorry that you came all this way for nothing, but you must understand that it's really difficult for me to remember all these details after such a long time. But, honestly, they both were roughly the same height and build. No, wait, one of them was wider and stockier, more mature type. Must be the soldier, yes of course, how could I forget! Once he showed me a photo, a little snap of a woman. "My wife," he said. Or maybe—"my ex-wife". That's funny— an ex-soldier with an ex-wife, ha-ha! Not mentioning an ex-runner.'

'Hilarious,' murmured Arina.

'Why did the veteran show you this photo?' Luke asked.

'Ha! Why indeed? Wait! Because I was showing a picture of my pretty Emily. Right! This must be summer last year, because the running guy, Aaron, yes, he was talking about his wedding. You see, it's not too empty up there,' George pointed at his head and burst out laughing like a lunatic.

Luke waited patiently for the fit to die out before firing away another question.

'Do you recall anything else? For example, Todd's,' he corrected himself rapidly, 'the soldier's wife—what was her name? How did she look like?'

George shook his head, 'You are asking too much, mate! No, I definitely don't know her name. Her appearance…nothing special…me thinking, plainish…I can tell you more about the other girl, the runner's fiancée, however. She was stunning, she was a star! I even felt a little bit jealous. Don't take me wrong, I am very happy how my Emily looks, but her…she was a cut above!'

'A blonde barbie?' asked Arina tiredly.

'Nope! A dark girl, with glossy long hair and a milelong eyelashes. Sort of a Latino appearance, like Spanish or Italian.'

Arina and Luke exchanged meaningful looks. Fairuza, it must have been Fairuza.

Now, sitting in her rapidly darkening garden Arina was not so sure. They had jumped to this, seemingly so obvious conclusion too quickly, and hadn't bothered to check the other possibility. They hadn't shown a photo of Lisa Roberts to George Hunt. He was not a reliable witness, he was continuously confusing Aaron with Todd. Why not to assume he would have done the same with their other halves?

Probable, it was more than probable, it was the only logical explanation.

Who had a plain fiancée? Aaron. Kind-hearted, honest and faithful Aaron. Todd Fisher, on the other hand, was a very different person. Keeping in mind all the evidence they had gathered so far it became clear for Arina that it would be totally out of his character to share with anybody from his class a picture of an unattractive woman, with whom he was in a relationship.

More likely, it was Todd's wife or girlfriend (why would he boast about his ex?) who impressed George with her Latino look. They must find her. And also, they must see Aaron's uncle again. Enough dead ends and red herrings. Enough empty fruitless days. The truth is near, it's lurking from around the corner. It's just a matter of reaching it in time.

Arina put her hands together and interlocked the fingers. From a distance it looked like she was praying; in a way she was, but not in the conventional way.

Diary 4

I'm looking down at my hands and see blood on them. The blood is dried up and covers them with its crust like scarlet gloves.

I know it's impossible! But still…I cannot help myself. I'm closing my eyes, keeping them shut tight for a while and when I open them again—there is nothing. My hands are clean. White and clean. My palms are wide, my fingers are short but strong.

I am not mad, I am not like Lady Macbeth, rubbing my hands, trying to wash non-existent blood off them. I know that this is just my imagination playing tricks on me. Nothing more. Not a big deal.

I'm not a bookworm, don't get me wrong, but I've read this play. Gripping stuff. I didn't understand all of it, of course, but what I understood impressed me deeply. It went down into my head and stayed there. In a contagious sort of way.

As I've surely mentioned before, I am used to killing, and it hasn't bothered me too much. I live with it. I eat well and sleep well.

Until now.

This fool, this Pole, this silly naïve Marek, he has upset me. I'm thinking back—could I let him go? Just let him go back to his motherland? But how can I be sure that he would not start talking? There is no guarantee. You see?

I am not a monster.

I feel sorry for him, I will be honest with you, I do. It's an unusual feeling for me. It's disturbing and worse—It's steering me off my course. I'm losing my concentration, I've started making mistakes.

Take, for instance, this silly blunder with the bold girl. I must not go back to this disaster.

I should have cut the bitch's head off! And planted it in the stupid Japanese garden of our great detective. Can imagine her face when she sees the severed head towering over her precious pagodas.

I must not work myself up, I must not lose my temper. Later I will deal with her. Right now it's not so important. I have to stay focused. Focused and composed.

That's better. I feel how the red heat, the boiling rage is losing its grip on my heart and I can breathe again.

Let the dead bury the dead. It's Marek's own fault that he bumped straight into me. Coming out of the "Green Witch" for a fag, he should have done better. I can only compare it to walking out onto a busy road in front of a fast-moving 4x4. What do you expect? Boom! Smash! Casualties.

I simply followed the most primeval instinct—the instinct of survival. I acted to save my own life. Of course, I'm fully aware that they will not hang me nowadays but being put in prison would be the same for me as death if not worse. So, they are the same concepts for me.

What a brilliant idea to keep a diary, even an unorthodox one. It really helps! That was where my shrink was right. It does help!

My strength is back as well as my confidence. One shouldn't stop on one's way especially when the goal is so close.

I'm back to myself, I am in one piece again. And I'm ready for my next move.

Chapter 14

Angel, the Barbie girl, as dubbed by Lady Holroyd-Kugushev so aptly, was very frightened and very confused. She was biting her nails nervously and staring out of the large school window.

She was still at school despite the late hour. She was behind in her project, as she had lied, and needed to spend a couple more hours in the workshop, to finish some details on her riding jacket. Angel was doing Fashion & Textile Design for A level and was quite good at it. She was usually well ahead with her coursework, so it took her some hard mental work to come up with an excuse to stay late.

Angel would do anything to be at home instead. The old building was always giving her the creeps. But after the horrible death of Ms Kale, it became practically unbearable to stay within its frigid walls.

Especially on her own. Mr Oliver, the old guardian of the school entrance, was not counted by her not only due to his ancient age, but also because of his unfriendly, suspicious attitude towards almost all pupils.

And it was so dark outside the school workshop's huge bare windows! There were some lamp posts in the grounds of course, but their light was not enough to penetrate all this darkness billowing outside. And the huge oak, mounting like a giant ogre in the middle of the square in front of the main entrance, was casting uneven and ugly shadows which could hide anything or anybody.

The workshop was on the ground floor and that was not good. Angel stopped destroying her once beautiful long nails and had a few rapid gulps of the strawberry flavoured water from the plastic bottle.

There was no love anymore. It was just a mirage, a Fairy tale she told herself and believed in with all her heart. How credulous she was! How gullible! The truth is cruel—you can't trust nobody.

The workshop with its dressmaker's mannequins, headless and anonymous, partly clad in all sorts of whimsical garments, suddenly stopped looking familiar to Angel. There were too many dark corners, too many strange shadows in this place. The bright light given by the swing arm desk lamp, which resembled a squatting skeleton, was deceiving and made the mannequins look more animated than they were destined to be.

There were also a few dummy heads on their long swan necks, wearing colourful hats and scarfs. They were watching the girl from all sides, in an aloof, calculating manner like a small, privileged group of cronies.

Angel cleared her throat, it was the same—dry and itchy, the strawberry water didn't appear to quench her thirst. Her light cough reverberated boomingly and made her shiver.

I'm coming down with a cold, she thought miserably. What am I doing here? I should be in my soft comfy bed, under my favourite velvet bedspread covered in pink roses, with a mug of hot milk watching something comforting on the telly.

Angel glanced at the window again and froze. For a moment she thought that it was a ghost looking back at her, with black hollow eyes and white hair. Then she realised it was her own reflection.

She was shocked. Her beautifully proportioned heart-shaped face had acquired a lopsided puffiness and unhealthy palish tinge. It was like she had several gumboil swellings. In a feverish panic, she brought her trembling hands up to her face and started touching it carefully.

It was simply a distorted reflection, she understood after the thorough examination. There was absolutely nothing wrong with her perfectly moulded face. But Angel's heart was beating fast and loud for some time.

The time had almost come. It was five minutes to six, and the waiting became intolerable.

Why did she lie about Mr Statham?

She didn't! He was always very nice to her, attentive in a gentlemen's way. She was his best runner, his blonde shining star, as he used to call her. Perhaps she let her imagination go a little bit too far…but it's not a crime, is it? And he spent a lot of time with her, training her, talking to her. Much more than with *you* Miss Robinson!

And, honestly, one day, in August last summer, she believed that *everything* was possible between them, her—Angel and him—Aaron. Oh! It was such a beautiful day, a proper summer day! She was able to wear her best blue frock and show her beautiful long legs fully.

She had met him after his physio class at this snazzy practice called "Better Life". It was a brilliant idea of hers! It was like a proper date! He even took her to the café for a cold drink. She couldn't remember its name but it was a really trendy vegie place.

It was doubly nice of him to remember that she was also a vegetarian. She smiled.

How did she know about his secret? Ha! Bet you didn't have a clue that Aaron was attending these classes, did you Miss Robinson?

All right, it was a pure accident that she learned where Mr Statham went twice a week. She overheard. No! No way she was spying on him or eavesdropping! She was just walking past when she heard Mr Baxter offering him a lift to the Pilates class. Only then did she stop and...yeah...listen a bit.

Making up a story was not too difficult for Angel. She was good at it, at making up convincing stories. Angel's dad was suffering from back pain. That was not a complete lie, occasionally he had some aches and twitches caused by sitting at his desk for too long. He was looking for a physio clinic and couldn't find anything he liked. Almost true! He will have to—in a few years' time—he certainly will! So it was natural for Aaron to suggest for Angel's dad the place he was going to. Even more natural was for Angel to ask to have a little look at this practice.

So, what's wrong with that? No need to send her these horrible, *horrible* messages! It's not funny anymore! They have to talk! Clear the air between them!

Okay, she's sorry—it was a slight exaggeration when she described their relationship to the private detectives. But she was *very* stressed! The old woman was awful, she hated her from the first moment they met. Angel was used to such a reaction from other women though. Nothing new in that respect. The man was not too bad but clearly under the lady's influence (whatever her foreign name was).

But then she had changed her story, right?

'Are you satisfied, Miss Roberts, now?' Angel cried out loudly in despair, 'no need to be so angry with me! I've lied, Okay! Lied! Aaron...sorry, sorry! Mr Statham had never promised to marry me! I've just thought...doesn't matter now. I've imagined this, that's all. Where are you? I don't want to wait any longer. My parents will be worried about me, I must go home now! Please!'

Angel looked around. Her heart was again beating so fast now, it was going to pop out of her chest any minute.

There was some soft rustling coming from the far corner of the enormous room, as if a draught was playing with a long dress or a scarf.

Then, like a scene from a nightmare, one of the mannequins started moving as if in slow motion, in a way soaring, silently, in a black cloud of trailing cloth, the wide brimmed hat perched on the stump. Closer and closer. Under the hat she already could see a brightly painted mouth.

And from nowhere—the handless and legless mannequin grew all four limbs. Its faceless head transformed into a clown mask. White powdered with red circles for cheeks and shining vampire lips.

Angel screamed. And then fell. Her poor, undeveloped heart couldn't cope with the incoming horror. It stopped beating at once. The beautiful girl was lying like a full-sized doll with widely open glazed blue eyes and the mass of the long blond hair streaming down on the floor.

****

'What awful news!' Arina replied to Luke, her voice broke and she went silent, stroking Chernomor absentmindedly.

'Poor girl,' Luke continued, 'it was her heart, sudden cardiac arrest, or SCA, they're saying. It could have happened any time apparently.'

'Is it a sort of heart attack?'

'No, it's a different condition. With a heart attack it's blood flow which is stopped getting to the heart. In the case of SCA—it's the heart malfunctioning. In other words, the heart itself stops beating.'

'How sad. And she was so young…'

'Unfortunately, it's not as rare among young people as you might think. More to the point, young people, or even children, who are involved in serious sports, for instance athletics.'

'Oh! What was she doing by the way, so late at school, have you found out?'

'Yes, Angel said that she wanted to work on her project, a jacket or a coat, that sort of thing, to finish some details.'

'Hm, have you checked with her teacher if that was the case?'

Luke shook his head.

'She didn't need to stay behind to catch up with her work, she was a star pupil actually.'

'Yes, and…' Arina looked at Luke expectantly.

'No, it's not what you're thinking, there was nothing fishy about it, I've been assured. Angel was a perfectionist at everything to do with her fashion and textile course. And this condition…it's called hypertrophic cardiomyopathy, it often goes undetected.'

It was Tuesday the 25th when Arina learned of the sad news. She was still unconvinced, it was simply too convenient for the death to be just an accident.

'Who did find the poor girl?' she asked frowning at her thoughts.

'Her father. He came to pick her up. Because she was not outside the school gates as they agreed and she was not answering her phone, he had to call the school. The porter answered. Do you remember him? The old gentleman at the entrance?'

Arina nodded.

'Mr Oliver, his name, said that there was nobody at the school except himself. The father, who has been known for his short temper, didn't believe him and insisted on coming into school immediately to look for his daughter. After a heated discussion which lasted a few minutes, Mr Oliver lost ground and gave up the castle.

'The furious father stormed his way through the school to the workshop where he discovered the corpse of his beloved daughter. Then he himself collapsed by her side unconscious. After ten-twenty minutes, Mr Oliver couldn't be more precise, he decided to check out what was going on. It took him a little bit of time to get there as his pace was not as fast as it used to be—those are his own words.'

'I've fathomed it out, thanks Luke! If anybody was there, they could have easily escaped many times over. That part is clear.'

'When he eventually got there and saw the two bodies lying next to each other, he almost fainted himself, but somehow managed to stay conscious and called the police.'

'What a waste of a young, beautiful life!' Arina commented sadly, but her resourceful brain was already working on something else.

Luke was not blind and seeing this familiar, vacant look from the sparkling blue eyes, asked carefully, trying not to disquiet Lady Holroyd's train of thoughts.

'What is it?'

'Luke, we need to check something with the gardener. I'm afraid you will have to see George Hunt once more and show him something. A photo.'

'Oh!'

'I've been thinking and, don't look so alarmed Luke! I came to a different conclusion about the photograph he was talking about. You remember?'

'Ah...'

'Good. I think it's time to dig into Todd Fisher's past. And I believe that the Latino beauty will be a good start.'

'Who? Fairuza?'

'No, Luke, it was not Fairuza on Todd's photo.'

Arina explained her new idea to Luke.

'I can see the sense here,' he agreed rapidly, his eyes shining keenly over the rectangular spectacles.

Chernomor woke up and scrutinised Luke with his shining moon-like eyes. Then he yawned and closed his mouth with a clatter.

'If you do it tomorrow morning Luke, yes? We need to find her A.S.A.P.'

'What about the last guy from our list? John Broader from Otley.'

'Of course we'll see him too. All in good time. I don't think he will bring us anything noteworthy though.'

****

The house in a leafy area of Harrogate was a big detached one but in a horrible condition, almost dilapidated, with white paint peeling off its walls, leaving ugly damp patches behind. A roof, covered with moss, was gaping forlornly with missed or broken tiles. The garden was also unkempt, littered and ugly. The place looked uninhabitable. The private detectives thought that they had been given an incorrect address. But they were to be proved wrong.

The Latino beauty did occupy this property, only she didn't look so beautiful anymore. It seemed that she had been slowly decaying alongside her house. Of course Mr Hunt might have exaggerated her appearance but not to this extent. She looked at least a decade older than her birth age of thirty-seven.

She had wrinkles furrowing free across the narrow forehead and a distinctive smoker's pucker—deep, needle-like lines were surrounding the thin lips. Her high cheekbones were unnaturally sharp and jutting out, emphasising the morbid expression of her artificially tanned face. She was wearing her long black hair, dull and greasy, loose and it made her look like a Native American from an old-fashioned match box label. She also had a low, almost masculine, broken voice. Her name was Laura and, of course, Lady Holroyd-Kugushev was right—she was the ex-wife of the ex-soldier, the deceased Todd Fisher.

It took them just two days to track her down. Of course the notorious Supt— Peter Crawnshaw had his finger in the pie.

Laura Fisher looked uninterested, cold. She also didn't seem over the moon that they had managed to find her. It was not like she was hiding or anything like that, she just didn't want to be involved.

Laura was dressed dowdily and didn't appear to be bothered with her appearance too much. Her nails, brightly varnished in red, looked incongruous and messy as if she had dipped her fingertips in blood.

She didn't invite the detectives inside, so they had to content themselves with sitting outside at the rotten, rickety picnic table, presumably retired from a local pub many years ago. They also had to put up with their hostess chain-smoking cheap, fetid cigarettes.

Very soon they realised how hard it would be to obtain any useful information from her, she was clamming up at every question, answering as evasively as possible.

They had already learned from the scanty records that Todd Fisher was an only child, with the father dead for some time, and a demented mother who lived in a nursing home. He didn't have any cousins or obvious friends. The only living connection left between him and this world was her—Laura Fisher. And she was not cooperating.

'Yeah, I know that he's dead,' she said gloomily not letting go of her stinky cigarette even for a second. 'What? I don't know, how on Earth could I know why he did away with himself? No idea! If you were to do your homework before coming like a bolt from the blue, you would know that we had been divorced for a long-long time,' she drawled the end of the sentence disdainfully.

'We're aware of this,' Arina retorted automatically and glanced at the filthy first floor window, partly disguised by the equally filthy curtains. Something caught her attention, something strange and out of place.

Her heart lipped heavily. The light net curtain, smudged and torn, was fluttering slightly. But the window was fully closed, she was sure of it.

'Why in this case, if you had been separated for a long-long time as you stated, was Todd Fisher showing your photo to his friends from the Physio Clinic just last year?' Luke asked quickly.

Laura smiled scornfully, which looked more like her baring teeth.

'I bet it was "the beauty queen" photo. He liked to show off, to boast in front of his mates. When there was nothing else to brag about, he would fish out my old snap as a trump card.'

'Sorry Laura, what do you mean?' Luke asked perplexed.

'It's simple, it's my old photo which I used when I was entering a Miss England Beauty Pageant, hm, when I was seventeen. I didn't win, obviously, but believe it or not I was not far from the top three,' she looked at the detectives who were too late in hiding their astonishment and scowled again, 'it's difficult to imagine that now, isn't it? I'm not stupid, I am not under any illusion how I look now. I'm aware how much I have changed since. I smoke too much, I've been a user of...you know...smack...'

'Heroin?' Arina asked turning her eyes again from the bothering window to look at Laura.

'Yeah, but not anymore. I'm clean now, swear!'

'We believe you Laura,' Arina said soothingly, 'but what about your husband, sorry, your *ex*. Was he a user as well? Is this how it all started?'

Laura uttered a sad snigger, 'No, he was too smart for that. He was a dealer and I was his first client. His guineapig,' she sighed and lit another cigarette, her hands now were trembling slightly.

Arina cleared her throat and glanced at the window just in time to catch a glimpse of the dark shadow sneaking behind the torn net curtain. She quickly checked with Laura, no, she didn't notice anything. Or pretended not to notice, thought Arina and asked aloud, 'Please, continue about Todd. You were saying that he was a dealer.'

'Todd liked to be in power, always liked. When you're a dealer you're a God to users. That suited him pretty well. I don't know if he stopped later. I don't know. I'd not heard from him for ages.'

'Do you know why he left the army Laura?' Luke asked with a frown of concern on his amiable intellectual face.

'The same reason. The big H,' she took a deep drag on her cigarette and went on, 'they couldn't prove anything, of course, just rumours...'

'Why "of course"?' Arina entered into conversation again.

'What?'

'You said that they couldn't prove anything, *of course*. Like you were sure that they wouldn't find anything against him.'

'As I told you before, he was a smart fucking bustard, excuse my language. Anyway, why are you so interested in him. He is dead, right?'

'Are you not sure about that Laura?' Arina said lowering her voice and looking straight into the woman's eyes.

Laura narrowed her still startling dark blue eyes, the colour of frozen blueberry, and just shrugged her bony shoulders. Then said in her low husky voice, 'Sure, he's dead all right. If he wasn't he would have made my life a misery again.'

'Even after the divorce?'

'Even after. Much less than before, that's true. But still…I had to be on my guard all the time.'

'Please, tell us a little bit more about your life together?'

'Why? I don't like talking about that part of my life. What do you want to know exactly?'

'You are helping our investigation very much Laura. We are looking for any clues, for anything really to aid us in solving this complex and puzzling case. We appreciate that it might be a very hard and uneasy topic for you to discuss,' Luke tried to reassure her.

'Yeah, yeah, I've heard this millions of times, your lot always want something from me, always demanding something. Asking and asking endlessly all these irrelevant, silly little questions. Trying to catch me out on something, trap me. Waiting for me to make a fool of myself, to lose my footing. Fat chance!' She produced a forceful yawn.

Luke was slow with his response, and Arina took the lead.

'We are very sorry to upset you so much! Please, accept our apologies, please!'

'Okay. But be short. I haven't got all day for you. I have my own life to live, if you want to know. I have actually quite a busy lifestyle,' she tilted her head back in a way of, say, the Lacota Indian accepting a challenge from a rival tribe.

'How did you meet Todd? And how long were you together?'

'The last year of school. When we were both about sixteen. I'm actually a few months older than him. We got married a couple of years later. And divorced…let me think…I was twenty-nine then. You can work out the total yourself.'

'Eleven years,' Luke summarised, 'eleven years of marriage plus two years, so you knew each other for some time…'

'What do you mean by this?' Laura snapped.

'Nothing to be worried about Laura, just building a mental picture of Todd's life, that's all. When did he join the army?'

'At twenty-five, I think. Those years are not so clear for me. I was in a bad state then. I took the beauty contest failure to heart. And then everything went wrong. I didn't win. I chained my life to this bastard. Drugs came along at what couldn't have been a better time. Then we lost our only child.'

'Oh, I'm so sorry,' Arina said almost inaudibly.

Luke just shook his head.

'Yeah, I'm okay now. I can talk about it. It was a cot death. But everybody, everybody blamed me! Who else? A junkie mother, of course! Surely not an exemplary hero soldier (if they only knew!) fighting for his country in Afghanistan,' she smiled wryly and added after a pause, 'then he dumped me. Walked out on me. It was him who started the divorce process, not me. Did you think the opposite? No! I didn't have the guts to do it. I was a real waster then.'

It was an uneasy moment. Then she continued.

'What else? One day I woke up and realised how sick I was with myself. I decided to try to do something about it. It was five years ago. Now I'm a different person. I'm totally free of my habit. I've got a nice job at a tanning salon. I've got a place to live. It was the only good thing which came out of our marriage—this house we bought together when we still had money. Todd inherited something from his family and I did a lot of modelling those days. When I was still young and beautiful. I know that the house now needs a lot of work to be done on it, but that's in the future. If I'm still here. The most important thing is that I feel free. I'm free…'

'That's great Laura! We're so pleased for you that you managed to get through this hell,' Luke said carefully, 'now, before we go and leave you in peace, just one more question, please. Do you remember when Todd left the army and…sorry, second question has just climbed through. How did he get his injury? And what was this injury exactly?'

Laura didn't answer at first. She suddenly looked tired. Her skin under the fake tan turned palish with a tinge of an unhealthy sallow.

'He retired a year or two before his death. He was helped on his way, as I told you before, under the usual pretext of an injury. I believe he really had a sort of an accident there, like a fight or something like that, I honestly haven't got a clue. I remember he had a limp. Cannot help you more.'

'Thank you very much Laura. You helped us tremendously, honestly! Good-bye and take care,' said Luke.

'Thank you Laura,' said Arina and added in an offhand manner, 'have you got a cat or any other pet by the way?'

'What?' Laura looked baffled, 'no! As a matter of fact, I am intolerant to pets. To any pets! Funny you mentioned that, it was one of the main topics in our endless rows with Todd. He always wanted a dog. It's strange, though, when I'm now thinking about it. I don't think he actually got any dog after we divorced. So what was the point? Maybe he lied and never wanted a pet. Just pretending, making this all up to annoy and upset me. How would I know now?'

Chapter 15

Arina was walking late through the shopping centre. Strangely, it was deserted. Was it really so late? Shop windows were still brightly lit but were shops open? And what was she so desperately looking for to come here in such a rush?

It was a windy and starless night. The wind was howling like a crazy dog. The streets were poorly lit, it was not easy to run. Why was she running? The wind was so strong, it was pushing her back, it was slowing her down. She had to stop.

Arina stopped. She was looking at the windows of a fashion boutique. There were several mannequins dressed in stylish dresses and hats on display. Suddenly Arina became interested. All those mannequins had featured faces. Arina smiled to herself—much better than modern headless dummies!

The more she was staring at them, the more details were revealed to her. Not only did the figures have featured faces, but these faces were actually more realistic than usual. They also differed from each other!

Then a weird thing happened. The faces started to look familiar. And then something chilled her to the bone. Arina was looking at a motionless face of former Todd's wife—Laura.

'Unbelievable,' she whispered.

The mannequin with Laura's face slowly and laboriously, like its hinge joints were rusty, turned its head to look straight at Arina.

Laura (because it couldn't be anybody else but her!) opened and closed, and opened again her icy blueberry eyes, fringed with enormously long, false eyelashes. Her black straight hair was freshly washed and lustrous once again. Her face and nails were impeccable. She was garbed in apparently expensive, stylish garments and accessories.

Despite all this she doesn't look happy, thought Arina, her face resembles a distorted mask, this is all just a pretence.

Laura tried to say something but Arina couldn't hear anything. And her attention was already distracted by something else. By another mannequin, with long blond hair and doll-like, fixed, blue eyes.

'Angel, is that you?' Arina asked in a false, toneless voice, which sounded alien even to her.

The blond mannequin cocked her head to the side. She was wearing a wide-brim black hat and something long and silky with wide sleeves. She jerkily brought the right hand to her glossy plastic mouth to cover it. She looked more wooden and lifeless than Laura.

Because she is already dead, guessed Arina and cried out softly.

Other mannequins started gathering together, which was extraordinary, bearing in mind that some of them lacked their legs, they were supported by tripod stands instead. And there were definitely more of them now than it seemed to her at first.

Were they hiding behind the curtains, deep in the darkness, inside of the shop?

Somebody else was gesticulating to transfixed Arina, somebody who she also recognised. The dressmakers dummy with short fluffy hair, scarcely covering the head, was Roxanne. This one was clearly not happy, she was wrinkling her baby-smooth shiny forehead and moving her lips in a vain attempt to say something.

Suddenly Arina understood what Roxanne was trying to say.

'Danger!'

Now all mannequins were repeating the same word after her, moving their lips in unison. But the strange thing was that they were not looking at Arina herself, they were staring at something behind her. It made Arina's hair stand on end.

She started turning back. Slowly, very slowly she was turning her head to see what was behind her.

She heard a rustling, the strong wind was dragging an old newspaper, lacerating it on the way. One of these flying shreds of paper was blown in her direction and clung to her face, pasting all over it. Arina tried to remove it but with a sinking fear she realised that she had lost feeling in her arms, both of them were hanging by her sides like overcooked Bucatini pasta.

She couldn't see anything and it became very difficult for her to breath. Arina tried to shout for help but the paper was already sucking inside of her wide-open mouth. To free herself she started shaking her head violently.

Ghastly thoughts were infesting her skull, digging into her brain like earthworms.

How awful it must be to be executed blindfolded! Or worse—with a filthy bag pulled over your head.

Then, somehow, she was not sure how, either her efforts were a success or the wind took back what it had imposed on her earlier on; almost literally "the scales had fallen from her eyes" and she was able to see.

The mannequins were right.

Danger!

Danger in the shape of her deadly foe was all this time right behind her back, hiding amidst the newspaper debris, awaiting her. The figure in the black mackintosh, with a deep pointed hood stood so very close to her.

Arina tried to run but her legs didn't obey her. She looked down and saw that there were no legs anymore—they had become tripods. Arina was growing into the ground.

The figure laughed, its jeering malicious laugh reminded Arina of something and she screamed in horror.

The hood was slipping back now, revealing the murderer's face.

Arina was looking at her Death and Death was gazing back at her.

'After all, you didn't disappear, did you, the missing marathoner? You've just become a killer,' Arina whispered.

Aaron answered her with a high-pitched laugh, the laugh of total lunacy.

****

In her ears when Lady Holroyd-Kugushev came back from her deep slumber to reality. She stayed in bed for a few minutes ignoring the bellowing phone. She was shaking. The aftermath of her vivid dream, or more precisely a proper nightmare, was still with her, and she found breathing to be a laborious and painful task.

The landline phone continued to ring. It was strange—not many people would call her on this number, unless it was something very important. So important that it couldn't wait until the morning. As usual her mobile phone was switched off for the night.

She raised her heavy, confused head and looked at the bedside clock. Five-forty-five am.

'What! At this time! Unbelievable! That is absolutely unbelievable! Appalling!' she shouted aloud, pretending to be annoyed and angry, but deep inside she knew that it was not the anger which made her heart to beat so fast. It was the fear.

'Yes,' she answered eventually.

'Princess Kug...Kugushev? I'm sorry to call you at this time but...'

'Who is it?' Arina asked automatically because she had already guessed who this old, wobbly and very nervous voice belonged to.

'Sorry, it's...Aaron's uncle calling.'

'Lord Mount-Hubert, how can I... What happened?' she tried to sound confident and efficient but the dread of last night and a pure premonition of something terrible and inevitable, which was going to happen to this old and very ill man, betrayed her attempt.

'It's Aaron...he is...he is a monster! You were wrong about him, it is him who is the murderer. And he is going to kill me! I'm next on his list,' he stopped and coughed violently.

'How did you know?' Arina asked and then added rapidly, 'do you want us to come round? We can be with you in a few hours.'

She could only discern heart-breaking whizzing noises from the other end. Then the old man managed to pull himself together and continued in a weak, almost inaudible voice.

'No, don't come! It's too late. They are together in this.'

'Who? Lord Mount-Hubert, who are together?'

'Aaron and...Barbara...my nurse, do you remember her?'

'Yes, I remember her. I noticed that she was very keen for us to leave as soon as possible.'

'That's correct. She was frightened that I would start talking!'

'Sorry, I don't understand you. What do you mean?' Arina, still in the remnants of the horrible dream, felt confused and tired of people muddling with the truth, leaving in their stories empty holes, or simply lying through their teeth.

There was a restrained growl on the other side of the phone line, which was promptly followed by a harrowing coughing fit. When the gentleman was able to speak again, he sounded like someone who was at death's door or even—half-way through.

'Aaron promised me something…you will think that I'm just a stupid old man who clutches at straws…'

'I shall not, now, please Lord Mount…'

'Oh, for pity's sake, would you please address me using my first name—Charles! There is no time for formalities!'

'Okay…Charles, and you can call me Arina.'

'Much better than that unpronounceable gobbledegook,' he said and added rapidly, 'please, don't be offended, this applies to both of us.'

'Continue, I beg you!'

'It's not easy for me, you must understand! As you possibly guessed I'm not a well man. To be frank with you, I'm very ill. I was diagnosed with lung cancer a year ago. And I have other serious health issues, so my prognosis is not good. But, you know, one always hopes…and then Aaron came to me with an offer…'

'So, you have seen Aaron since his disappearance?' Arina asked, sounding harsher than she intended.

'No, I didn't lie to you when I said that I haven't seen him for all this time, I didn't lie about it. But…he…we communicated more than once since…Aaron phoned me occasionally or sent short letters. He said that my house might be watched and it would be better for him not to show up here for a while. Do you remember the story I told you, that he was involved with the schoolgirl who was threatening him with blackmail?'

'I remember very well, Lord…sorry, Charles. She is not a threat to him anymore, she won't blackmail him or anybody else.'

'What? How do you know?'

'She passed away. Angel, the girl's name was Angel, died on Monday.'

'What? What?' the words were coming out with a great effort like rusted bullets, there were also some hissing and clanging noises in the background.

'Are you all right? Sorry, I didn't want to…' Arina faltered, it was difficult to think what to say in this situation.

'I'm back, I'm still kicking, not sure about alive. It was my oxygen cylinder. What an almighty noise it makes! You were saying… this girl…how did she die? Was she…'

'It was not an obvious murder, if that was what you were inquiring about. She died of sudden cardiac arrest. But it could have been caused by fright.'

'I see,' he said lifelessly, 'how sad.'

'So, there is no need for your nephew to hide anymore,' noted Arina coldly, 'if, of course, that was the real reason. But you were saying that he is a monster now, right? How did you come to this conclusion?'

'Okay, okay, I'll tell you. At first, I believed him. I'm desperate you know. And he used to be such a nice lad, so why not? I'm rich, I have plenty of money, so why not?'

'I'm lost here Charles, please, would you kindly explain to me what happened? Sequentially, if you don't mind.'

'He said that in America they found some treatment, still at an experimental stage of course. But if I wished to try it, it wouldn't cure me of course, but it should delay my…my departure. It's kind of a targeted therapy, but much, much more effective than the usual one. It would be expensive obviously. *Very expensive* as it happened. I was to pay in instalments, to help with their research, final research…He, Aaron, promised me that by Autumn, at the latest, I would receive the treatment.'

'And did you?'

'Yesterday.'

'Have you taken any? Sir?'

'I have. But I didn't like the taste. And I didn't like the expression on Barbara's face. So, I spat it out. Secretly of course.'

'Oh! What was on her face?'

'A ravenous expression. She was gloating at me.'

'Hm, what do you know about this medication yourself? Did Aaron provide you with any information at all?'

'Yes. There were…erm…articles, a lot of them, which he sent to me.'

'What sort of articles? What magazines were they published in?'

'Oh, no! They were printed from American medical sites, internet web pages, that sort of thing.'

'Did you yourself see them on your computer?'

'Not exactly. I cannot say that I use my computer very often, that's true, but I am not a dinosaur either. I know how to switch it on and off and so on. But one has to be careful nowadays, all the internet is infested with viruses.'

'It's a simple enough question—did you see it or not?'

'Yes, on my…how it's called…the little thing…a small computer…a tablet, yes, I saw it there.'

'How did you find the site,' Arina continued her interrogation mercilessly, 'did anybody help you? Barbara, perhaps?'

'Barbara... funny you should mention her. You're right—it was Barbara. But it was *me* who asked her help. Aaron sent me all the instructions but they were short and so technical, so complicated...of course it was not too difficult to predict that I wouldn't be able to do it by myself.

'It was all staged! I can see it now. I used to have so many people around me, my secretaries, agents, advisors who would deal with all the dull technicalities, leaving to me the brain work. Now, when I've got old and ill, I have nobody. There are obviously people who are managing my finances and legal issues, but it wouldn't cross my mind to ask one of them to help me with this petty thing. How blind I was! How trustful!'

'Did you speak to anybody from America yourself?'

'No, it was always Aaron. He was the link.'

'Did you go along with this idea, or rather let your nephew involve you in this business because it was Aaron who was behind it? In other words, if it was someone else, not Aaron, you would have never ever agreed to it. Is my assumption correct?'

She heard more coughing, then a word "yes" was mumbled.

'Do you see where I'm heading?' she asked after a long pause. When there was still nothing from Lord Mount-Hubert, she repeated the question.

There was silence on the other end. Not a cough, or rustling, or any other movement. Nothing.

Then from nowhere, a hushing sound, a hiss.

'What? What are saying?' Arina whispered too.

'Somebody tried my door. I locked myself in of course. But somebody tried to come in,' his voice was trembling but his mind was clear as always.

'Where are you?'

'In my study. There are solid wooden doors with old-fashion bolts. They are not easy to force.'

'Why did you do this?'

'Because, my lady, I'm not as strong as I was, and I don't want Barbara to force these horrid, colour-of-baby-urine pills into my throat when I'm asleep. Okay? What a whimsical creature I am!'

'I see...but I beg you to call the police. How long are you planning to hold off the siege?'

A distinct chuckle reached Arina's ears.

'As long as necessary. I'm well provided, you know,' the old man said proudly, 'I have a small bathroom adjoining to the study, and I have been smuggling some biscuits and other non-perishable bits and pieces. On top of this, I always keep a spare set of my medications, enough to last for a week or so.'

He sounds like a scout who earned his final Challenge Badge, thought Arina wearily and said aloud, 'You're playing with fire! Once again I'm begging you to get help from the police. I know somebody from the top, a superintendent actually, who can keep an eye on things, to make sure that everything is done properly.'

'Hm…but then again, the killer might escape and we will be left just with the silly cow Barbara. No proof, nothing. No! We must not reveal that we *know*. I can play my role easily. No doubt—you too.'

'You mean setting a trap?' Arina asked slowly.

'Yes, my lady, I was right about you, you grasp things quickly,' he chuckled softly, 'we will decoy the bastard and then, and only then—set your police on him. How does that sound?'

'Risky!'

'That's my girl! Oh, sorry if I offended you. Inexcusable blunder on my part,' said Lord Mount-Hubert without any trace of remorse in his voice.

Cheeky old codger, Arina thought.

After ten or fifteen minutes of a lively discussion they exchanged farewells and hung up. The call was over, but the problem was still there, and anxiety settled firmly in their hearts.

****

Arina took a few deep cleansing breaths and went to run a cold bath. The icy water made her brain function better. A cup of strong coffee helped her to shake off the rest of the drowsiness. Like wisps of filthy clouds, they were disappearing one after another, revealing an unobscured purity of her mind.

The plan was ready. It had been crystallising in her head for some time, maturing, waiting for the right time to hatch out. And the right time had come.

Arina smiled. But her smile was not a merry one, it was a composed sublime smile of a warrior who was prepared to go to the end of her destiny to confront Evil.

When Luke arrived at ten o'clock sharp, he found his boss fully dressed and ready to go. Arina was wearing her usual uniform for this time of the year: the long black coat and a pair of smart, knee-high boots. The cowhide haversack was hung over one of her slender shoulders, swinging freely. With her aquiline nose, sharp chin and hollow cheeks she more than ever reminded one of a hawk. Luke noticed that she had also lost some weight, and it made her features sharper and more significant. There was nothing new about her losing weight during one of their cases. The more complicated a case appeared to be, the thinner she got.

This Saturday they were going to meet the last man from their list of the "Better Life" Practice participants. His name was John Broad, forty-one, he lived in Otley and used to attend the Thursday Pilates class together with Aaron. He worked as an assistant store manager at the Pharmacy in the same town he had lived all his life in.

'Doesn't look too exciting,' started Luke, testing the water, as they drove for almost fifteen minutes without a word, 'this our last guy, John Broad. I don't think we will gain anything new. Erm…'

'One never knows,' Arina replied and added enigmatically, 'it's not so important for now.'

'Why?'

'Stop asking silly questions Luke! Better occupy yourself with driving us safely to our destination. I need to think.'

Another twenty minutes went past. They were almost there, when Arina came out of her thoughts with a loud "Halloo". Luke jumped in his seat and by a pure miracle just missed the curb.

'Sorry for that, Luke! Good reaction, by the way! Now listen! Better pull over here for a few minutes. That's right! I'm going to tell you something important. It's about how we are going to catch our murderer.'

Chapter 16

John Broad met the private detectives with a polite smile and showed them into the living room.

'The wife and kids are out for a couple of hours, so we can talk in peace,' he giggled, 'that is a very rare occasion in this house.'

Mr Broad was of an average height and average build. His features were also so insignificant, that it would be almost impossible to recognise him on a second occasion, if such an event ever took place.

John Broad offered them tea, coffee, or something stronger. Biscuits, buns, a sponge cake, or something more substantial. He was unstoppable. He was incapable of keeping his mouth shut for any length of time. Though he was emanating benevolence and hospitality enough to embrace a small army, this didn't strike the right note for Luke. His behaviour on the whole had a false tune about it, Luke thought testily.

Eventually Mr Broad prevailed and disappeared to the kitchen with a smile of triumph. Luke had been persuaded to try a homemade cupcake stuffed with cherry jam and generously sprinkled with pink icing sugar—the latest creation of Mr Broad's daughter. Arina held her ground and confined herself to a cup of black coffee only.

Their host returned in no time with a large tray laden with all sorts of pastries. He obviously hadn't lost hope of treating them with more than had been agreed upon.

Arina was getting more and more anxious, Luke could see it. She was fidgeting about, hardly touching her drink, flickering her eyes from one side to another, her mouth set in a determined straight line. Luke knew those signs too well. His boss was losing her patience, which was not great at the best of times.

Luke uttered a polite little cough and thanked Mr Broad for the delicious feast greatly. Then he started to ask the usual questions. Unfortunately, Mr Broad couldn't help much. He was very upset himself. His face turned into a mask of sorrow in one quick moment, as if somebody had used a tumbler switch to turn off the happy face and replaced it with the face of the sad clown Pierrot.

'I'm so, so sorry! Deeply sorry! Would you care for more of these cupcakes or would you rather try something different? I would strongly recommend this sponge cake with glazed pears on the top. I'll share with you my little secret! It's my favourite! But please, don't tell the children. I pretend that I like all their cakes equally. Hm, Lady Holroyd, I hope that you have changed your mind and will agree to have *something* to eat. What about these small pancakes with chocolate mousse? No? Then, perhaps, some Belgian waffles with fresh strawberries? Sorry to hear that you dislike all waffles. Let me think…I knew it! You wouldn't say no to the smallest and the nicest of all—the flapjacks with orange bits. I knew that! How many would you like? Only one? Hm, sorry, the second just slipped in, didn't want to separate from his little brother.'

Luke tried very hard not to laugh, seeing his boss's stony face when she was forced to have these flapjacks, which actually didn't look too bad.

Mr Broad was so pleased that Luke helped himself to more of his delights that he tried to think again. This time harder. And after long arduous brainwork he managed to dig up something of use at least.

'It was the last time I had seen Aaron, a week before his wedding. On our usual Pilates class, which was running on Thursdays, but you already know this.'

'Let me see,' Luke quickly checked the dates for the last year on his phone and came up with the exact date, 'that must be the 17th of September. Please continue.'

'He was so very happy, beaming with happiness. We usually didn't talk much, but on that day he wanted to share his good mood with someone, and there were not many of us around. Somebody was ill, then the doctor, the radiologist, Roger, I think that was his name, had a conference in Manchester. The retired jockey, he was there but you know he is not a really sociable type. So there were not many of us to choose from.

'I remember, we were in a changing room when he started talking. At first, how nervous he felt before his wedding. And here he found the right shoulder to cry on. I could understand him well, I still remember my Big Day pretty well. Then he started saying (he couldn't stop grinning) what a grandiose surprise they had prepared for his wedding day. That his fiancée would fall off her chair when…'

'Wait a minute,' Arina interrupted, 'did you say "they"?

'Oh, yes! The whole idea was not only his, but mainly belonged to his best friend, his best man actually.'

'Who do you mean? Who was…supposed to be his best man? So far, nobody has been able to answer this question, which we found to be a little bit strange.'

'No, that was the point! They kept it secret. Aaron and the chap from his physio class. Sorry, I cannot remember his name. They were preparing something very funny for the wedding day. Like a prank I think. And Aaron asked me not to tell anybody.'

'Why did he tell you? What do you think?'

'I don't think he meant to. It was like he spilled the beans, you know…then realised this and became sort of worried.'

'Why was he worried?' Arina asked sucking her teeth.

'Oh, I'm not so sure, maybe because his best man wouldn't be very pleased if he found out. Aaron himself was usually carefree, he trusted people. He just asked me not to tell anybody before the wedding. Or Todd…oh, gosh, that was his name, the best man,' Mr Broad smiled proudly, 'that's funny how this name just popped out!'

'Or Todd would do what?'

'That was not serious, you must understand. It was said in a jocular way.'

'What? Can you repeat what Aaron said to you? Please!'

'If Todd found out that their plan had been revealed to somebody else, he would have killed him.'

****

'It's me, it's Barbara,' she said and regretted this immediately. Of course, he would know who was calling him. It was absolutely unnecessary. It might annoy him.

There was a long pause. Too long?

'Hi Barbara! Is everything going as planned?'

His voice was muffled as usual. Distorted. It could belong to anybody. It didn't have a face behind it. It was a disembodied voice. One thing she was certain about though. It didn't belong to Aaron Statham.

'Almost, but I…'

'What's wrong?' his voice lashing out, the anger was spewing out of him like scalding lava.

'It's…it's your uncle…he is not well…he has taken a turn for the worse.'

'Yesssss, go on,' it was almost a hiss.

Barbara moistened her lips nervously. They were as dry as sandpaper. She must not lose it now. Don't rush! Don't overdo it. Keep your voice under control.

'Lord Mount…'

'No need for namessss!' another hiss, this time—with aggravating irritation.

'Sorry. I'm just under a lot of pressure! And not a word from you for a while.'

That's good, more natural. Keep your fear at bay.

'He is in a bad state. This time it's serious. He will not survive the week.'

'How long has he been taking these pills?'

'Hm…'

'Has he started taking them at all?' it was like a bomb exploding into her ear, so loud the shout was.

Barbara winced and recoiled from her phone with a jerk. It almost slipped out of her sweaty hands.

'Of course he has! What do you think? That is highly likely the reason for his sudden deterioration. But…'

'Hush! Don't say too much! I understand. What else?'

'He wants to see you. Before…you know, before he…'

'I understand. I anticipated this. Let me think.'

Barbara almost stopped breathing.

'I suppose I have to show him my respects. *After all*,' he giggled almost inaudibly. 'Tomorrow. No, tomorrow I will be busy. The day after. On Thursday afternoon.'

'He might not last that long.'

'He has to,' another dry giggle.

Barbara shivered. This was almost too much for her. The man on the other end was undoubtedly mad, and this belated understanding filled her with horror.

Barba looked into the watery, but still shrewd eyes of her employer, who was watching her intensively all this time.

She silently mouthed to him—what now?

He understood instantly and with his jerky arthritic hands gave her a clear message to finish the conversation. And to do it now!

Barbara cleared her throat. Bit her lips and licked them several times. They were still as parched as a snake slough.

Lord Mount-Hubert gave her an encouraging nod.

'It is very important for him to see you. You know…he…he has asked for his solicitor. It's about the will,' the words were pouring out of her, she couldn't stop them, 'if you want to get anything, anything at all, you better not delay with the visit.'

The mentioned old man was shaking his head desperately. What had she done?

'It's not your business—what I want or don't want! It's not for your pea-sized brain to decide. I will come when it's convenient for me!'

Had she spoiled everything? But they wanted her to be herself, behave naturally. That was what she did.

Lord Mount-Hubert was shaking his fists at her and swearing wordlessly.

The person on the other end finished the call.

Barbara was near to tears, large beads of sweat were rolling down her forehead.

'He will kill me! He will! In a horrible, torturous way! He promised me before. If I ever betrayed him…' Barbara didn't notice that she was speaking aloud.

'No, he will not!' he spitted out fiercely, 'Barbara, calm down! Now! Please,' there was almost empathy now, which was unheard of, 'I'm sure that he took the bait. You haven't done too bad. Under the circumstances…you…in short, well done Barbara. For saving my life,' he chuckled embarrassed.

This was an awkward moment for both of them. Barbara pulled herself together first. She was a professional nurse with long-serving experience after all! Barbara helped herself to a couple of paper tissues and dabbed her face with them.

'I'm going to bring some tea, sir,' she announced and received a satisfied growl.

Barbara was making tea and thinking back to when Lord Mount-Hubert eventually got out of his fortress and made her an offer. The offer was very difficult to decline, especially as it had a great likeness to blackmail.

Simply, if she continued to plot against him on the side of the homicidal imposter, she would be in the hands of the police in no time. End of career, end of freedom. Dishonoured, penniless life afterwards.

Scenario number two. She helps her old vulnerable patient and the private detectives. Helps to catch the lunatic. A very handsome reward is guaranteed straightaway. Plus, another considerable sum will be awaiting her in his amended will. A clear conscience and everybody's respect as an extra bonus.

It didn't take long for her to make the choice.

****

He took the bait. He must have done.

These words were circling in Arina's head all morning. Morning before the *finale*. Wednesday morning, the 1st of November, Arina went for a walk around the reservoir. To clear her mind. To prepare. The air was raw, chilly. Above her head the sky was milky, with invisible clouds, full of threatening rain.

Arina was wearing a pair of her favourite, well-worn walking boots and a navy anorak with a bright orange padded lining, which made it warm and cosy. The path was muddy, with a lot of deep puddles on the way.

Of course, it differed from Austria walks very much—there were no Alps, to start with. But still the surroundings were not too bad. On her left, through the lacy autumn foliage, she could see the rippled lead waters of Eccup reservoir. From her right, the path was safely guarded by pine trees, spruces and larches running up the hill.

Weoo-weoo-weoo!

Above her head a couple of black dots were getting bigger. Two red kites were soaring over the nearby fields, diving down slowly, mewing to each other occasionally. They were obviously looking for prey. Alive or dead. More likely for this time of the year—their finding would be carrion.

A dead body hidden in undergrowth. Arina shivered.

Weoo-weoo-weoo!

The two red kites were joined by another couple. They were all gliding together now, circling over something precious waiting for them down there, only visible to their excellent eyes. With their ethereal majesty, the birds looked as if they had flown into our world from some prehistoric age.

Without noticing it, Arina was slowing down her pace. Apart from occasional kite calls it was so quiet here. There were very few people today on this usually popular route. Maybe some believed the extraordinary forecast, which seriously promised the first snow to fall this afternoon? Snow on the first of November! Must be a joke!

Arina smiled to herself. Rather, she tried to smile, only to produce a pathetic shadow of her normal smile.

Why was her mood so down? She should be exhilarated. The case was solved. She knew the murderer. The motive. There were some details lacking, surely. But tomorrow—everything would come to an end.

Tap-tap-tap!

Out of nowhere, there were booming steps behind her.

Tap-tap-tap!

Somebody was approaching her fast.

Arina wanted to scream but the scream died out inside of her suddenly dry throat. Her vision was catching up with her. One of many.

Tap-tap-tap!

She turned back. A tall masculine figure was running fast towards her. His bright lime green trainers were moving with a robotic rhythm. She tried to distinguish his features, anticipating the worst.

A long-distance runner was a few metres away but she still couldn't see his face. Was he wearing a dark stocking over it?

Her heart had stopped beating, Arina was sure of this. It was sitting there, inside of her chest wall, doing nothing, a useless clod.

The faceless runner was next to her. He slowed down and raised his arm.

Arina squinted expecting a blow on her head. Instead, he waved to her politely. The black athlete, wearing a black woollen hat down to his eyebrows, smiled and ran away. By the time she had come to her senses, he had vanished around the next corner like a ghost.

She shivered again. Got a pair of gloves out of her pocket and put them on. It was getting much colder, the snow might not to be such a joke after all.

Arina resumed her walk. It was quiet again. Just high-pitched mewing up in the sky. There were six or seven red kites by now circling tirelessly among the heavy clouds, disappearing behind their disguising covers time from time.

She needed to concentrate on the case, but her thoughts were wandering somewhere else. She was thinking about her late father.

He had died when he was ninety-seven, a good age as they say, but not good enough for her. He was fit and kept his sharp mind till the last minute of his life. That was thirteen years ago. The next year she lost her husband. One after another with no time to prepare oneself. Prepare for what? For an immense loss?

Of course they were always with her. She could feel them, their presence, when she wanted. Two of them, two of the greatest men she had come across in this life so far. Unlikely she would ever meet anybody near their match in the future.

An elderly couple with a lively white poodle appeared from the opposite direction, walking energetically. When they met, they smiled to each other. The grey-haired couple were wearing matching hats, gloves and coats. They even smiled identically, their plump pink cheeks were wrinkled symmetrically. They exchanged the usual jokes about the weather and expected snow, then departed in their own different directions.

Their intentional bonhomie and over the top friendliness reminded Arina of Klaus, the retired NATO general, as he had introduced himself at their first meeting in this Tyrolean guesthouse where she had stayed in September. Unbelievable! It was less than two months ago, but it seemed so much longer. Time was playing its usual trick with her, stretching or shrinking itself as it wished.

He was a very dangerous man, Arina was sure of it. When will she get some news about him, she wondered. She didn't have any doubts about it, she knew her son-in-law too well, sooner or later he would get to the bottom of this.

But again, these thoughts made her anxious, filled her with worries and foreboding. She had had enough of this frigid walk. She wanted to be home *now*. But stopping in the middle of the route was not her habit. She had to complete the walk, no matter the cost. Anyway, she was more than halfway through it already. It would be very silly to turn back at this point.

It started snowing. The weather reporter was right for once. Big flakes were falling down to the ground, not setting there yet. The temperature was not low enough. But soon it would be.

The first snow of the year. It had always been a special day for her and her father when she was a little girl. In the evening he would close the curtains tight, light candles, no electric light was permitted, and then he would bring a box upholstered in a goatskin. The rest of the year it was kept somewhere well hidden. Only once a year, on the day of the first snow, the magical goatskin box was allowed to be opened. Surely, it was magical because of who lived there.

Arina would sit still, waiting for Prince Alexander Kugushev to put the box in front of her and take a seat opposite. She would then be handed a tiny silver key, which she would have to insert into a tiny keyhole. Turn it twice. Slowly and carefully push the curved convex lid up and there in the soft nests made of blue cottonwool they would be waiting for her, her small fairy zoo. Perfectly carved out of stained-glass animal figures were twinkling at her their red, yellow or black eyes. They were from China, as father told her, they had travelled with him a long way from Shanghai to London, with a short detour to Paris. He never told her more about their origin.

So, there was a family of red dragons. *Papa*-dragon armed with a pair of white sharp fangs and black spines on its back, *mama*-dragon and four miniature baby-dragons. There were also a group of milky-white rats with red beads for eyes, a family of green snakes with red twisted tongues and a light-blue ox with a pink mum-cow, surrounded by their four calves.

Arina would take these figures out of their box, one at a time, and display them carefully in four groups. She was allowed to play with them for an hour. Then the ceremony would be repeated in reverse order. All the glass animals would be safely returned to their beds until the next year.

By mutual agreement this annual event had been stopped when Arina turned sixteen. It was however resumed when her little girls were old enough to be trusted to touch these delicate animals. Iris was first, of course. She was introduced to them at the age of three, two years after she was joined by Sasha.

When the girls grew up, they decided not to stop the family tradition but move it to Christmas Eve instead. They couldn't rely anymore on snowfalls, which had become so irregular and unpredictable. When the head of their clan died in Autumn 2003, on 24th of December the same year they all gathered together around the magic box in remembrance of him. But when they opened the box, it was actually Arina herself who was in charge of the ceremony, they discovered that the box was full of sparkling multicoloured powder, not a single animal figure could be found. It was as if they couldn't outlive their Grand Master and followed him, leaving behind just dust.

Arina sighed, then clenched her teeth together and continued her march through the blizzard. She was totally alone with the raging elements, she must not let fear creep into her heart, she must not let sorrowful thoughts distract her.

Diary 5

I am so close now! Ha-ha! Very soon I will be rich!
No! Wrong! I will be very, very rich! Ha-ha!

The uncle, my uncle appeared to be not as shrewd as one had thought. Don't judge the book by its cover, how true that is.

I have saved quite a lot already. It's true, thanks to his naivety and desperation (how on earth could he have been a successful businessman in the past, I really don't have a clue!). But now a real jackpot is awaiting me. A massive one!

I must not be too excited, I must control myself. There are still a few…hm…a few loose ends which need to be tied up. One of them being Barbara. I don't trust this bitch anymore.

Should I not come to see him tomorrow? That would be wise, I think. But then, I would not get what I deserved, what I worked so hard for. And that is unfair.

I'm not a greedy type, don't get me wrong, but I have reached the certain age when one would like to live a comfortable, easy life. But to do so, one would need a lot of money. A lot! Believe me, I know something about what makes the world go round.

Damn, it's snowing now. I hate snow! A traitor! I have to be careful not leaving any footprints behind. It's melting for now, so fingers crossed, I might be lucky…if I don't have to wait too long.

But again—how can I be sure? She is so unpredictable. Between me and you, I think that she is mad. Batty. Honestly! Touched in her head.

I am stretching my arms with my palms facing up, then turn them down, up and down, up and down. My hands are steady like steel. They are not trembling. I'm made of steel myself, I'm a very strong person. I don't mean physically, though I'm not a weak one. I mean that I'm of a very strong character, determined, focused.

And I am very patient, I can wait and wait. Time doesn't mean very much to me. I can fill it in easily. It's like lying in wait for the…prey. Ha, this comparison is really funny. And it's actually true, if you think about it for a while. Which I do a lot. Especially recently. I have all the time of the Universe in my hands.

Snowing heavily now.

Damn! Damn! Damn!

Stop! Stop now! I'm telling you now, you stupid, stupid, stupid bastard! I hate this weather! I really hate it so much!

Now, listen to me! You have to control yourself! You have to calm down! At once!

I must calm down. I'm so close...so close to my target. I've planned everything so well, so perfect. I cannot mess up now, I'm almost there.

I'm calm, I'm composed, I'm in control of the situation. I'm in control. I have conquered my rage once again. I'm in control.

I hear some movement outside. I hear some stamping. Like somebody trying to clear snow from the boots. Then somebody is walking to the front door, opening it. Somebody is coming inside.

After all, it cannot be anybody else but her...

Chapter 17

First, boots off. Anorak off, needed to be hung up somewhere warm. Hopefully, the heating was on. Then, hot bath to run. Finally, a glass of something strong. Good old whisky would do.

Arina was talking to herself. The walk around the reservoir took the whole two hours, which was unheard of. She was cold, hungry and tired. Moreover, she was frustrated. What was supposed to be a relaxing easy walk, suitable for peaceful meditation and restitution of the inner balance, turned out to be an irksome endurance test.

She checked inside her walking boots and, as she expected, they were wet. Thanks to a pair of thick thermal socks she was wearing, her feet had kept dry. Arina inspected her favourite boots thoroughly and sighed. Unfortunately, she had to start thinking about their replacement. Not right now of course, but in the near future.

Arina couldn't stand changing something she liked, something she's got used to for a long time. Anything new was usually worse than its older predecessor.

She unlaced the boots, took out their soles and placed them on top of the hot radiator in the hall. The boots were left to dry underneath the radiator.

Then, still in her thermal socks, she walked into the kitchen and hung her anorak on top of the door which led to the hall. Then she froze, and not only figuratively.

The other door, the door to the back garden was ajar, and the wind was bringing inside armfuls of snow freely.

'Bloody cats,' Arina whispered looking around.

But there were no cats to be seen. That was a little bit strange. They would all usually meet her by the front door, or at least one of them. And others would join shortly.

She listened. Silence.

'Brahms, Brahms! Nero, Nero! Chernomor, my dear!' Arina called them, but again—not loudly, just audible.

Nothing. Not a single mew, or approaching tapping of fast little feet, or sound of scratching against the nearby furniture. Nothing. Like the house didn't have cats. Like it was a cat-free house, a house she didn't recognise anymore. A strange, unfamiliar house.

Something had happened to them. Something awful had happened to her beloved creatures. And this door, why was it open? She knew very well that she had left the door closed, even locked. As usual. As always.

Suddenly Arina had an epiphany. Luke, it must be Luke of course, why didn't she think of this before? He had come to see her, to give his moral support for tomorrow. He had used his own keys and let the cats out. Or more likely, the cats had let themselves out. Silly man! And now he is trying to get them in before the boss arrived. Too late my friend, too late. You will have to pay for this. She almost laughed, relieved.

Arina put the kettle on and looked in the fridge. She was starving. Luke was probably starving too, simply because he was always hungry except for the short intervals which followed his meals and usually didn't last more than an hour.

Arina dipped her right hand into her thick grey bob and messed it about. The fridge was almost empty. Why didn't he warn her? He should have been well aware of her habits by now. She had just simply forgotten to do some shopping. It's the end of the case, for God's sake! Her mind was pretty well occupied with more important matters.

Then she remembered something, which made her heart skip a beat again. Luke hadn't popped in to comfort her before the day of reckoning. He was going to his dentist, as he had told her yesterday, or the day before, or doesn't matter when. His back tooth had been troubling him a lot for the last few days and needed immediate attention. And this attention Luke and his tooth were receiving now. His appointment was booked for half past one today, which would be in five minutes time.

Arina closed the refrigerator silently and quickly looked back. The door, which led to the living room, was open wide, which was how she would usually leave it. But the room itself was dark, all curtains had been fully drawn. And it was not her who had done it.

He was hiding there, somewhere in the darkness. The murderer. He was waiting for her, waiting to kill her. To shut her up forever.

She couldn't afford to lose her head, she must play it cool. Arina tiptoed out of the kitchen to the hall.

As quiet as a church mouse. What a ridiculous expression!

She found it where she had left it. On the wall shelf by the front door, where she kept her keys, gloves, small change and all sort of bits and pieces, was her mobile phone. Old and battered, but still useable. Luke hated it. With his taste for fancy-schmancy things, he would always make a face after one glance at this primordial device, as he called it.

The first thing she did was to switch off the sound. Secondly, she typed a short message saying: "HE IS HERE. CALL POLICE. CATS MONITOR!" Her fingers were so stiff and clumsy, it took her a few attempts to make it readable. Finally, she sent it to Luke.

Arina turned around, half-expecting to find the foe from her dreams standing behind her back. There was nobody. She put her phone into the fleece she was still wearing and tiptoed back to the kitchen. Again, as silently as she could. The thermal socks served the purpose well.

She knew that the wise decision would be to leave the house right now. To run away when she still had time. Any more delays would cost her life. But she couldn't do it, of course. How could she? To leave her cats behind in the killer's hands? To betray them? Never. She was not capable of doing that, and that was why she slowly came into her living room, which had been occupied by her deadly enemy.

She was sure that he would not jump out of darkness, attacking her straight away. By now she had learned his character enough to know that he would postpone with killing. He would want to enjoy her fear, her confusion at first. He would need to keep her alive for the time being, even if it wouldn't be a very long time.

'Where are my cats?' she asked into the darkness and received a snigger in response.

She was peering intensively into the gloom trying to make out where he was hiding. Her eyes were adjusting annoyingly slow, so she repeated her question, trying to sound as if she was still in charge of the situation. It didn't work, he sniggered again, this time even more derisively.

Arina took two more steps and then suddenly she saw him. There he was, standing by the furthest side of the fireplace, partly hidden, leaning his elbow against the mantelpiece casually. He was wearing something long and bulky—

the black mackintosh with a pointed hood described in detail by Roxanne, the black mackintosh from her own visions. But this time the deep hood was half-down, revealing a ghastly patch of the face.

'I haven't seen you cats. They were probably wise enough to hide somewhere,' the murderer giggled, 'I don't hurt animals usually, it's not my habit. But if it is absolutely necessary, I might be forced to help them on their way, you know, to meet their Creator.'

Arina shuddered in disgust and wished that she had a proper rifle handy. The bigger, the better. She was not afraid anymore, she was furious. It was as if the knowledge that her cats were safe tripled her inner strength.

'What are you doing?' screeched the intruder.

'Is it not obvious? Switching on the light. I cannot see a damned thing.'

'Oh, I see, you want to show how brave you are, fine, I'm not worried about the light. It doesn't matter much now. It really doesn't,' he uttered another one of his revolting giggles.

Arina slumped into the nearest chair she could reach, her legs suddenly gave way. She could see his face properly now and that filled her with horror.

'You can sit down too,' and added after a pause, 'Todd.'

His face distorted even more, like a cornered animal he bared his teeth at her.

'I'm not going to stay here for long, don't you understand?'

'I understand that. But I also think that you will stay long enough to find out how I cracked your crimes, one by one. It was not difficult really. It was easy, you know…as easy as shelling peas.'

Todd Fisher didn't say anything at first, he was twisting his mouth angrily.

How anybody could had taken him for Aaron, thought Arina. Of course, their heights were similar and their build was very similar too. Clearly Todd Fisher had made a great effort of losing his excessive weight, because in all the photographs she had seen he looked so much bigger than he was now.

'It was the reason why you had to stop your physio classes in the summer last year. You were slimming yourself down rapidly to get in Aaron's shape!' she exclaimed aloud.

Todd looked at her, right in her eyes. His dark grey, almost jet-black eyes lacked any expression, they could be easily mistaken for the eyes of a dead person, or a mannequin. Or a purely demented man.

'You will not leave this house,' he stopped himself abruptly and stretched his worm-alike lips into a sneering smile, 'sorry, a correction, you will not leave this *room* alive.'

He had obviously worked hard on his short army haircut as well. To match Aaron's style: he had let his dyed blonde hair grow, he made it look tousled and lively, with a long strand falling over the right side of his forehead. His face was also quite broad and generally reminded one of the features of the man he had murdered. At first glance, in a poor light one could have easily been mistaken. She had been wrong early on, he did look like Aaron. Only like the Aaron who had turned to a merciless killer with a heart of stone.

'Shall we wait and see about it? Let us not jump to conclusions…just yet.'

'Do you still hope to escape? Are you so naïve, or just stupid?' Todd spluttered out, his wide face, all bones, not a gram of fat on it, shiny with sweat, was twitching with frenzy. But his eyes, his eyes stayed the same, expressionless, dead. The discrepancy was eery.

'I don't think you actually planned to kill him at first,' Arina started meditatively, 'I think you liked him. You wanted to be his friend, only you don't know what that means, Todd. You wanted to be with Aaron, to be *included* in his circle. But it didn't work out, did it?'

Arina looked at him. His face was unreadable again, his jet eyes—blank. But then, like a robot, which was put into motion, he slowly nodded. Then he again very slowly detached himself from the wall and walked to the nearest chair which was next to the dining table. With his long mackintosh and dark shadows spreading across the thick carpet on the floor it seemed that he was silently soaring.

Todd sat down, put his elbows, clothed in the crunchy rubber material, upon the table and rested his chin on his two big hands clasped tightly together.

'Go on now, I'll listen to you for a bit,' he said through his teeth.

'Somehow, during this time you learned about his ill uncle. Very rich and terminally ill uncle. Wouldn't it be nice to be in Aaron's shoes, you thought once. Just for a tiny moment. Just to feel yourself privileged, whose future is secured. Just to play a little game. Just for fun. Perhaps, you started thinking what would *you* do if you were him. Firstly, of course, you would break up this ridiculous engagement. Not only was Lisa not the right person for him (for you): too old, too plain, too common. But it could also jeopardise your inheritance. We are convinced that Aaron told Lord Mount-Hubert nothing about his upcoming wedding.'

'Here you are wrong!' Todd cried out with a gloomy satisfaction, 'the fool even tried to invite his uncle to that wretched event. Luckily, the old sod had enough common sense to decline the invitation.'

'Luckily for you, perhaps,' Arina started in her usual sarcastic manner, but was rudely interrupted in the middle of the phrase.

'Hush! Stop talking nonsense! I am the one who is in charge here, I decide when you speak and when you're silent. Not you! Do you get it? You're still alive because I'm letting you. A little bit more respect! Now, listen lady, here are my conditions. Every time you're wrong, like now, I will deduct a minute from your life. Ha, the only problem for you is that you have no idea how many minutes there are in total. That is a tricky brain teaser for you, ha!' he snarled like a hungry impatient wolf.

****

'Now we're coming to the time when you decided to change your appearance,' Arina continued like as if nothing had happened, calm and composed, at least on the outside.

Todd Fisher was snarling again but didn't say a word.

'You slimmed down pretty well and pretty fast. I think you were helped on the way by somebody...somebody professional? After all, you were in the right place for getting healthier, for getting slimmer... Right! Couldn't be better, couldn't be more convenient. What do we know? We know that your physiotherapist—Julia Bower disappeared. I think, no—I am convinced that she is dead, killed. And you did it!'

Todd Fisher didn't say a word. He stopped snarling, however.

'You murdered her just recently, why? Because she knew your secret! Because it was *her* who helped you to shed off the extra pounds,' Arina stopped for a second, she was thinking on her feet, suddenly she could see through all this, like in a crystal ball, all the pieces were coming together and this was all making sense now. 'You *didn't* plan to look like Aaron. It just happened! Julia Bower, as your dedicated and thoroughly professional therapist, advised you to lose some weight to help you with your health issues, whatever they were. You listened to her, because you wanted to look better, you wanted to look good. You

202

have got a very strong will and determination. Together you were reaching the goal fast. And then, one day, somebody, maybe it was even her, noticed that you began to look a little bit like your best mate Aaron. And that was it. That was the turning point for you… and for your future victims.'

'It was Julia who noticed, you're right on that,' Todd broke the silence.

'Good. Where are we now, what is the time? Probably still in July, yes, it's July 2015. Aaron is amused, it would be real fun to have his best man (by then you're his best man, I'm sure of it) look like his twin brother. From now you are stopping the physio sessions. You don't want others to see the metamorphosis. Julia is still okay, she poses no threat to you yet. This situation will change, of course, in a year's time. But let us leave her for now. You have two months in hand to plan how to kill Aaron Statham, get rid of his body and become him. It's a challenge, no one is arguing.'

If eyes could kill, he would have burned through me, Arina noticed to herself and continued audibly.

'Now it's the last day of Aaron's life, the day of his wedding, the day of his brutal death. Based on a lot of statements and some other evidence, I came to the assumption that Aaron Statham was able to run,' Arina held a short pause, didn't get any response and proceeded, 'of course, his running was nothing like before the accident, but that was a start. He was able to do what he had always loved to do again, what he had been craving for all these months became a reality. He decided to keep his miracle recovery secret from his fiancée, he wanted to make a wonderful surprise for Lisa on their wedding day. Only you, his best friend then, the best man, the closest person to him at the time, knew about this. He let you into his plans with his open heart. He trusted you wholly. And you betrayed him.'

Arina hear a bloodcurdling snigger.

'If you think that you put me to shame you couldn't be more wrong! It's laughable, it's so bloody laughable!' his voice sounded strained, like a rusty mechanism which had never been oiled.

'At first, I thought you killed him on the road, on the lonely country lane, where he was doing his last run, in the early hours of the extremely foggy September morning. I believed that you hit Aaron with your car so hard that his body went flying up in the air…'

'How? Witch! How did you…' Todd managed to control himself again, this time with difficulty. He was breathing heavily now, glistening grains of sweat appeared on his forehead and on the wings of his nose. 'I never believed in this mumbo-jumbo, in this crap, the figment of an old spinster's mind, as I always thought. But you…did you really see this?'

'Yes, I did see this in one of my earliest visions. But you didn't kill him on the road in the end, did you?'

'No.'

'It was all in your imagination, wasn't it?'

He gave an almost invisible nod.

'Let me think for a minute. Yes. He was running that morning, that very foggy morning after it rained all night. It was indeed very early. In order to be fully ready for the ceremony he went for his run much earlier than usual. No other cars, no witnesses. You stopped to pick him up, as you agreed the day before. But instead of taking him home, you killed him on the way. Probably, I'm guessing here, you gave him one of you drug concoctions in which you are such an expert.'

'Laura, bitch! She has never learned to keep her big mouth shut! She's got a loose tongue which needs to be shortened one day! My mistake! I should have addressed this before,' he growled.

'It was you,' Arina said quietly, 'behind the fluttering net curtains, in Laura's house. You were hiding there when we were interviewing your ex-wife.'

'It's not only *her* house, the house is mine too!' Todd barked losing his temper again.

'So, that is where you are living Todd. Clever, very clever.'

She could see that he was pleased. His mood changed instantly, he was already grinning arrogantly.

'I don't think that Laura knows anything about her secret lodger, unless she is a great actress…' Arina said.

'Of course she is not! She is incapable of deceiving a child, silly bitch!' Todd giggled, 'the house is big enough for me to live there without any risk of bumping into my beloved-half-of-the-past.'

'But you didn't expect us, Todd? You couldn't, could you? Without your smart little listening device, you ended up shorthanded.'

Todd uttered his usual high-pitched theatrical laugh.

'It doesn't matter now! I've found out everything I needed to, and I have dealt with every single obstacle accordingly. I was ahead of you all this time, silly amateur detective! Why, at your old age, you wouldn't do what other normal, old women do? Looking after grandchildren, for instance. Oh sorry, you haven't got any,' he sniggered, 'or gardening, or knitting, or I don't know, but not mixing with something which is too complicated for your elderly brain? And too dangerous…But it's too late now Lady Holroyd, you haven't got a chance to follow my friendly advice anymore. There is nothing left for you now, unfortunately.'

'Now you have achieved half of your plan: you killed Aaron, or made him unconscious, I don't know for sure but I'm inclined to assume that you just knocked him out with a very powerful drug,' Arina proceeded undisturbed. 'He is in your car. What do you do? I would go for the simplest solution. You are bringing him to your place. To this wrecked caravan home that you had been living in since your divorce on the outskirts of Harrogate.'

'It was not wrecked, it was old, but modernised and fitted with everything I needed. It suited me well,' he muttered.

'Of course it suited you well,' Arina agreed meekly, 'to start with, you could leave Aaron's body for as long as you thought it would be necessary to make him practically unrecognisable, without raising any suspicion. Nobody would notice anything, simply because there was nobody around to spy on you. The place was deserted. You were well prepared. You're a very organised and meticulous person altogether Todd.

'It's still very early, there is no traffic, you get to the caravan in no time at all. Aaron next to you on the front seat, he looks like he has had a good night out in case anybody would be interested. But nobody stops you, nobody asks any questions. His head is touching your shoulder slightly. It's not unpleasant. I think you felt sad for a moment. Were you attracted to him sexually?'

'That's not your business!' he barked, 'even if it was so, it didn't change anything!'

'I understand, you are putting your own feelings to one side, your goal is much more important. As I said before, you are an exceptionally focused man. You're there, you're taking Aaron out of the car, you're bringing him to his final resting place. To the execution site. I believe he can walk himself but with your help, and he is staggering like a drunk. You're safely inside. Now you need to change his clothes, to change him into yours. It's not a very easy task, his running outfit is damp, but not an unpleasant one. You might need to increase the dosage, but not too much, you must not overdo it. He has to be alive. The hook and the rope are ready, you took care of them before. The trap door on the floor is unlocked, it would be easy to push it down with the hangman's feet. I didn't guess here, I've read the report, where it is said that because the roof in the caravan was too low, the deceased, in order to hang himself freely, opened the trap door underneath. Did he die quickly?'

'You talk too much. Yes, he died quickly,' the murderer answered, his voice suddenly sounded tired.

****

Arina shifted in her chair, making herself more comfortable, at the same time quickly glancing at her intruder. Without a doubt, he looked exhausted, his pallid sweaty face resembled his own death-mask.

'After you hanged Aaron Statham you wrote a suicide note and left it in an obvious place. You were leaving now for good, but personally, I'm convinced that you came back once more, later, just to make sure that everything was how you meant it to be.

'You're on your way to Aaron's flat. You have to drive fast, you don't have a lot of time. On the other hand, you have to be very careful on the road, not to attract too much attention. I'm sure that you're getting very tired by now. And, of course, you're wearing his running track suit, which is wet and uncomfortable. It also carries his smell. The smell of the man you hated and loved at the same time. The man who you have just murdered.'

'What a pack of rubbish! What gibberish! Hate and love, pff! You should write soppy love stories, it would suite you better. I didn't have any feelings towards him. Do you not get it? I didn't love him! I didn't hate him either! That was irrelevant. He stood in my way to the wealth and, therefore, he had to go. Simple!'

He is lying, how clumsily he is lying, Arina thought and smiled in her thoughts.

'You're in Aaron's flat,' she stated matter-of-factly, 'it doesn't take too much time for you to gather what you came for. You're familiar with the place and the owner's habits. You know where to look for his passport, his credit cards, etc. You've already got hold of Aaron's mobile. It is from this number that you will send your texts to Lisa, pretending to be her unfaithful betrothed. Your glance might be caught by the morning suit hanging in vain, with its elegant white carnation buttonhole…'

'You're very thorough, lady detective, no, lady sleuthhound—suits you better. You're rarely mistaken. But look where you now are, you walked into my trap willingly. Hm…I didn't get something… how did you know that I was hiding here?'

'Elementary. I had left the curtains undone, you closed them. It was not a very smart move.'

'I didn't, silly woman! I'm not so stupid! The room was already dark, the curtains fully drawn. You probably forgot that you had done them yourself. And I'm getting bored with you. As I said before, you talk too much. Your time is ticking, your minutes are running low.'

Arina smiled thoughtfully, the hands on her wristwatch were showing 2:42, then she continued undisturbed, 'So far so good. Everything went like clockwork. You're in charge of the situation, you're in control. You're contacting Lisa and asking her to forget and forgive you. You're writing to Lord Mount-Hubert with your cooked-up story. Nobody suspects anything fishy. Aaron's body is waiting for the time to be revealed. You're waiting too. Meantime you're working on *your* uncle. Taming him. You're lying low, you're in a safe place. I'm not hundred percent sure, it could be…yes! You're renting a small place, a flat? It's in the centre of Harrogate. And, by pure accident, it was your unlucky day Todd, you met somebody from your Physio class. And the timing couldn't be worse! You were supposed to have been dead for at least three months!

'"Your body" had been already discovered, thanks to an anonymous call, undoubtedly made by yourself. There had been a formal inquest into the matter, and the coroner's verdict concluded "suicide by self-strangulation (hanging)". Your ex-wife and the Physiotherapy & Pilates Practice "Better Life" had been informed. Foresightedly, you had left behind little clues you wished to be found, for example your "Better Life" membership card. You had a quiet funeral, you had been cremated and your urn had been buried by the side of your parents' grave. End of story. Except it was only the beginning.

'You were very unfortunate. How could you know that Cribble's Antiques was just round the corner from your so carefully chosen burrow? How could you know indeed that one day you would run into each other in a convenience store, which you used a lot, and he, Jan Cribble, used occasionally.'

That was the final straw for Todd Fisher and he slammed his huge fists on the table with a heartrending thump. His lips were moving, hurling inaudible curses, his body was twitching like in agony.

'That's how you knew! Oh, I should have killed him!' another heartrending thump, 'but he's gone away. He is in Australia! I don't understand, he promised me. Bastard! Fucking bastard! I will kill his pathetic brother instead. Torture him first, then kill him in a horrible, horrible way! And see how he would like it!'

'There, there, don't waste your energy for nothing. You will need it later. You'll have hard times coming to you soon, Todd, I can see it. It seems to me that your luck has finally run out.'

'Are you insane? Stupid woman! I could kill you right now! With these two hands! Do you understand or have you lost all your senses out of fear?'

'Maybe I'm insane, but shall we continue our little story? We haven't got too much time, have we? Both of us. So, never mind me, can we proceed? Good. It was a blow, meeting Jan. Did you know that at first sight he mistook you for Aaron? If you had kept your cool and restricted yourself to a short greeting, you might have obtained a valuable witness of the runaway bridegroom, perfectly alive and healthy. But you rushed and started talking. You didn't say anything important or incriminating yourself, you were chewing the fat, to put It bluntly. One thing you achieved however, you managed to put Jan Cribble on his guard.

'Highly suspicious individual at the best of times, Mr Cribble sensed that something was not right. It was not your voice, by the way, he wouldn't notice any difference as he has a tin ear. It was your behaviour which hit a false note. Aaron's manners were very different, even the thick-skinned antique dealer noticed it. I appreciate that you had been taken in by total surprise, you didn't have time to put on a performance, but it was a blow to your so far perfect plan. You were like an actor who was called onto the stage at the last minute to perform a role he didn't have enough time to prepare for.

'To give you credit, you reacted fast and you dealt with the problem without delay. I don't know for sure, Mr Cribble was quite discreet on this point, what did you use exactly, I'm inclined to suggest that there was some sort of racketeering involved.'

'Sort of...' Todd Fisher snarled.

'And perhaps some blackmail took place? Mr Cribble certainly had been associated with one or two shady businesses in his past. More than one or two? Thanks, I've got the picture. Anyway, your strategy worked. He didn't say a word to anybody, even better—in April, this year, he was gone, leaving his shop to his brother. You couldn't do more. It was impossible for you to get rid of him physically, he was too careful now, he was watching over his shoulder. Forewarned means forearmed, as they say. It was not your fault Todd, it was just bad luck.'

'I think that *your* luck is really bad, but never mind you, as you said, for now. Go on!'

'I'll be honest with you Todd. I'm puzzled here.'

'You and puzzled! Ha-ha!'

'No, I'm serious. I'm talking about the CCTV image. Was it you or was it Aaron's? I'm fully aware of how good you're at computers and stuff.'

'Go on, what do you think,' he giggled in his usual, offensive manner, 'you're so clever.'

'Okay, that's what I'm thinking happened. It was Aaron, of course it was him, but only this picture had been taken before, maybe the day or several days before his death. You're adept at these things, and security cameras are one of your fields of expertise, as I learned from you CV Todd. So, it was Aaron on this video you tampered with.'

'I worked for this bloody branch. It was me who set their security cameras up after all, so yes, you're right on this one. But you must admit that it was super clever of me, wasn't it?' his eyes beamed like a pair of freshly polished brass buttons.

'And it didn't cross anybody's mind to check if the money had been withdrawn twice.'

'Of course not! Aaron (real Aaron from this footage) took out of the same cash machine some petty amount, like thirty pounds or so the day before his wedding. On the other hand, I, myself, took out exactly two hundred a week later, removed the CCTV's footage with my face, replaced it with Aaron's for the correct time of this withdrawal and hey presto!'

'And without proper technical expertise, nobody had seen any reason to carry out further checks. Your smart forgery worked out well.'

'I swindled them all!' he chuckled arrogantly.

'By the end of September you were doing really well Todd. You achieved almost all your goals and came so close to your main aim. But then everything went to pieces,' Arina held up her index finger to mark the point, 'Lisa was not content with the official version of Aaron's disappearance, she decided to contact us. How did you know about that? You reacted instantly!'

'Yes, how did I know?' Todd grunted.

'At first, I thought that you had fixed another of your smart "bugs" in Lisa's house. But then I rejected this idea. Lisa shared the house with her elderly mother, who was almost all the time at home, no, it would be too much trouble for you. Plus, it was not so important then. You had just hacked Lisa's email account. I'm not sure how exactly…'

'You cannot possibly know everything! Two minutes deducted!'

'What?' Arina exclaimed.

'Sometime in June last year, Aaron came to me to ask for some advice. Lisa's laptop stopped working properly, she also had problems with her email account. He was ever so pleased when I agreed to look into the issue. We all met at his flat. Yes, we actually met, me and Lisa Roberts, isn't it amazing? She didn't know anything about our physio sessions, of course. He introduced me as somebody's friend, a computer geek apparently,' he giggled. 'It was a cakewalk, a five-minute job, which I made last for over an hour.'

'Did you hack her email?'

'Ha-ha! I didn't have to! She gave me all her passwords and logins. No, I installed a few additional little programs, a few small smart friends who would report back to their Master promptly.'

'I see,' said Arina gloomily.

'You don't see anything, you stupid woman! You don't have a clue about what it takes to become a pro in computing! You really don't have a clue. Hours and hours of hard, boring, tedious work. When all your mates are going for a drink or meeting chicks. That's unfair! But life as a whole is unfair. For some, at least.'

Chapter 18

Luke was sitting, as stiff as a pikestaff, frozen to his chair in a dental practice waiting area. He had already been given an injection of local anaesthetic to his lower jaw. An extremely painful injection, mind you. Luke touched his left cheek with his trembling fingers. It was a strange feeling, like stroking somebody else's skin. Rough skin covered in large pores and stubble. Disgusting feeling. He thought he might be sick. He hated going to the dentist. He really did.

Unfortunately, the waiting area had been redecorated since his last visit, which had been back in July. He shouldn't have been near this hellish place for another three months at least, if it was not for the damn tooth of his! Luke took off his glasses and rubbed the watering eyes.

The dazzling white walls were hurting them. Ghastly, freshly painted white walls with botched monstrous daisies all over them. There were also a few ladybirds, the size of a baby's head, decorating the reception area frivolously. This would put anybody in a stupor.

Luke looked around, trying to distract himself. It would have been better if he hadn't. Directly opposite him an elderly toothless gentleman was slumped in a chair which was too big for him. His sunken, wrinkled mouth was moving by itself, his small eyes, deeply sunk in their sockets, were half-closed. He was moving his head from side to side, lamenting wordlessly.

The wall clock was showing one-forty. It was five minutes fast, as Luke noticed checking the time on his watch. He sighed anxiously. This place was getting on his nerves. The old man sighed too, but his sigh was accompanied by a whistling, unhealthy sound.

'A-a-a!' somebody wailed.

Luke jumped in his seat. The dozy man jumped too and opened his eyes wide.

'What was that?' he lisped.

'Somebody is being tormented, perhaps,' Luke forced a lopsided, totally false smile, 'in one of their torture chambers, you know, where they take all your teeth out in one go, erm...' Luke stopped short in embarrassment.

The toothless man looked at him with mild reproach and said nothing.

'I'm very sorry, it was thoughtless of me...I was just trying to joke...it was a very silly joke,' Luke mumbled, his face reddening quickly.

The man nodded politely and narrowed his eyes again, but not for long.

There was an almighty bang, more like a bomb explosion. A door to one of the treatment rooms had been slammed open, and a very angry middle-aged woman stormed out. She was heavyset and was stamping her high-heeled shoes forcefully. The woman had great similarity to a goose in rage. She was also hissing out some very uncomplimentary words about her dentist. The latter, a young man with a disturbed face, was trotting behind her. After a short but lively discussion the patient was escorted back to her destiny.

This episode didn't improve Luke's mood, neither did it bring any more serenity to the toothless gentleman who, fully awake now, continued his moans but in a more forceful and agitated manner.

'Mr Weir!' somebody shouted at Luke's ear.

This time Luke almost fell off his chair. An elderly, very serious looking woman in a nurse's uniform was standing next to him. She was wearing round spectacles on her long nose and was looking at him sadly. It was the dental nurse attached to his dentist. The time of his execution had come.

Luke tried to stand up but his legs went numb. He rubbed his sweaty palms on his black corduroy trousers instead. He opened his mouth to say something, to make an excuse to delay the inevitable but the dental nurse beat him to it.

'Mr Weir, we are very sorry that we are slightly behind time. It will not be too long now. Our apologies again,' she smiled sourly and walked away as quietly as before.

On one hand, Luke was pleased with the delay, on the other hand, he started worrying that the anaesthetic would wear off.

Time was dragging so slowly, that it looked like as if somebody had glued the wall clock's hands to its face when Luke closed his eyes for a minute or two. One thing had happened though. He was waiting on his own. The old man must have already been taken in because, at some point, when Luke glanced in his direction there was an empty seat, the toothless patient was not there anymore.

I must have nodded off, Luke figured as he yawned nervously. Then he decided to send a short message to Arina and reached out for his phone, expecting to find it in his trousers pocket as usual. It was not there. With his long sensitive fingers he searched rapidly through the rest of his pockets: four in the thick brick-red jacket, two chest pockets in his colourfully striped rugby style shirt, all the trouser pockets again—no luck. Luke jumped to his feet and scanned the floor under his chair—nothing! He swore under his breath, in his before-dental-appointment dismal state he had left the phone at home.

His heart sunk, he couldn't explain to himself why he wanted to contact his boss so desperately, to check on her. On the spur of the moment, Luke decided to get out from here, to cut loose.

Luke quickly looked around. The two receptionists were busy with answering phones, nobody was paying attention to him. He took his outdoor jacket and, without putting it on, casually walked to the front door. He almost made it.

'Mr Weir! Hey, Mr Weir, where are you going? We are ready for you now!' the dental nurse called out, as if she was trying to stop a naughty pupil who had decided to play truant.

In half an hour Luke was released. Still shaken, an old-fashion drill machine at the very end, to finish off the procedure, was horrendous, he began to feel an enormous relief. After all, it was not too bad. Why was he always so fretful before, that was a deep mystery even for him.

Luke came out of the dental clinic and was startled. He didn't recognise the place. For the time he had been inside everything had changed. Streets, cars, houses, trees and bushes were all enswathed with a white puffy duvet, like they were too cold to withstand the bleak weather and needed some extra covering to survive.

Almost immediately he regretted not bringing his car. In normal weather the distance between his home and the dentist would be a pleasant fifteen-minute walk. But certainly not in these conditions, and the snow continued falling heavily.

Luke gave a little shiver and zipped his brick-red down jacket fully up. Then he started walking very carefully. He had already slipped once, when he had been going down a few icy steps on the way out from the dental practice, and almost fell down. He had probably twisted his left ankle, as it was already hurting. The

213

dull, nagging pain was trying its grip, humouring it, preparing itself for a proper attack.

In his fashionable, thin-soled sneakers, which rapidly were soaking through, Luke was plodding along a non-existent pavement, trying very hard not to think that he might be already too late.

Too late for what? Don't think! Keep going!

By the end, Luke was practically dragging his wounded leg along. With his glasses plastered with snowflakes he could barely see where he was going.

Like one of the three blind mice. What rubbish he was thinking of! Luke rubbed his frozen numb hands together. Of course he'd forgotten to take his gloves with him, how typical! He imagined that it was Arina mocking him, in her usual condescending manner. He attempted to smile and flinched immediately. His lips were bleeding, he didn't notice that he had been biting them for some time.

For the last few metres Luke was basically crawling. He couldn't believe that, as a boy, he used to enjoy the long snowy winters in the Shetland Islands where he had spent most of his childhood.

****

Time was running out for her. She finished her story, the murderer listened to the end, now it was his turn. He grinned. He was savouring the moment with the snarl of a hungry wolf. He put his big hands on the table, the rubber mackintosh scratched ominously.

'Now, what shall we do with you?' Todd purred and leaned with his chair backwards, then brought it forward and smiled.

He looked calm, almost sane, and that's what made Arina very frightened. She thought for the first time that she might not survive. She tried to guess what the time was without looking at her watch, she didn't want him to see that she was checking it.

Then they both heard a barely audible rustle. Todd Fisher pricked up his ears immediately. He started peering in the direction of the sound, like a cold-blooded hunter tracking his unfortunate prey. He was totally silent, he didn't move a muscle, he was ready to pounce when the time came.

Arina saw the bushy tail first and her heart sunk. Then the big fury head appeared, and Brahms revealed himself proudly out of the darkness. Arina shouted at him, trying to shoo the cat away but she was too late.

With an ear-piercing shriek, Todd Fisher grabbed the first thing he could find, which was an apple from the fruit ball, and lobbed it at the poor cat. The apple, smashed to a pulp against the wall, not reaching its destination. He missed.

Only Arina sighed with relief, hoping that Brahms had run far away, the latter reappeared with a savage growl. He didn't waste much time and, with his ears flattened against his head, ran straight at his offender.

Then everything happened in the blink of an eye.

Arina heard an almighty scream, Todd's features were distorted, a black hole in place of his mouth. An almost comical expression of childish disbelief settled on his face. Todd slowly bending down, trying to reach for his wounded leg. Another almighty growl from down on the floor.

And then, balaclava men were everywhere. Masked men, armed to the teeth. Like a scene from an action film she had never watched. Arina's perception of what was happening in front of her became disturbed. It was like she was looking at all of this from somewhere outside, like prying through the window, peeping into the room. She was not taking part in the events anymore. She had been transformed into a spectator.

Somewhere in the background she could see the very pale, very worried face of Luke. It was out of focus, it was jerking up and down like on old videotape.

Todd, handcuffed, restrained by two muscular policemen, without balaclavas but stuffed into their bulletproof vests. Todd still in a state of total dismay and shock, still wearing a babyish pout as if he was cheated or tricked into losing the game. With his trousers torn and legs bleeding he was catching confused looks from the police.

The first sense which returned to Arina was the sense of smell. A strong and rich honey scent, a smell of expensive and mature whisky. Somebody was holding a tumbler with amber liquid to her nose. Somebody with spiky ginger hair and rectangular glasses, behind which were hiding very concerned eyes.

The next thing which came back to her was hearing. A deep purr came through to her, like the bubble she was encased in had suddenly burst, and the outside world poured over her, absorbing her, returning her to reality.

'At least…Luke…you…came not…too…' the words were coming out with such a huge effort that Lady Holroyd-Kugushev couldn't finish the sentence, so exhausted she had become.

'Shush Arina, please, don't speak yet. You need to rest. Have some water,' Luke put the whisky away and held out a glass of water instead, his hand was shaking.

Arina shook her head and mumbled something.

'What? What did you say? What are you pointing at? Ah, got it! You want the other glass? Yes? Are you sure of it? Do you think it would be wise to…erm, in your condition… Okay, okay, if you insist.'

'Better!' Arina uttered after she gulped down a good half of what was there.

'I was so worried, I am so sorry Arina. I actually thought I was too late.'

Arina gave a wave tiredly. Then she glanced around.

'Is he…Have they taken him away?'

'Yes, don't be worried.'

'I'm not anymore,' she paused, then with shining eyes added, 'he still didn't get it. You know Luke, how we caught him,' she chuckled, the colour slowly was coming back to her hollow cheeks.

Luke grinned. It was a pleasure to see his boss coming around so quickly. He felt enormously proud and privileged to work with such a remarkable person. But he must not show his feelings so openly. He was fully aware how Arina hated any sentimentalities.

He grinned again and felt how the heavy burden, which had been wearing him down for all this time, was lifted from his shoulders. A strange desire came upon him, a desire to embrace Lady Holroyd-Kugushev. The next second he was greatly ashamed of himself and stole a surreptitious look at her. Whew! Arina was occupied with her cats, gathering around her with a loud cacophony of mixed purrs and mews. She didn't seem to notice anything.

'Do you want to lie down? You must be absolutely knackered,' Luke suggested carefully.

Arina looked at him, a mischievous smile was hiding at the corners of her mouth.

'We can make a tender, devoted carer out of you, Luke,' she said and winked suddenly.

Luke smiled back with uncertainty.

'Do you know what,' she continued in a much stronger voice, 'I'm dying of hunger and I'm dying to talk about what has happened. There are other things I would not mind doing, but going to bed—pff! Absurd! You should know me better, Luke!'

****

'I wonder,' Arina said reflectively and stopped.

They had just finished a scrumptious omelette cooked by Luke. He used all the ingredients, all the leftovers he could find in Arina's kitchen. He chopped a couple of ancient onions, sliced a few mushrooms and one half-rotten tomato. He fried them in a big frying pan, adding time from time generous pinches of salt and pepper, paprika and rosemary, and basil. Then he beat the whole lot of eggs. Eight in total. At the end of cooking he sprinkled the omelette with cheese flakes, those which hadn't turned green yet, and served the food with tinned anchovies and a few more or less fresh-looking parsley leaves.

'Just as well we had this smart baby monitor connected to my mobile. Do you remember how you disliked the idea at first?' Luke giggled.

'No need to remind me,' Arina snapped but then added in a more amiable manner, 'yes, of course, I was so lucky to have this baby, hm, cat monitor. A real example of amazing modern technology. Fitted and fixed by *you*, Luke!'

'He…Todd couldn't guess in a million years that he would be caught thanks to such an innocent gimmick as a baby monitor, used for checking on cats by a cat-sitter. Meaning your humble servant. Ha-ha! You should have seen his face when they told him!'

Arina chuckled and finished her second mug of aromatic almond tea. Luke confined himself to a cup of very strong Arabic coffee, a jar of which was kept by Arina for Luke's consumption exclusively.

'It seemed to me that, I know how bizarre it sounds, that after all, it was he himself who brought Todd Fisher to justice. You know Luke, if he hadn't tried to be so super clever, we might never have got him.'

'Did you mean Ms Kale, the principal?'

'Her as well.'

'I still feel awful about her death. I blame myself so much,' Luke said with desperation he rarely showed.

'Please Luke, calm yourself down now. It was not your fault, okay? Have more coffee or whatever you fancy but don't interrupt me. Please! Good, have some brandy. No, I'm fine, I don't want anything.

'Ms Kale. That was a tricky one. I really couldn't get that one. It cost me an extra five minutes,' she smiled wearily, 'on his punishment scheme.'

Luke nodded gravely.

'Todd wanted her to be his witness, the person who believed that he was Aaron. That Aaron was alive and well. He set the whole scene up so well, him hiding under the trees under her window. So desperate, so unfairly accused. Poor, poor Aaron. Tricked by nasty, ugly Lisa to that *unholy* wedding. The wedding which couldn't go ahead. Simply because it was so wrong! Ms Kale herself gave away her feelings about this engagement to us at the first meeting. She didn't hide her attitude. She was supposed to be on his side.

'And then everything started going to pieces, his cleverly erected tower of lies had already been rotting from inside. But Todd was oblivious to his mistakes, small and insignificant at first glance, they eventually led to more serious ones. One after another he was taking wrong steps.'

'Sorry, Arina, I'm a little bit lost here, can we go through some of his crimes once more, please? No questions about Julia's murder, that one is clear. But then—the principal. We met her, and our meeting was pretty useless as I remember. Why her? Then, in her muddled phone call she didn't give away much. She was vague. And after this he waited the whole week before killing her.'

'Firstly Luke, he knew nothing about this call. He was convinced that she was going in the direction he indicated for her. He was watching her, he was sending her short pitiful notes. He was swaddling her in his deceit, he played with her like a spider with a fly, only planning to let her go free at the end. His aim was simple. Ms Kale tells us that Aaron is alive and well, that he is begging not to look for him. He doesn't want to hurt Lisa more but his decision is final and should be respected. The inquiry has to stop. Everybody deserve peace, right? He is not an exception. Ms Kale always had a soft spot for him, for Aaron, she would believe anything he said.'

'But it didn't work, did it?' Luke asked.

'No, it didn't. Ms Kale was not stupid, and she had a good memory. He underestimated her. And this cost her, her life. She noticed that something was not right, she smelled a rat, to put it bluntly. Todd was not sure on this point. It could be that he limped on the wrong foot occasionally, when he was stalking her in the bushes under her window. It was a long wait and his left leg, unlike Aaron's, was always the weaker one. Or something in his writing alerted her. Who would know now? But she demanded to meet with him. She said she wanted to clarify a few things before helping him. It was not Todd who chose the day by the way, we were wrong on this. They met at the crack of dawn on the 11th, the outdoor activities day, remember? She thought she would be safe, she thought that there would be some people around, preparing things for the event. She was unlucky. There was nobody in the area at that time.

'He didn't plan to kill her at first, as we know now. It was her reaction which alarmed him. She was not a good actress. The fear and surprise were easily read on her face. Then she cried out something like, "It's not you! You are not Aaron! Who are you?" With these words she basically signed her own death warrant.'

'And Angel?'

'Poor, silly Angel. Always snooping around, always worried to be left out, always drinking in all gossip, like a sponge absorbing water. Of course, it was inevitable that their paths would cross. He tried to scare her off. Sick bastard! Pretended to be Lisa, he was sending her text messages full of menacing stuff. That is why she was so different when she was interviewed by Roxanne. But it was not enough for him. Todd arranged this macabre spectacle for her, only not knowing that her heart would stop.

'He was really furious by then. Marek's murder put him off balance. Again, he didn't plan it. He was quite regretful about the whole business. Next, the attack on Roxanne. And he failed. He felt so humiliated by this, he almost lost his mind right there, in the park. By this time, he had stopped thinking logically. Rage overtook him completely. He was moving to the edge fast.'

'Did he tell you why he tried to kill Roxanne?' Luke asked, trying not to sound too involved.

'Oh, her... his usual paranoia, I suppose. Oh, maybe, thinking now, it could have been her preliminary profile she started on him that he found to be too close to the truth or too humiliating. He was still listening to all our talks, you remember? Anyway, who knows for certain? He was not very talkative on this topic.'

'Do you know how he killed Marek?'

Arina sighed and stroked Chernomor, who cuddled himself in a big furry ball next to her mug.

'Trustful, open-hearted Marek. He believed instantly that it was Aaron in front of him and followed him to his car without a word. Todd played his cards well there. Made big warning eyes, finger to his mouth, a sort of conspiracy theory, go with me and don't ask questions. Marek listened to him because he was his friend, his mate. He didn't know us, he had met us on that day for the first time. His whole life experience taught him not to trust strangers too much. Todd killed him as soon as Marek got inside his car. In his usual way, he stuck a syringe full of poison into Marek's forearm. No delays, no hesitation. He told me that he usually kept about five such deadly dosages on him.'

'What did he do with the body?' asked Luke lifelessly.

'He actually buried him. Somewhere in the woods, on the outskirts of Harrogate. In a weird way, he felt obliged to do it.'

'Arina, can I ask you something? It has been bothering me since I came here…'

'Fire away!'

'How…how did you guess that Todd was here?'

'Oh…that…' Arina smiled mysteriously, 'there were two things. One—the kitchen door was ajar. You know me, I never leave doors open or unlocked when I go out. And it made me suspicious straight away. It was Todd who came in that way because it was easy for him to pick the lock, which was very old and very fragile, and sneaked through the back door without anyone noticing. He closed the door after himself of course, but the cats must have opened it later because they didn't feel safe with him in the house. Except poor Brahms who was fast asleep at the time. My saviour, my hairy hero,' she murmured to the latter, who made himself very comfortable on his owner's knee and was purring with a deep rumble.

'It was so brave of you to stay Arina, you know, you are a really…erm a hero yourself.'

'Oh, stop it Luke!'

'And what was the second thing you mentioned, which gave him away?'

Arina didn't answer at first. She finished her tea. She tugged and mussed her hair a bit.

'Never mind about the second thing. I will tell you one day Luke,' she said eventually, 'just let us drop it for now.'

****

Time passed, it was into the middle of December now, not too far from yet another Christmas. The snow, which had fallen at the beginning of November, had long gone. The streets of London, wet with drizzle from the early morning, were freezing fast as the temperature started plummeting.

He came out of the Corinthia, a luxury hotel where he stayed on his frequent visits to London and swore under his breath. Even in his Magnanni loafers with double monk-strap he could feel how slippery it was under his feet. A thin, invisible film of ice was spreading everywhere quickly.

He turned into Northumberland Avenue and started his walk in the direction of the National Gallery. He was carefully making his way, time from time stepping down from the pavement onto the road.

His tall, slender figure in a long, black, elegant coat was attracting the attention of the rare passers-by. He was used to this and it didn't please or annoy him anymore, he simply was not bothered.

He reached his destination at twenty-five minutes to three, he was five minutes late and it infuriated him. He was not used to being late. He walked briskly through the empty rooms of the art gallery, aiming for the Italian section. He was wrong. He found her in the South Germany and Austria room, by Albrecht Dürer's painting of Saint Jerome.

Arina didn't see him, she was fully absorbed by the painting. She was as beautiful as ever, perhaps even more so. Maybe because of her expensive designer clothes she was wearing or due to her freshly cut and styled hair. He didn't know but she looked stunning.

'Are you particularly interested in St Jerome?' he asked at last.

She turned her head and smiled vaguely.

'Not as much as in his lion. Just look at his wise, beautiful, noble face. I don't have the heart to call it snout, Peter.'

Superintendent Peter Crawnshaw smiled back.

'How are you, my dear mother-in-law? Are you doing well?'

'Very well, thank you. The old lord became very generous in the last weeks of his life.'

'When did he die?'

'Four days ago.'

'Oh…he still outlived all those doctor's predictions. Yes, what was I saying? You look absolutely smashing!'

'Thank you Peter. It's difficult not to look good in all these luxury garments I could afford thanks to Lord Mount-Hubert's cheque he sent to us for catching the murderer of his nephew.'

'Was it big, if you don't mind me asking?'

'Massive,' she chuckled, 'and he also didn't forget Lisa in his will. As I said, he became a different man in those last days of his life.'

'How strange,' said Supt Crawnshaw thoughtfully.

'Indeed.'

'Where is Luke, by the way?'

'He went to his parents in Scotland for Christmas. More likely to heal his love wounds.'

'What?'

'Yes, poor boy, he was smitten by your protégé. Roxanne. He needed some time to recover.'

'I cannot believe that! What did he find in her?' Crawnshaw exclaimed earnestly.

'I don't have a clue either!' Arina agreed eagerly.

Suddenly the room was filled with noises, voices and general bustle. A large, lively tourist group from China burst in.

'Shall we go somewhere *more private*? I need to tell you something,' suggested Peter Crawnshaw.

'Hm…do you have anything in mind, which is not very far from here? I'm quite short of time today, you know. I'm meeting Richard at five, before his concert. In the Royal Albert Hall.'

'Oh, is he here? I didn't know that he was back from wherever he had been touring,' he noted acidly.

Arina just smiled and shook her head slightly. They came out of the gallery and started walking slowly and carefully, she was forced to take her son-in-law's arm.

'Where are we going?'

'It's a very old and famous pub, called "The Marquis", nearby. And actually—there we are—we're here.'

'It's really nice! Strange, I've never been here before,' Arina said and lifted her crystal flute filled with the pub's most expensive Champagne (it's the time for a very special drink, Crawnshaw said making an order).

'Cheers!'

They clinked their glasses. They were sitting by the fire in a small private section in this already very busy pub.

'Why do you not like Richard?' Arina asked.

'He is too pompous, too arrogant, overconfident and all together—an extremely annoying specimen!'

You're describing yourself, my dear, Arina thought floutingly and shook her head again.

'Plus, he is much younger than you!' with this Parthian arrow, the Superintendent retreated to his drink.

'Richard is fifty-six by the way, so it's not a massive difference. I'm just enjoying his company and his music. He is a very talented cellist and a very interesting, widely travelled person. And I don't know why I should be accounting to you, I'm not going to marry him! That is out of question.'

'You're not? That is wise!' he said smiled widely.

'Peter, you were going to tell me something.'

'Oh, yes, I'm sorry! It went out of my head. It's about your German acquaintance and his so-called daughter.'

'Klaus? What did you find out?' Arina asked lively.

'You were right about him. He a first-class crook. He is on the Interpol wanted persons list. With a Red Notice, actually.'

'Gosh! And his daughter, is she involved too? She must be!'

'Firstly, she is his mistress, not his daughter. Secondly, yes, she is also on their list.'

'What did they do? And why did they want to kill me? I cannot believe how right I was about that *sweet couple*!'

'They are known for befriending elderly people, mainly women. Then, there can be a few different scenarios. They are quite ingenious in their own way. There were cases of sudden deaths and all money had been passed to them, as the nearest and dearest, even if they had only known the victim for just over a year. There were some fake investments or all sorts of donations to non-existing charities, again with great benefit to those two. The list of their crimes is long, believe me.'

'But why me?'

'That was interesting. We think that they saw you as a threat. They thought that you were after them. That you had been hired by one of their unfortunate victim's relative or friend to spy on them. And they panicked. They tried, fortunately without success, to stage an accident.'

'Oh my God! Is there a trial now or…'

'Unfortunately, the police managed to arrest only Krista, it's not her real name but let's call her that for now. The *general* escaped. Vanished. We're thinking that he might be somewhere in Argentina but we don't know for certain.'

'How awful!' Arina exclaimed and finished her glass in one gulp.

'And how lucky you were,' her son-in-law said quietly, 'you're just not bothered about the danger which you attract, it seems to me. Take the last case, for instance…'

'I'm absolutely fine, I'm careful, don't be worried. Yes, thank you, you can pour me another glass of this heavenly ambrosia,' she interrupted him lightly.

'What are you plans now, what are you going to do with this,' Peter Crawnshaw grinned, '*lottery win* of yours?'

'I'm going to travel. I'm going to Russia! Believe it or not, I've never been to the country of my ancestors. I'm going to Saint Petersburg in June.'

The Supt was lost for words, he just looked at his lively elderly relative-in-law in a way of great amusement.

'That is a surprise!' he managed to say eventually, 'and what does Luke think about all of this?'

'Luke? He doesn't know yet. Anyway, what is it to do with him. I'm going on my own.'

'What?' Crawnshaw cried out.

'Would you like another bottle, sir?' asked an insinuating voice.

'Yes!' Lady Holroyd-Kugushev and Superintendent Crawnshaw said in unison.

The End